S0-CEX-426

Novels by Thomas Savage

Midnight Line_____

Midnight Line _____

a Novel by
THOMAS SAVAGE

Little, Brown and Company — Boston - Toronto

COPYRIGHT © 1976 BY THOMAS SAVAGE

ALL RIGHTS RESERVED. NO PART OF THIS BOOK MAY BE REPRODUCED
IN ANY FORM OR BY ANY ELECTRONIC OR MECHANICAL MEANS IN-
CLUDING INFORMATION STORAGE AND RETRIEVAL SYSTEMS WITHOUT
PERMISSION IN WRITING FROM THE PUBLISHER, EXCEPT BY A RE-
VIEWER WHO MAY QUOTE BRIEF PASSAGES IN A REVIEW.

FIRST EDITION

T 02/76

LIBRARY OF CONGRESS CATALOGING IN PUBLICATION DATA

Savage, Thomas.
  Midnight line.

  I. Title.
PZ3.S2652Mi   [PS3569.A83]   813'.5'4   75-28252
ISBN 0-316-77141-4

Designed by Susan Windheim

*Published simultaneously in Canada
by Little, Brown & Company (Canada) Limited*

PRINTED IN THE UNITED STATES OF AMERICA

*For my sisters — Isabel and Patricia
with love*

*Midnight Line*_____

I

AT NIGHT the entire East Coast shrinks and fits neatly within the circumference of a radio dial. Philadelphia, New York and Boston become a single city with a singular population — those kept awake by their loneliness, their anguish, their shame, their pain. They are the listeners and the talkers, their language most often the simple speech of the high school dropout, the speech of the radio talk shows.

Talkmasters preside.

Each has his own following. Each has his peculiar personality.

One talkmaster boasts he has no formal education — but now look at him — intimate of doctors and lawyers and others whose money has bought them the leisure to talk the night away as guests on his "show." By her first name he addressed a woman of a certain age who has so successfully written of an old poodle dog who shares her life that she is moved to write with spectacular success a kind of novel about sex in the office and sex backstage. She and the likes of her and the doctors and the lawyers talk about witches and flying saucers and the advantages of freezing over embalming. At intervals the talkmaster pauses in deference to his sponsors and recommends a drinking water said to be free of detergents and sewage. He speaks a good word for a shop that sells sparkling stones few can tell from diamonds, and of shoes cleverly contrived to fit the human foot.

Another talkmaster is a displaced Southerner with the puzzling southern inability to pronounce the pronoun "I." His gift is that of gab. Excited or enthusiastic, his voice leaps and crowds into the upper reaches of his throat and stops just short of a giggle. His deference to the ladies is antebellum. His similes and metaphors spring from the virile language of the football field, the distant golden times of fraternities and college proms when Betty Coed was queen and chins were high and good men sat in high places. His guests are proud unwed mothers, sometimes models seen on the covers of magazines, pilots of airplanes who write books about how it is to be up in the sky. He chats with naturalized foreigners who love America as the land of opportunity. He talks with poor people who have become rich people without entirely losing their innocence. He pauses to recommend rooms in a clean if cheap hotel, and speaks well of a scent which, if applied to certain crucial areas, make women most attractive to what he calls "the opposite sex."

One talkmaster is a sadist, surely. He punctures dreams and holds opinions up to ridicule. He waits for calls from the ignorant in the night who have got hold of some idea from Bible or tabloid and wish to air it as original. Alas, they have not got hold of English grammar. The double negative, the tricky third-person singular, the puzzling difference between "lie" and "lay" and their use of "anyways" betray them as idiots who have no right to any idea at all. He cuts them off in midspeech and leaves them to regard the silent telephone in their hands.

Certain talkmasters appeal to the sportsminded, knowing well that sports outrank religion and even sex as the opiate of the people, that since the lives of many are empty they must identify themselves with men who throw or hit balls or pucks and thrill only to goals reached by men they will never touch or speak to.

One talkmaster runs what he calls a "fun" show. His audience, sick unto death of reality, does not wish to be led along the unpleasant paths of politics, crime or domestic rows. Rather, it prefers to talk and listen to others talk of men who have seen and even spoken with creatures from outer space, the power and benefits of hypnotism and what vitamins promise — virility and youth. They hear their talkmaster use his Celebrity Phone to call Las Vegas or Miami, for it is there that the ignorant rich take their old bones in air-conditioned cars and recapture youth over the gaming tables or, grotesque in revealing bathing garments, lounge beside the pool, entertained by the Celebrities who sing and dance and crack jokes at considerable profit.

But these talkmasters are but followers and imitators of the greatest of them all, Tom Westbrook. First among them, Westbrook was feared by shady politicians and dishonest police. He was adored by housewives who sometimes called in to say they loved him. He was the simple friend of men who gardened and puttered around the house on weekends removing screens and cleaning drains. He was opposed to cruelty of every description, from the slaughter of birds and animals by poison or firearms, to the dismemberment of cat or dog for the questionable purposes of science. He was the enemy of those fiends who lurk in parks and halls and gratuitously expose their genitals.

His good deeds were many and legendary. He advised would-be suicides to flush away or to vomit up the pill, to apply the tourniquet just above the fresh-slashed wrist. He urged the despairing to take hope and open their eyes to the beauty around them. His compelling voice held them on the wire until the telephone company traced the call and the police carried them off to the sterile ambience of the hospital where they might think better of life or at least consider seriously the horrors that lay just behind it.

Westbrook's mounting influence at City Hall prevented the poor from being cast into the streets. He advised wandering young people to return to their homes. A quality in his voice, an urgent inflection, hinted that he, too, had once been young and troubled, that one needed only to hang on, to "hang in there" — as he had learned to say. He suggested that the impulsive act is prompted by the heart and not the head, that the head must prevail. And his files were thick with letters from the grateful. These he sometimes read over the air, deleting the signatures. No one on his "show" was known by other than initials or a first name. Mr. A. Mrs. B. Confident in their anonymity, Mr. A. and Mrs. B. spoke their minds.

Politicians listened. Sponsors listened. From the stroke of

twelve until six the next morning thousands upon thousands in thirty-eight states attended "Midnight Line" and comfirmed Tom Westbrook's peculiar power at WBOT, Boston.

On the fifteenth of August, shortly after midnight (if his mother's memory was correct), Tom Westbrook was to turn fifty-five. His mother had once mentioned the hour 2:00 A.M. as the exact hour of his birth, an hour more night than day, for day requires the sun or the promise of its imminent appearance. He had heard that most births take place in the early hours of the morning when a woman's body is more relaxed and she can put her whole mind to the thing at hand, and there was no good reason to believe his own birth was any different, especially since he had his mother's word.

Over the years he retained the simple affection for his birthdays that one does for what is peculiarly one's own — the smile in the mirror, the pipe that bears the thoughtful intaglios of one's own teeth. But, as for a child of one's own that has not turned out so well, he had come to regard his birthdays with a certain irritation. Birthdays in the past had promised more. And except for birthdays, he would not now be mired in middle age.

Fifty-five. Older than middle age.

He ate his breakfast when most men sat down to dinner. He showered and shaved when other men began a second cocktail; when others considered dessert or had already gone on to highballs (as they do in New York City), Westbrook brushed from his teeth traces of his breakfast.

He could have worked days, had he wished. He had only to say the word, so absolute was his power.

Long ago in high school, he had learned to type. Out of the red-backed copybook beside the old Remington machine he had typed over and over:

Habits are at first cobwebs; at last, cables.

How true! For his breakfast seldom varied. Toast, coffee, orange juice. Correctly described, his breakfast was orange juice, coffee, and toast, in that order. He did not care for coffee until he'd had his juice — if only a sip. He had found that orange juice prepared his mouth for the comfortable, onlooking taste of his coffee. But with breakfast in mind and the recent nagging concern that he was falling into a rut, he sometimes bought strawberries or even blueberries to carry home when he finished work in the early morning. He bought them not directly after work but after he'd had his "dinner" in one of the big hotels, a meal that amounted to other people's breakfast. The big hotels afforded a menu hearty enough for one who had eaten little but a doughnut and coffee for some eight hours. At the hotels he might choose a small steak, finnan haddie, chipped beef in cream — one hotel he knew browned the butter slightly before the roux was prepared — or kippers with a side order of home fries. His mother, when he was a child, often recommended a bigger breakfast than he had felt like eating, but he liked a big dinner which was now comparable to other people's breakfast. The true breakfast people in the hotels, drugged by sleep or preoccupied with business shenanigans, were quieter than a lunch or dinner crowd. Their tongues and inhibitions had not yet been loosed by drink. Cocktails be-

fore dinner and even cocktails before lunch (in certain lei-
surely occupations) were acceptable, but the man who drinks
before breakfast is on his way out.

In Westbrook's experience, acceptable strawberries are
available only in the first fine days of July; before that, the
berries are not entirely ripe except for those on top, arranged
there to dupe the unwary. Late in July, if the summer is
normal, the hidden berries are perhaps overripe or grow a
musty gray fur. As for blueberries, blueberries are better as a
concept than as an actuality; the wild variety had the happier
flavor, but were seldom available. A dealer had confided that
the young people who used to pick berries out in the woods
would no longer work for a reasonable wage; they preferred
to move into the city and go on welfare. The cultivated berries were larger, prettier in the bowl, but the flavor was dis-
appointing. One's eyes anticipated what the tongue denied.

Now, a decision to buy berries for the next evening's
breakfast opened a regular Pandora's box of confusion. The
market district — the only place open at the early hour he got
off work — was far across town near the wharves in the
shadow of Custom House tower, to the top of which he had
repaired years before to get his first look at the city — his city,
now. Since he found the subway depressing in the morning —
the faces of the passengers stamped with the futility of facing
yet another day — his alternatives were walking or taking a
limousine. He no longer kept a car of his own; he had passed
through the entire sports car business, another segment of the
fulfillment of early dreams, beginning with an MG and end-
ing a few years later with a Jaguar. He smiled now at the gray
suede sports cap he kept in souvenir of that time in his life.

He had learned to raise his hand in greeting when he passed another sports car and never to raise his hand to greet the driver of any automobile of domestic manufacture. But vandals had knifed the leather upholstery of the little black MG and others even more vicious with scarlet paint under pressure had sprayed FUCK on the side of his gray Jaguar. When he had lived on the Hill there were parking problems, words with the police and with neighbors. Dead batteries, snow. Now his lack of a car was no secret. His lack of a car was something of a trademark, and allowed many indigent listeners of "Midnight Line" to identify with him.

It was admittedly absurd to spend three dollars on a limousine simply to be carried to a box of forty-five-cent fruit; it was equally absurd to walk there. A big brown bag of berries was a minor embarrassment when he stopped later at a hotel for his "dinner." Should he check the berries with his topcoat and umbrella? Take them into the coffee shop while he ate? A stranger had once sat on them.

Truly it was a relief at last — comparable to his relief at ridding himself of his own car — to have, at least tentatively, settled on the classic breakfast of orange juice, coffee and toast, a relief to accept the frozen juice and to long no more for the fresh juice that required not only shopping for and buying oranges that were sometimes woody inside, but also complicated modern squeezers. The heavy glass hand-squeezers he recalled were no longer available. His attempt to describe one had left a young clerk shaking his head. Those old squeezers had, in truth, removed only a part of the juice and left one with the untidy problem of pulp and seeds. A more complicated squeezer, called a Dazey, crushed rather than reamed out the fruit, and was so harsh in its action it extracted not only the juice but the bitter oils lurking in the rind.

And it was a relief at last to have accepted instant coffee, bad as it was. He had retired the drip pot and the percolator; neither could be washed carefully enough to remove the rancid oils that attacked and ruined each fresh brew. To his cleaning woman he handed over the last of the glass machines that made fair coffee but sooner or later shattered in the hand.

But why shouldn't a man who paid almost a thousand a month for an apartment in a tall new building have a right to a decent piece of toast? Westbrook liked good bread. He often said so. The appeal of, the longing for, good bread is atavistic — it is not for nothing that bread is described as the staff of life. But that bread available is so often a weak staff — even a dangerous one: he had no use for what he described as mattress stuffing, and had once read that certain dogs, in a controlled experiment, had been fed exclusively on commercial bread, and they had all died.

Fairly good breads had appeared on the market and almost at once had gone commercial; nothing remained of the original idea but the wrapper. He had once discovered a small shop where an enterprising woman came each morning with loaves of bread baked in her own oven, each golden loaf wrapped by hand. It had seemed as if a new day had dawned, that a real bread in even a small market heralded a new era — an era without plastics, fake leather, chromium trim and Madison Avenue deceit — not a new era but an old era of white picket fences, the sound of old-fashioned lawn mowers, of lemonade and band concerts in the park. Dwelling on such homely images, he smiled to himself — he was at bottom a very simple person, with the simplest of wants.

In that brief era of honest bread he had looked forward to making his own toast, watching the slice lower itself into the glowing network of wires; then, after a suitable length of time, he watched it rise slowly into view — hot, golden, fragrant and nutritious. He disliked those first automatic toasters that ticked away like infernal machines and hurled out the toast when you least expected it. He disliked the unexpected. He hated shocks.

But almost before he was ready to admit it to himself, he knew the newfound bread was no longer what it had been. He noticed that it was no longer handwrapped. The woman had got herself a wrapping machine. She had got herself mixed up with the pure-food-and-drug people — the new wrapper admitted that a chemical had been added "to retard spoilage." Spoilage. This bread, then, that had appeared fresh to the touch and to the nose, was not fresh at all. Except for an additive, it would be spoiled and no better for dogs or men than any other.

He had found it good policy, when he finished his "breakfast," to blot up the crumbs with a moist plastic sponge and, while he was about it, to wash, dry and put away his juice glass, cup, saucer and spoon. He imagined that his cleaning woman, on the three days she came to him each week, appreciated the gesture. Since he now buttered his toast directly with the knife he kept with the butter — he had learned to do this without transferring crumbs to the remaining butter —

there was no extra knife to be considered. Last of all, he retired the butter to the refrigerator, a machine that required no defrosting. Musing, he sometimes thought he might go again into English muffins, but since it was almost impossible to cut them into equally thick slices, the thicker of them got stuck inside the toaster and had to be aborted with a kitchen knife. He had read that a man had been so electrocuted — the wife had come upon him dead. If he used the thinner slice in the toaster, the other slice was wasted, and although God knew money was no immediate object, he disliked getting no value for money; he disliked abandoning any principle he had once honored. But sometimes there appeared on his lips a rueful little smile when he considered his passionate concern for tiny details — what was it but a striving to give point and reasonable complication to a life that was, in truth, a life without complication and which sometimes struck him as one that had largely passed him by.

Where, at fifty-five, was he going — and why?

Alas. He had passed as through a curtain the age when life offered challenging complications. The spice had lost its flavor.

And now it was time for the bathroom. His bowels were reliable. He could say that for them. Yes, pleased with his bowels, he subscribed to the Chinese opinion that one was only as fit as one's bowels. His had been unfailingly faithful, thanks, perhaps, to his attention to the leafy vegetables, bulky foods and proper mastication. A man named Fletcher recommended that each bite of food be chewed fifteen times. Fruits, too, had their place. Many men his age were dependent on pills, on milky liquids or turgid oils. Until just recently, his medicine cabinet housed but few drugs, and even now they were but mild ones.

His was a pleasant bathroom. Living on the top floor of a building many floors higher than those around it, he need not draw the draperies to hide his evacuations and ablutions. Through the windows each evening he might see the scarlet reflection of the setting sun on the gilded dome of the State House. One wall of the bathroom was a huge mirror that might have proved embarrassing to a man less well formed than he and — until recently — he had felt no reticence in performing before them a tight schedule of exercises developed by the Canadian Air Force that required tension but virtually no movement. Instructions for performing them had appeared in the *Reader's Digest*. But his hair was graying.

Wall-to-wall carpeting of a warm yellow covered the floor and absorbed his wet footprints, leaving no trace of his passage. Two deep basins were sunk in white marble that rested on ebony chests deeply carved with symbols of the Manchu Dynasty and bound in brass and with brass pulls for the drawers that once, perhaps, had sheltered bolts of silk. The tub was of deep blue porcelain; sliding doors framed with gold plate converted it into a shower should he wish the water to fall on him instead of his being immersed in it. On the whole, he preferred immersion, as more relaxing.

The deep blue porcelain toilet scarcely murmured when flushed — thus no one beyond the closed door need be aware of the disposal of his feces. The toilet was so low that the effort to rise from it showed in the face; one sitting there and suddenly called upon to defend his life might be destroyed before he could get to his feet.

The single disorder in the room was the feature section of the Sunday paper he had abandoned that morning. He leaned now to pick it up. His name was prominent on the first page; as usual, there was no picture of him. No picture of him as a grown man existed.

The care of his teeth was no casual affair. He preceded the actual brushing of them by setting into motion a device his dentist had recommended, a machine that forced swift needles of water through the spaces between his teeth, removing lingering traces of meals that might ordinarily have remained there and fermented. His dentist was opposed to dental floss; if absentmindedly used it pulled out the fillings. Only recently Westbrook had known the real if small despair at feeling with his searching tongue a hole where none had been.

"When you grow older," his dentist had said, "as you age, fillings fall out."

As you age.

Teeth cleansed, he moved into the living room; there he smoked a cigarette. He sat at the mahogany partners' desk that had once belonged to a Brahman, and there he thought to answer his mail.

On that desk were two birthday gifts, returned to their boxes after he had inspected them. Only two people within three thousand miles knew the importance of August fifteenth. Both were women. Both had wormed the date out of him. He had noted the interest of women in other people's birthdays — how they loved buying gifts. How long they took in choosing appropriate cards. On several August fifteenths, each woman in her own time had entered his apartment while he was at work with a key he had himself reluctantly turned over to her for her own use. Each, in her own time, had cooked a birthday dinner and surprised him with gifts. Each expected to spend the night, and did.

Although both now called him from time to time, he no longer saw them, and he had repossessed his keys. In any event, he had had his lock changed, should anyone have had extra keys manufactured while her original key was in her possession. Both women had again embarrassed him with gifts meant for old times' sake. Out of curiosity and not for old times' sake he had opened them when they arrived, refusing to accord them the importance of opening them precisely on his birthday anniversary. As he pulled off the decorated paper he wondered what they had thought would please him — they whom he no longer saw.

The most recent of the women had offered an outsized flask of a cologne made in Italy and available only at a few select men's shops. Since the woman knew he had long settled on that scent and would therefore make certain he had an adequate supply, her gift was not so much a gift as a souvenir, an awkward attempt to recapture an old intimacy, a reminder that it had once been her pleasure to kneel before him and anoint his entire body with the fragrant liquid. But old times were over. It had pressed in upon him that she was much too young for him. He had heard it remarked of another man his age and of an equally young woman — and in a public place — that "he was old enough to be her father." Where once he had been pleased that he could attract anyone so young, he now wondered if he were not now simply a father-image, and he recalled how in a certain bar she had once glanced again and again at a young man her own age who laughed and talked and touched a young woman.

May and December. Well, anyway, October.

The thought was offensive that he be regarded as ridiculous, and although he had been careful where he was seen with her — dark, modest bars where no one went — he began, like an outsider, to regard himself as foolish in prolonging a relationship that could never end in marriage. His one marriage had not worked out. Neither could a second succeed, and for the same reason. He could not — could no longer — sire a child.

So he spoke gently, and had used a paraphrase of the very words that had troubled him, and he smiled.

"Find yourself a man your own age," he'd said, and had felt at once a relief, and a wry pleasure in the renunciation. Like most men, he was uncomfortable in the presence of tears, but he refused to listen to any nonsense. Twenty-two years is a vast and disturbing gulf. "Why," he'd said, "when I'm entering late middle age, you'll still be a fairly young woman."

The second gift on the polished surface of that partners' desk was the more thoughtful, as he'd have expected. The second woman — the first in point of time — had known him more intimately, had been closer to the real Tom Westbrook. She not only knew the date of his birth, but was acquainted with his eating and sleeping habits, his taste in music, and where he enjoyed being touched. Caught up in a brief emotion he thought was gone forever, he had even for a small space of time considered marriage to her, and had allowed her to believe he so considered. But armed with her belief, she began to make plans; among them was his giving up his apartment (on the Hill, then) and moving into the country. That had alerted him. Moving into the country meant she wanted and expected more than sex and companionship. She wanted children, and his failure to impregnate her would render him a laughingstock, particularly since he had deceived her into believing he was fertile by insisting she use a contraceptive device when they lay together.

This woman had now presented him in a chaste box a set of solid gold cuff links from Shreve's. Gold, in these times. Engraved with his initials, they were not impulsive, like the cologne. His own experience with Shreve's — he bought odds and ends there and they had supplied him with the steel die that marked his stationery as his own — his own experience was that initialing required at least five weeks. Everything of so personal a nature requires at least five weeks. Shreve's would not be hurried.

Clever of her — the initials. But for the initials, he'd have returned the gift, and she might have passed it on to another man, or even returned it to Shreve's for a refund, explaining (and he smiled at this) that the one for whom she had intended it was dead. In a sense, he was.

This woman, this older woman, had been the more difficult, had more arguments, was more tenacious, possibly because she was no longer young and saw the specter of loneliness stand naked in the near distance. His own strength, he often thought — he had once thought — was precisely that he needed no one person. But alas, that very strength had attracted many people. Still did.

Her beginning to drink was the beginning of the end. No man is comfortable with a woman who becomes suddenly not herself. A perfectly sober woman's changes in personality are difficult enough. But the loose mouth, like an open purse — the eyes that squint against some fancied brilliance, the exasperating repetitions of word or phrase or idea — these are insupportable. Drunk, she had even threatened blackmail. Most uncharacteristic of her.

And quietly he had pointed out to her the futility of attempts at blackmail. In his position, he was not likely to be damaged by rumors of sexual irregularity so long as it was not perverse. He was not a high school teacher or some professor at the beck and call of PTA or board of governors. He was not a scoutmaster nor was he a minister of the gospel.

"And what's irregular about it?" he had asked her. "I'm single, you're single, and this is hardly the age of Victoria."

And this woman, this mature woman, like the younger woman later on, began her awful weeping.

"We've been so close," she cried.

Ah-ha! But not so close as she'd thought. And he thought it odd how the young, in weeping, look so much younger; and how the old, in weeping, look so antique.

When at last she saw he was unmoved, she went quietly across the room and removed from her purse a sheet of tissue and dabbed at her eyes, a pretty, feminine piece of business meant to prolong the fact of her tears. Just as the filled ashtray means nervousness, so the wielded handkerchief means sorrow. When she had finished, she looked at him strangely, as if seeing him for the first time. There had been something accusing, something almost like a smile on her lips.

"Do you know what you are?" she asked.

"That depends," he said. "That depends on who is doing the judging." And he had reached out to touch her. She drew away.

"I'll tell you what you are," she'd said. "You are a God-damned priest."

He was surprised by her use of the hyphenated adjective, especially in connection with the word "priest." Surprised, because one of the few things apart from sex they shared was their mutual dislike of profanity. Profanity, he had maintained, she had agreed, was the last resort of the ignorant.

But the woman was right. He was like a priest. Had a priest's responsibility. Having a priest's responsibility, it was small wonder he felt more and more the priest in his relationship with women. Ah, yes, he could understand why the Church insisted on the celibacy of priests. Priests cannot allow females to stand between them and their dedication. Yes, he was dedicated. Hoped his dedication to his vast if somewhat ignorant audience justified a certain segment of his past. But then, had not many priests come to their calling because of irregularities in their past?

"Now," he'd said when her tears were absorbed and she'd taken a cigarette and paused for him to light it for her, which he did, "now, if I were you, I'd hike into the bathroom and get yourself fixed up a little. I'll have a drink ready when you're through." As she moved from him, he patted her arm.

"You really believe those people out there need you," she said. He saw no point in drawing to her attention an article in the most recent *Journal of the American Medical Association* pointing out the place of talk shows in the lives of many people — forum, confessional.

He simply smiled at her, and spoke almost humbly. "Yes, and I need them."

And now so much later she still remembered his birthday, possibly grateful to him for how things had turned out. He admitted to feeling a trifle sentimental. Perhaps there was, after all, something to "auld lang syne." A man grows older. The past stretches behind. What lies ahead? At least, one is sure of the past, has known it and has overcome it. Used it. Here and there in his apartment in this drawer and that one were other birthday gifts, all either initialed or of so personal a nature they'd have meant little to another man — raw silk pajamas because cotton disturbed his skin. A sterling Zippo lighter that never failed to offer him its flame.

He removed his eyes from the gifts on his desk, and spent the next few hours reading over and answering his mail.

Half an hour before midnight, he left the apartment.

Only a few years before it had been his pleasure to walk to work. Walking, the soles of his shoes communicating with the sidewalks, he felt a heightened intimacy with the city — his city in a real sense. He was a power and a friend and an influence to thousands upon thousands who trod those same concrete paths. Boston had been good to him, the seat of his power.

But then almost overnight the streets grew dangerous; too many people discontent with not having enough; too many people wanting more than they had or deserved — both despair and greed breed violence. Each morning's papers advertised the muggings and stabbings of the recent night. Crimes went unsolved; their perpetrators still walked abroad.

Now each night the same limousine waited no matter what the weather. The black Continental was privately owned; during the day it was at the service of successful out-of-town salesmen and visiting executives who required more panache than was offered by the common hack. Lord knew how many fares Frank, the owner of the machine, had passed up to be certain that the car would wait as usual half an hour before midnight.

The car glistened. The windows were freshly washed, the passenger space smelled perpetually new — Westbrook suspected some kind of special spray. The ashtrays were clean. In ordinary cabs Westbrook had come upon the unpleasant leavings of strangers.

"Good evening, Frank."

"Evening, Mr. Westbrook."

They maintained a pleasant little formality in spite of Westbrook's knowing something — a good deal — about Frank, the patch of tomatoes in the backyard, Frank's wife's fear of the water and of high places, their plans for retirement to a town on the South Shore nearer their retarded son, a boy of twenty with the mind of a six-year-old. At Christmastime Westbrook handed Frank a hundred dollars and a bottle of good Scots whisky to make the gift more personal and Frank's wife some good piece of costume jewelry from Bonwit's, an establishment she was not likely to know except by reputation. The boy could manage simple kits not much more complicated than Tinkertoys for the construction of airplanes and ships — never any more complicated year after year — and Frank had been kind enough to furnish Westbrook with an enlarged snapshot of the boy, signed by the boy himself in simple block letters FROM BILL. It is seldom one sees such innocent eyes and so guileless a smile. The boy spent the holidays and his birthday with Frank and Frank's wife (who worked in a supermarket doing her part to put together the money they felt was necessary to insure that after their death the boy would not be at the mercy of charitable institutions).

"Oh, he can do lots of things," Frank told Westbrook. "He can shovel snow and pick up around, and all like that." And Frank's eyes mirrored the innocence in his son's eyes in that snapshot, and his face took on the same curious sweetness that one might expect in a friendly dog. Wasn't it strange, as the years passed and he removed himself more and more from direct human contact, that Frank, his driver, had emerged as the one left who knew the most about him — his preference for berries, his brand of cigarettes, his expensive, conservative style of dress?

Now Frank hopped right out and opened the door of the car as if it were a private limousine, which in a sense it was. Driving, Frank did not smoke unless invited, and was silent except to answer questions, sensing that human speech is sometimes distracting.

The eve of Westbrook's fifty-fifth birthday anniversary was hot and humid. The papers had warned of the heat that, moving to the East across the anonymity of the Middle West, had dried up streams, left animals thirsting and crops wilted. Something about disaster areas and the government. Westbrook was grateful that his personal metabolism precluded his feeling the heat. He seldom sweated. His choice of garments was never governed by the warmth of the material of which they were constructed. In the warmest weather, jackets and ties were easy on him.

The streets, preceding midnight, were almost deserted. Frank was taking what they called The Shortcut through a slum neighborhood of brownstone tenements, once the dwellings of a solid middle class that had fled before the strange speech, pigmentation and personal habits of those who had advanced into the city wave upon wave from the frightful conditions of their former lives. Human shapes sprawled on stoops, perched on fire escapes, leaned out from open windows. Streetlamps now here and now there revealed a profile or picked up some cheap bit of jewelry. In the still air there lingered the odor of meals recently cooked for men, for husbands, brothers or lovers returned from second shifts as night watchmen, dishwashers, janitors. The heavy stench of fat, garlic and herbs suggested a colorful poverty and a peculiar relationship with God.

Westbrook snapped his sterling Zippo and brought the flame to a cigarette. "Cigarette, Frank?"

Frank seldom spoke without first slowing the car, knowing that speech might divert his attention from the traffic and the stop lights ahead. "Sir?"

"Cigarette?"

"Thanks, Mr. Westbrook." Frank reached a hand back without taking his eyes from the street before him.

And then the traffic light turned red.

Frank stopped the car so abruptly that Westbrook felt himself thrown somewhat forward. The narrow street was a reminder that once the streets of Boston had been cowpaths. The first-floor windows of the tenements on each side pressed so close that Westbrook could hear the angry flushing of a toilet, and then a fit of coughing so violent the cougher must have been left leaning against the wall for support.

And then — and then from the window opposite came a man's voice — cold and vulgar and level. The window was open, but the man — bent on violence — or the woman — expecting violence — had drawn the yellow shade as if reducing their figures to shadows were sufficient disguise.

"I know what you are," the man said. "And I know where you been." A shadow moved. Sound of fist on flesh and bone. A cry and a groan. The sound hung in the air.

Surely Frank had heard it all. Westbrook would have been grateful had Frank turned with a cynical or comical remark that might have dismissed the incident as common enough, to assess it for what it was — merely another reminder that jealousy and infidelity are everywhere and lead to blows, and are especially common among such people as lived here in tenements or on the edges of nameless towns in shacks and trailers, all those with no Name and no Money, living from hand to mouth and from bed to bed and day to day, who must substitute booze and drugs and violence for hope.

Now, Westbrook was uneasy in the presence of poverty, and yet he himself had saved far too little. His sometimes compulsive spending he justified by reminding himself that as a single, childless man he had no reason to make long-range plans like Frank's. He was responsible only to himself and those few friends he cared to help.

"She had it coming," Frank might have said.

Had it coming.

"Women," Frank might have said.

But Frank remained silent, and silence underlined the incident. Both Frank and he had suddenly become part of the confrontation beyond that dirty yellow shade. He felt that in hesitating he had forfeited his own right to speak, to make light of the thing, but he now felt bound to react in some fashion — maybe because, being human, he could not ignore the human condition. Thus, he leaned forward to crush out the cigarette he'd been smoking when he first heard the man's voice, the guilty cigarette that had prompted him to suggest to Frank that Frank smoke, a suggestion that had made Frank slow the car, and thus they had been halted by a light and had become a party to a brutal tableau.

. . . leaned forward to crush out the cigarette that had led them to this point. It was not a pleasant harbinger of a man's fifty-fifth birthday anniversary.

. . . leaned forward, and was amazed to discover that for the first time the ashtray was so stuffed with a stranger's burnt-out butts there was no room for his single one. He wondered what Frank's excuse might be. Too busy with the tomato plants? Plans for the future? And it takes but a moment to clean out an ashtray.

He flipped the cigarette into the street.

The light turned green.

Shortly, Frank was opening the door of the limousine.

Westbrook got out, as he had time and time again, but now he felt a compulsion to alter the direction of his life, if ever so slightly.

"Frank," he said, "you'll be free at six this morning?"

"I'll see that I am."

"I want to go to the market for berries," Westbrook said.

"You can count on me, Mr. Westbrook," Frank said.

But not, Westbrook thought, to remember to empty the ashtray.

Frank drove off around the corner, the taillights of the car a reminder of another red light. Westbrook turned and walked into a building known as the Tower, something of a symbol of the New Boston, his Boston. Except for a prowling security officer, the vast lobby of square columns and polished granite was deserted, alive with a vaulting, cathedral-like silence. His footsteps echoed on the walls and multiplied as lighted candles breed and multiply in a hall of mirrors.

He entered the empty elevator. He rose in it, his face suddenly expressionless, as aloof and withdrawn as if even in an empty cage he must protect his identity. Thirty floors up the door slid open. A second security officer spoke softly and raised a hand in greeting and walked deferentially ahead to open the heavy glass doors into a carpeted reception room large enough to accommodate two islands of functional Scandinavian furniture spaced to insure the privacy of conversation. The heavy clear glass ashtrays were clean, ready for the use of authors, wardens of prisons, directors of mad houses, clergymen, fund-raisers, politicians and sponsors.

Westbrook, as was his custom, raised his eyes to the full-length portrait that dominated the room, a fine likeness of the former manager — his old employer. It had been painted from photographs and snapshots shortly after the Old Man's death, and paid for by voluntary contributions from everybody including the charwomen to whom the Old Man had sometimes sent candy and flowers and to whom Westbrook still did in memory of the Old Man.

The Old Man had grown up with radio, had first broadcast from a single room over a grocery store, had been his own engineer, had solicited his own advertising for the upstart business called Radio. The Old Man had been as common as an old shoe. A visiting Englishman, it was said, had mistaken the Old Man for the janitor. It was the Old Man who had discovered Westbrook, had noted the attractive quality in Westbrook's voice, and had brought him to Boston from a struggling little station in Connecticut where Westbrook first worked after coming East from Montana. The Old Man had recognized Westbrook's as a voice that had only to recommend a product to sell it. It was a far more commanding voice than the intimate whisper used by so many to sell laxatives and panty hose. It was a trained voice with music in it, and not precisely the voice he was born with. A professor of speech at Harvard had pleased Westbrook by remarking that he thought it interesting that Westbrook had no accent at all, if by accent one meant a local peculiarity of tone, pitch and slovenly vowels.

The professor had just accepted a canapé of thin-sliced ham wrapped about a dab of cream cheese. "Your voice is pure phonetics," the man insisted. "I doubt that anybody hearing it could place your hometown within a thousand miles."

Hometown, Westbrook thought. What a curious, homely phrase on the lips of so polished a professor with leather patches on his elbows, and how it brought back to Westbrook, somewhat without welcome, Grayling, Montana.

"I shouldn't go so far as to say that," Westbrook smiled.

To a degree, the Old Man had looked on Westbrook as a son. They lunched often together — when the Old Man lunched out at all — in a dismal little hole-in-the-wall the Old Man fancied because the stew was good. It was over a lunch that the Old Man had asked him point-blank what, in his opinion, would get radio out of a bad rut. Radio, unable to rely on novel visual effects, was losing ground to television as once the phonograph had lost ground to radio. It is so much easier for the rabble of the world to use their eyes than to use their ears.

"What's the answer, Tom? Shock stuff? controversy?"

"Controversy, yes. But we'd have to get around the FCC. But I've got a hunch there's another answer." Westbrook's answer seems obvious now, just as the paper clip seems obvious in the wake of its invention. "The answer is, let people talk."

"Talk?"

"Just talk. People want to talk. People hate silence. When they talk they feel they're being something, contributing, no longer ciphers. Making their voices heard is something like their writing their names on toilet walls. They're creating when they write and they're creating when they talk, and in forming opinions they're even creating when they listen to other people."

"Hold on," the Old Man said. "How many would talk, speak their minds, the minds they want to speak — with a million others listening?"

"The law doesn't require they give their full names," Westbrook said. "You can get by with initials. Mr. Adams won't speak his mind, but Mr. A will, and so will Mrs. B."

The Old Man grinned and said he'd be a son of a bitch. "And it would be cheap, too."

Westbrook had laughed out loud at that. They'd often joked about how tight the Old Man was. Oh, he often brought his lunch to the station in a paper bag, the cold grease of a joint of fried chicken soaking through. "No more expense than my salary as moderator, or whatever you want to call me, and the price of a few new telephone circuits. I don't think we'd even need an engineer, but we'd have to look into the unions about that."

Together they worked out a program, the first of what was later called a talk show. It was heard at first in the daytime, but Westbrook knew that the night is the lonely time. He knew that darkness magnifies loneliness, that in the night voices long to call out to other voices.

That was the beginning of "Midnight Line."

Now the Old Man was dead, and his likeness up there on the wall. The network, with headquarters in New York, had brought in a man over the heads of equally efficient men

Westbrook knew and could work with. As the station's biggest attraction, as the Master of "Midnight Line," he was riled that he had not been consulted. And the new man was not a New York man as might have been expected. No. The new man was from right there in Boston. This new man was Old Boston and, smiling, Westbrook had disliked him at once. The man's name was Edwards. Sewall Edwards. Oh, yes, Edwards was efficient. God knew he was. Edwards had spent previous years untangling the murky affairs of insurance companies. He looked on radio as a business like any other — not as a business that was at least half public service and heart — a lifeline to the lonely and disturbed.

Westbrook believed the man had been hired to lend an Old Name to a comparatively new business. A rough-and-tumble business, appealing chiefly to the middle and lower classes, the lace curtain and the shanty, the new Frigidaire and the bottle-of-milk-on-the-windowsill — perhaps radio did suffer from a lack of respectability in the eyes of some people.

And Edwards was respectable. It was rumored that he counted Jonathan Edwards himself among his ancestors. Ah-ha! Westbrook had seen photographs of Sewall Edwards in the papers — he and his wife at the yacht club; he and his wife in the lobby at Symphony. One photograph in the Sunday supplement that particularly had irritated Westbrook was of Edwards attending his Harvard reunion. Edwards had his arm about the shoulder of his son. The boy, perhaps fifteen, was surely bound for Harvard, and without doubt already knew how to bring a sloop about. What irritated Westbrook was that this display of fatherly affection was deliberate, done for the cameras, meant to reveal a side of Edwards that Edwards felt unnecessary to show to those who worked under him.

The Old Man's office had originally been a storeroom. It had no windows; the only air came from a shaft that housed a dumbwaiter and was moved about by an electric fan. The light came from a naked bulb overhead and a brass goose-necked lamp on the desk. And on the desk was the Old Man's Remington typewriter with the carriage return on the right-hand side that must be approached with a motion something like the backstroke in swimming. That and the two wire In and Out baskets and a small safe over in the corner where the Old Man kept locked up his good Scots whisky. Westbrook and a handful of others were privy to the combination.

Now, Edwards at once had furnished for himself on the top floor of the building an elegant little office reached only by private elevator. Mahogany paneling, Persian rugs, hurricane lamps. A tall clock told the phases of the moon. Paintings of sailing ships that other Edwardses had sailed to China.

From this upper room — Upstairs, they called it — Edwards sent down bulletins by a lackey (a relative of his, it was said) who tacked them up on a new bulletin board and woe to him who did not heed them. Those who did not heed them were "called Upstairs" — a euphemism for being discharged, fired, sacked. Those unfortunates got their first and certainly their last look at that precious little office.

Bulletin Number One: the staff, from file clerk up, was to appear for work half an hour early, for possible briefings. Briefings. Westbrook hated the word. Everybody was to sign in so the man Upstairs would know where everybody was. WBOT had become a factory.

In the old days, the good old days, everybody arrived at the last minute, huffing and puffing with excuses, but they did arrive. Except for Westbrook, the employees were rather poorly paid and thus felt they had a right to treat their jobs somewhat cavalierly, and like newspaper reporters they felt themselves a strange breed, and were proud of their difference from other men.

Bulletin Number One, was it? Well, Westbrook continued his old haphazard pattern.

Bulletin Number Two: the new policy of the station was to be based on Good Taste. It was Edwards's belief that the public nurtured a nostalgia for the past. Instead of competing with television, he would take radio back to the dark ages. He revived a Theater of the Air. He negotiated contracts with orchestras that played in big hotels, searched for new Ben Bernies, comedians with stooges. He planned stories for children, expecting stories to compete successfully with television cartoons and space-age heroics. Ah, but Westbrook could imagine Edwards as a child, a golden-haired child listening rapt while someone, some nanny, read from *Treasure Island* or the Jungle books or maybe *Billy Whiskers in France.*

"God help us," Westbrook had remarked to one newscaster, "it wouldn't surprise me if he revived 'Amos n' Andy.' But of course nowadays 'Amos n' Andy' wouldn't be in Good Taste."

It was clear that Bulletin Number Two about Good Taste was aimed at Westbrook. Only recently "Midnight Line" had concerned itself with police brutality, a subject that struck close to City Hall. Two blacks had been hosed down until they had almost drowned. It was not Bad Taste that Edwards minded, the hypocrite. What Edwards minded was disturbing City Hall and The Powers That Be.

And so Westbrook's immediate response to Bulletin Number Two was to broach the subject of homosexuality on "Midnight Line," and for the first time in radio history the word was thrown out over the air, and that word was heard in thirty-eight states. It pried up a stone and out from underneath something pale and terrible crawled forth into the sunlight visible even to the chaste eyes of Middle America.

Mr. A. called in to say that if a queer touched him, he would knock his teeth out. Indeed, he had been approached by one, and indeed he had all but kicked his teeth out. That's all Mr. A. had to say, but he'd say it again anytime, anywhere.

Mr. C. thought perhaps Mr. A. was overreacting to the situation, that perhaps he kicked teeth in because he was afraid of the same thing in himself?

Mr. A. had no way to answer this ugly charge, since callers were forbidden to phone in more than once a night.

Mrs. B. came to Mr. A.'s defense: if her own son were that way, she'd rather see him dead.

Mrs. D. wondered, if it came to that, if Mrs. B. would be the one to kill him?

Mr. F. identified himself as a psychiatrist. He had successfully treated, so he said, a number of homosexuals. By successfully, he meant that on leaving him they had married. He saw no reason for people to remain homosexuals. If they did, it was perverse of them, and they simply didn't want help.

Mr. G. likewise identified himself as a psychiatrist. He said Mr. F. spoke sheer hogwash. If they didn't want help, why had they come to Mr. F.? Mr. G. said deviants could no more be changed than the color of their eyes could be changed, that marriage was no escape and only compounded the tragedy and often led to suicide, as Mr. F. damned well knew.

And then the Love that dare not speak its name was itself — speaking.

The queers called in, called from the public telephones in the bars where they went to meet and to choose each other. The telephone picked up the faint music of "My Funny Valentine." They called from their hideaways of ice-cream-parlor chairs, Tiffany glass, paper lanterns, arrangements of peacock feathers and Marlene Dietrich recordings. They told tales of childhood, every day a small Gethsemane, of hiding from the other boys at recess, terrified of the jeering mob who cried out "Sissy!" because of the way they walked and pronounced the letter S. Sissy! And on them were pinned girlish names, Clarice, Minerva — yes, the mob recognized them before they recognized themselves in their failure at games and their running from fights, their unaccountable interest in fabrics and in flowers. And then later wondering whether it was worth it to touch — to touch — and risk the kick in the teeth.

And when did they know — when did they know they were what they were that the mob instinctively knew?

Mr. X. said he knew when he was fifteen.

How did Mr. X. know?

He knew because he wanted to kiss a man.

But it was worse than the public had imagined. The Kinsey Report said one in seven was queer. One in seven?

Mrs. S. had the figures right there before her. Almost twenty-nine million people were queer. Whom could you trust to be not queer? When seven men gathered together in a room or on the subway, one of them was queer.

No one could be trusted. Why, Mr. Z. had been married twenty years, had three daughters and a son, and no one knew but his lover.

Bad taste? Two big papers in Boston and two in New York thought otherwise.

TOM WESTBROOK'S TALK SHOW SLAUGHTERS A SACRED COW.

Westbrook could not but despise Edwards for not calling him Upstairs. It was clear it was not Bad Taste Edwards was worried about now. It was losing an audience.

The following of "Midnight Line" swelled. Westbrook had given the people out there a glimpse of a real if shadowy world, and had comforted troubled mothers who, unlike Mrs. B., did not care to see their sons dead, no matter what. So many, it seemed, were in the same boat, and as shipmates at least did not despise each other.

HAS WESTBROOK FREED RADIO?

Had radio suddenly shot ahead of television because anonymity is almost impossible on television?

And now Westbrook, and partly for reasons of his own, attacked the laws against abortion. Abortion! The very word evoked images of Dickensian squalor — the dark alley, the drop-light over the kitchen table, dirty hands, hatpins and hooks fashioned from coat hangers, blood poisoning and murder and the unborn child. Furtive graves where the wind sighs and the whisper of money changing hands.

Westbrook was not called Upstairs. Edwards knew that the power of the Little People, safe and strong and terrible in their anonymity, was greater than the formal power of priests and bishops and judges. To fire Westbrook would bring down around Edwards's ears the wrath of ten million troubled insomniacs who knew the world was sick beyond belief, but it was still the world, and theirs to inherit.

On the now-deserted reception desk just under the portrait of the Old Man, a vase held three roses. Each morning at nine a florist delivered them, an outward and visible sign of Edwards's Good Taste — not a dozen, nothing gaudy like that, but three, possibly an expression of some arcane Trinity Edwards revered. Three perfect roses. Visitors would take away a memory of them — singular because they were so few.

Edwards, Edwards the Brahman.

But it was not simply atavistic dislike of Edwards and the elegant little office upstairs and three perfect roses somewhat passé now as midnight approached — not simply this that compelled Westbrook to discuss what he pleased over the air and to arrive for work precisely when he wished. It was far more complicated than that. For more than twenty years now, Westbrook had been followed — dogged — by a shadow that insisted he was a man who had always been free to act exactly as he wished.

Now on the eve of his fifty-fifth birthday, the shadow still with him, he walked down a corridor past glassed-in cubicles. In one of them a man sat reading news into a microphone. The news was as usual: birth and deceit; coupling and death.

He walked on down and entered the last cubicle. It was as austere as the confessional, as functional as the death chamber. On the desk was a small black box, a console housing little lights that glowed when the telephones were alive. A switch, and several buttons. One of them, when pressed, stopped the tape on which a caller's voice was recorded just ten seconds before — it was the tape and not the actual voice that was heard on the air. Thus, profanity and abuse that might otherwise fly out all over America could be halted, silenced. Many of his callers thrilled at speaking foully. They exposed their language as others might expose their private parts.

The desk was in perfect order. Westbrook kept it so himself. Aware that objects on his desk had been moved, if ever so slightly, perhaps by the janitor, he had had the lock on the door replaced. He alone had the key.

He sat down. He glanced at the clock high on the opposite wall. Three minutes to midnight.

From a drawer in the dark he removed a fresh pack of cigarettes. He allowed himself exactly twenty cigarettes each working period of six hours and was so scrupulously fair in allowing himself each one, he smoked the last and carefully crushed the empty pack just as the hour of six fell due.

The warning on the cigarette pack could not be ignored, however small the print — maybe because of the smallness of the print — that the Surgeon General had determined that cigarette smoking is dangerous to your health, but he hoped to some degree to circumvent the opinion of the Surgeon General by smoking a brand with a triple filter: one filter to retard the tars and nicotines, a second to render less harmful certain lethal gases, and a third to dilute the dangerous smoke with healthful air. As a further safeguard, he used a disposable filter that cooled the smoke by a process that was not clear to him. Perhaps the Surgeon General, aware of how cautious he was, would give his own smoking the green light.

But recently the unpleasant thought kept intruding that he really should give up smoking; having constantly to consider the delicate balance between the pleasure of smoking and the possibility of death made him nervous and irritable. He would not, perhaps, so have disliked the idea of death if he were convinced he had any sort of immortality. Sometimes on a clear evening the everlasting stars and planets in their perfect order and infinity rejected the finality of death, but then, there are the hateful changes to hair and skin, the loss of teeth and the withering of flesh. There are the obituary columns, and the earlier frantic giving to charities.

By this I will be remembered.

Who would remember him? Not his audience — not really. Not after a short period of time, for they were fickle. He was a realist. Who would remember him? The woman who had sent him the cuff links? He must remember to call her.

He lighted the cigarette with his silver Zippo. In three minutes, he spoke.

"Tom Westbrook here. Welcome to 'Midnight Line.' "

Out in the dark they reached for the telephones, the sick, the troubled, the crippled, the brokenhearted, the lonesome ones who for company and for therapy and hope depended on Westbrook and on "Midnight Line."

II
_____

THEY CALLED from their beds; they called from all-night bars and from telephones down the hall. They pulled in at pay phones, struck by some word of Westbrook's that sparked memory or prejudice. They reached out their hands for the telephone — hands that had touched hands, hands rendered clawlike with arthritis, hands that made love, felt the hot cheek of a sick child, or touched in prayer; hands that guided the old to the chamberpot and once, long long ago, had crushed a fragrant leaf between thumb and finger and lifted it to the curious nose. Young hands, veined hands soiled with liver spots, hands to comfort and to murder. The long thin hands of Mr. C.

"Mr. C., you're on 'Midnight Line.' "

Some years before, when his audience had yet no character of its own, Westbrook like a schoolmaster had assigned topics for discussion. He guided their thoughts and their tongues, suggested something read in the papers that might move them to thoughts of their own — local politics, housing conditions and the soaring price of red meat that Americans regard as their birthright. As an announcer, he had been trained to avoid dead air, the silence with nothing going on in it. Familiar topics would lend them the courage to call in and keep the air alive.

When he had established himself as a man with vast patience that they took for understanding — when they felt they could trust him, he introduced livelier subjects of a more personal nature. Monday, he announced, they would talk about adoption. Should a child ever be told it was adopted?

Ah, he had never believed there were so many adopted children — grown up now, and longing to talk. They had longed for or loathed the image of the mother who had abandoned them, or hated the shadowy father who had caused the mother to abandon them. That mother who had loved the father more than she had loved them.

And the long-lost mothers called in. How they had grieved, especially at Christmastime. A mother still hung up a stocking for the lost child.

His audience leaped like fish to the bait of Honesty. Behind initials, safe from the cold and searching eye of the Internal Revenue Service, they admitted to cheating, and anyway they didn't like what the government did with the money, handing it out to people who wore better clothes than they, people with no pride, with their hands always out. All these people moved into the city and spoiled the neighborhoods. It was no wonder how everything was — a President who got rich in office and had swimming pools and special lighting and golf carts the people paid for, and lying and paying out hush money. What kind of example was he to the American people? They should be allowed to deduct him from their income tax.

Mr. C. did not cheat on his tax because he was afraid to cheat. His brother-in-law had a nice little business and a snowmobile he used in New Hampshire, but he had been caught and ruined.

Mrs. D., at the age of ten, had stolen from her mother's pocketbook, and she later stole Fatima cigarettes and went to a girl's house and they smoked them and played a record called "I Met a Million-Dollar Baby in a Five-and-Ten-Cent Store." They don't write music like that anymore, and the young people today are all losing their hearing. After that the Depression came and they all went to live with Daddy's people outside of Lincoln, Nebraska. No matter what direction you looked, there was nothing.

They cheated on their wives and on their husbands because they were lonely or nobody understood or they were sick of everything because you thought things were one way and they were another, because nobody told you the truth. They had not told the truth because it would only hurt the husband or the wife or the children, and what people don't know won't hurt them.

At the end of six hours on the air, Honesty appeared to be but a relative term. Sometimes you were honest and sometimes not. You lied because you wanted to save somebody's skin, very often your own.

As time passed, then, the followers of "Midnight Line" no longer wanted a schoolmaster. They no longer needed the group security they had found in discussing a common subject. Now each wanted to be heard as an individual. Each wanted a single confidant, a priest. "Midnight Line" became an open forum.

As the exact hour of Westbrook's birthday anniversary approached, the air crackled with life. The five little lights before him glowed.

An educated woman called. She was prompted to raise her voice because the President of the United States, having surrounded himself by criminals (as she saw it) as advisers, had committed yet another indecency. Why was the House, she asked, so tardy in starting proceedings to oust the man from office and jail him? The House as a whole was apparently a true reflection of the mediocrity who elected it.

J. W. agreed. The President himself was a true mediocrity — but not a timid one by a long shot. In a nation of timid mediocrities, even small guts loomed large and gave the President the desperate courage of a cornered rat, the sharp little teeth bared, the tiny eyes glittering with hate.

Mrs. P. identified herself as a young housewife. What that profession required of her she left to the imagination, but certainly it entailed more than moving about the house straightening flowers and pillows and bearing food home from the A&P.

Wishing to be more in the thick of things, she had vowed to walk to Washington to protest the war in Viet Nam. Westbrook recalled her brief publicity, her picture in the *Globe* as she moved out in sturdy shoes, bearing a Cub Scout's backpack containing her toothbrush, her comb, and her money and emergency food. Heftier rations she expected from sympathizers along the way, and in their houses she would spend the nights. She traveled Routes 9 and 20 through Marlboro with its lovely old homes, its pillars and fanlights, landmarks of a gracious, easier America.

Over the weekend, she made forty miles.

Ah, but when we set out to do fine things, we run into snags, the imponderables — the bad dogs. The dogs, being beasts, could be expected neither to understand the nature nor the importance of her journey. Rather, they wished to molest her, snapping and snarling; not even her gentle sex recommended her to them. In Worcester, therefore, she paused at a hardware store where she equipped herself with a device shaped like a phallus that shot forth crippling fumes, and a hunting knife.

On Sunday her husband, a good man, if not so hotheaded politically, drove out in his car to accompany her a while.

How were her feet? he inquired. How were her heels holding up? What did she require?

Nothing, she assured him, and her heels were splendid. And things at home? Did the plants want water? Had he got to the dump Saturday, and who was there?

But traveling with her was awkward. In no gear would his vehicle crawl slowly enough to accommodate her mild speed. There was nothing for it but to shoot ahead of her and wait and smoke, or wait until she got ahead, and then overtake her. Certain other travelers were curious, suspecting she had perhaps been turned out of the car following domestic trouble, the wrong word at the wrong time; or perhaps she had lost something, an earring, say, and searched for it along the way.

"The dog misses you," he told her.

The third night out, she was turned away from several houses, even from those whose tenants were aware, through television, of her pilgrimage, for no matter how pure people's beliefs might be, however inflamed they were over the progress of the war or the President's imperial activities, the arrival at night of a stranger destroys the order in a house. The bathroom requires explanation. A stranger is liable to make toll calls. And make toll calls she did — embarrassed, hesitant, offering of course to pay, but knowing full well how people feel about toll calls even if they are not financially accountable for them. Toll calls!

When at last she crossed over the Connecticut border, her husband put his foot down. She had made her point, he said, and he worried. He didn't know what to say at the office. But it had all worked out all right. The following week a cease-fire was signed, or whatever you do with them, and she was proud of her part in it and saved the clippings.

A veteran of the conflict called in to say he had been left with no legs, from the hips down. His trunk alone remained. He would appreciate it if those who had time to write to him at the hospital where he must spend the remainder of his life would do so. Only at that hospital could they handle him. No, he could not agree with the housewife who had walked into Connecticut that the war was useless. If the war was useless, what was the use of his lost legs? If you had but one leg, as his friends had, you could learn to keep your balance on a false leg, or so they said. Strange to think of, now, when so much had changed, but he had once had a boat, a rowboat, and he had used it summers and weekends from the time he was a child. Why, he could still see the early sun flash across the flat surface of that pond. And he knew secret places on the shore — you know how a kid has secret places? Rowing had so developed his arms and shoulders that now he had but little trouble pushing himself about on the platform with swivel wheels the orderlies would sometimes help strap him into.

Anybody can understand how a man wants to marry and have a wife and kids to teach about boats and save up for them because that's what a man does, leave things better than it was for him. You see, that way, they have somebody and you have them. That's the way it is, you know.

All the time he was over there in Asia he thought about how she was buying things they would have together later in their house and she wrote him about them, the sheets and the pillowcases that in the states wouldn't be very interesting but over there it was. She was a teller in a bank and very pretty to look at. The bank liked her and paid her the same even if she was a woman.

Luckily she had been told what had happened to him before she came to the hospital to see him, so he didn't have to, and she could have got over her shock and it wouldn't show so much in her eyes. He could understand why it took her so many days to come to him, because she had to make up her mind. He was all shaved for her and with some Old Spice from a buddy that his girl had given him.

Well, she smiled and smiled and held his hand, but he noticed her eyes moved to where his legs would have been.

A man's legs are so much a part of him. They move him about to do a man's business, and without legs it is difficult to mate in the usual way, the burden is on the woman, and she would be thinking that she was not mating with a whole man instead of what he should be, a man who didn't need shoes.

He thought it over and because he loved her he quarreled with her the next time and called her a terrible name, about how he knew what she was up to while he was over there, a letter came to him about it, he said. He called her that name. He said he didn't love her, never had, only wanted one thing. It was the hardest thing he ever did. Oh, but he got nasty. She cried, and he cried when she left, but we must face things. He did sometimes still dream of her and of being married and having a wife and kids, so there would be somebody and they could all go out in the boat.

Once Westbrook had been married. Because he wanted a son, a Westbrook to stand between him and loneliness and death and oblivion that were the core of his nightmares, he had married.

There had seemed to be no hurry. At forty his skin was taut, his muscles hard, thanks to those exercises. He waited for the "proper" time. The proper time was when he had his feet on the ground.

For fifteen years after leaving Grayling, Montana, he did not honestly feel he had his feet on the ground. Two of these years he had spent at Emerson College, training his voice, tempering it, modulating it, learning breath control and how to pronounce all foreign languages. He'd read aloud, throwing his voice from his diaphragm, and while at Emerson he'd been approached by a woman teacher who was interested in the blind, and for her he read and recorded certain short stories selected because of their cheerful nature. The small fee she offered was the first money he had earned. He paid great attention to timing; he learned to isolate the important word, and to linger over a pleasant phrase that made a paragraph unique. Handed a routine piece of news, he could transpose it at once into something quite his own. He picked up tricks that set his style apart. A significant pause before the last word of a sentence — and then placing a rising inflection on the word, but careful to avoid a mannerism.

After graduation came eight years of barnstorming — Albany, Springfield, Bridgeport, Hartford — and finally a small local station where he was something of a big frog in a small puddle. His colleague there had been with the station ten years; it was clear nothing would become of this man whose booming, pompous voice smacked of old-fashioned oratory. The cruel called him Bryan, behind his back. Westbrook kept this fellow at a distance — he disliked the company of failures quite as much as he disliked poverty. Failure and poverty, like odors, cling to the fabric of clothing. Failures require special handling, and must be treated with the same difficult delicacy one accords cripples.

And then one day the Old Man heard Westbrook, and called him to WBOT in Boston.

He gave the Old Man a few months to get to know him and to appreciate his work. Then he spoke frankly to the Old Man of his desire to marry.

"I wanted to speak to you first," he told the Old Man, "because I don't want to get involved in anything so permanent as marriage without knowing my position here is secure."

The Old Man had looked at him a moment, and then said, "Well, I'll be God-damned if you're not a one. But you go right ahead, Tom. I don't make mistakes, hiring announcers."

Westbrook did not much care for drinking and preferred a good sherry when he did — Dry Fly in a cocktail sherry and Harvey's Bristol Cream in a sweet. Almadén out in California offered a fine domestic sherry — something about setting the casks out on the roof and letting the sun get at them. But now he accepted invitations to parties — a good many of them given and peopled by politicians who were on the make and intellectuals who were curious about the shady world of professional radio. Westbrook looked about him. He was attracted to Marge by her extraordinary grooming and attention to style; he felt he need not be ashamed of her in any group he cared to enter. Her dark hair shone from what he found later to be daily washings. Her hands and nails were perfect — the nails not so long as to indicate undue concern nor so short as to hint that she bit them. The seams of her stockings ran straight; her jewelry was simple and correct — she seldom wore more than a single piece at a time and earrings, never. She wore her glasses only for reading, and her engaging manner of holding them to her eyes like a lorgnette when she examined a menu, he found engaging. During her time in junior college she had been in love with Modern Dance — that showed in her easy walking style, her posing, her arresting an attractive gesture, as if listening for the click of a shutter. She might have danced professionally, but realized that to dance professionally meant abandoning a normal life. He admired her setting aside a brief if glorious self-indulgence for normal life — sex sanctioned by God, children, and well-balanced meals.

Before their marriage, she was at Bonwit's with reason to believe she would shortly be a buyer; he was proud she would relinquish her future for his, but as she said, a buyer's was not a normal life: the backbiting and the — well — the arrangements so many used to advance themselves.

She loved radio — he was reading news then. "Little did I know!" Little did she know she and the man whose voice she fancied would be one flesh.

One flesh! He was pleased she was a virgin now when everybody sleeps with everybody, but it was good to know the mother of his son had never been entered by other than he.

How had she remained a virgin until thirty?

She had laughed. "Too busy otherwise!"

Well, he'd been busy too. Too busy to marry until he was forty — in his prime. He confided his future plans, and how he'd told the Old Man about his plan to marry.

She had laughed. "What a funny thing to do," she said. "Usually a man falls in love first, and then might speak to his boss."

He disliked the word "boss." He preferred "employer." The word should have warned him of something coarse in her, but a man about to marry does not think straight.

Neither of them believing in God, they married at City Hall before a few people from Bonwit's and WBOT. Marge thought it would be fun to have a drink at the Merry-Go-Round Bar. Westbrook wondered if she feared being alone with him. He wanted to get on with it, had prepared himself for sex by reading a manual recommended by a doctor friend, and for days previous to his marriage he watched his diet, that his seed be potent.

For Marge and himself he ordered sherry.

"I don't know," she said, avoiding his eyes. "I think I want an Irish coffee."

Irish coffee! If there is a drink inappropriate at noon, it is Irish coffee. Was her poise a façade? Was this the first crack? Was she bent on badgering him? True, ordering Irish coffee may have been but a symptom of nerves; possibly she feared her first sexual encounter. He wished she had gone along with sherry until they were alone. Her sudden yen for the drink might be taken by his friends and hers as the first rift in their relationship, and her friends and his might begin to gossip. He loathed gossip, never indulged in it, never carried tales. It made him uncomfortable to think anyone noticed his personal life, let alone spoke of it.

They spent three expensive nights at the Copley Plaza upstairs over the Merry-Go-Round Bar. "As long as we're here, we might just as well stay upstairs," Marge said. "Then we won't have to move so far." These remarks were taken by her friends as unbearably witty. They writhed in laughter, and when their laughter had subsided they shrugged their shoulders, showed the palms of their hands and wagged their heads as if to say, Well, that's Marge for you.

Marge, indeed! She was drunk when she left the slowly revolving platform of the Merry-Go-Round Bar. She had removed and briefly lost her shoes.

Upstairs, their sex went well. He went after it slowly as the manual instructed, but her cries and pleasure were hardly virginal.

Their suite had a faded elegance — green plush and threads of gold enhanced the draperies. In the marble fireplace was a gas log. He liked things he had paid for to work; he knelt before it to light it. It looked as much like a log as the ironmonger's art allowed. Where the false knots protruded and along the ripply ridges of the false bark almost invisible holes allowed the escape of a combustible gas. Suspending disbelief, as one must in the theater or at night on viewing the miracle of the heavens, one might imagine a true oak log burning merrily and feel it cast off discernible heat, once the thing was lighted.

Marge, quite naked, sat up in the bed. "I wouldn't light it, if I were you."

He very nearly snapped, But you are not I.

"They blow up," she said.

Her remarks said she believed she had had more experience with good hotels and with gas logs than he had, and cast doubts on his knowledge of physics.

"We'll just see if this one blows up," he said. He lighted a match from the packet the hotel had furnished, and brought it close to the imagined log. He opened the butterfly valve.

The report was like a pistol shot.

Then came a knocking at the door.

And a voice requiring to know if everything was all right in there.

"Just a minute, just a minute," Westbrook shouted, and there was all that humiliating scurrying and dressing and pulling things up.

"I thought I heard a shot," the old bellboy said, sniffing to detect the odor of gunpowder, but it was clear that no one was dead, not even in the bathroom.

"It was only the gas log," Westbrook said.

"I told him not to try to light it," Marge said.

"They don't work good," the bellboy said.

But to Westbrook it was not the appearance of the old bellboy that was so awful, but the fact that when he leaped back naked after the explosion, Marge had shouted with laughter. He could see he was going to have a time with her.

However.

It was with Marge that he first explored Beacon Hill and Louisburg Square. They were so charmed by the location that they took an apartment on West Cedar Street, very small, but with an iron balcony one could crawl out the window and stand on, and a small fireplace they fed with small bundles of fragrant wood they bought on Charles Street for a dollar and a half for five sticks. Both realized they must move as soon as she was pregnant.

They talked. They thought perhaps something in the country, some nice old house in Sudbury off in the trees that something could be done with. They'd restore it themselves.

Respecting her virginity, he had not insisted on sleeping with her before their marriage, and thus he knew nothing of her personal habits. Since he knew nothing of marriage and had the example of his recently dead mother's passionate neatness before him, he was astounded at how untidy a woman could be. With Marge, it was apparently a matter of public poise and private disorder. She appeared on the street as if she'd stepped out from a bandbox. What she left behind, the awful machinery of her stylishness, was appropriate to a pigsty.

Item: she never shut a drawer. Over its lips as from an untidy mouth slopped her leavings. Item: she washed out underthings in the bathroom and hung them so they brushed against his bare skin as he passed in to bathe or to relieve himself. Because hair is of so personal a nature, he did not suggest to her that she brush her head hard before washing it and remove loose hairs that plugged the drain. Obviously she did not know as he knew that the normal head sheds eighty hairs each day. He could imagine nothing more offensive than human hair that is not attached to its source, and must be pulled from the drain with a hook made from a coat hanger.

She never capped a toothpaste tube, nor did she roll up the tube as the paste was used. Rather, she twisted it until paste escaped through the breaks. Uncapped, the paste hardened at the tip of the tube; too much pressure on the tube and the obstruction was released so suddenly the paste shot forth like an orgasm.

Cigarettes she stubbed out in ashtrays continued to smolder. She removed her shoes the moment she entered the apartment, sighing as she did so. She hopped on one foot while she removed the other shoe; she often went barefoot around the place the entire weekend. He had never much liked the shape of the human foot. Her expensive shoes, bought at a discount at Bonwit's, were in random piles on the floor of their common closet. It sometimes took her five minutes to find two that matched. She found his expensive wooden shoe trees amusing. These he inserted in his shoes as soon as he had removed his feet. Any man knows shoe trees maintain the singular shape of his shoes.

"I never knew a man who used shoe trees," she had said, grinning. "I thought shoe trees went out with Paris garters." Small wonder he wondered if she were, after all, a virgin, having known so many men she could set apart a group who did not use shoe trees. For the life of him, he could see nothing amusing about shoe trees.

"Well," he told her, "I never before knew a woman who needed three towels to dry herself." On their very wedding night, she had treated herself to three of the four bath towels the Copley provided.

She had simply laughed and grinned.

Westbrook liked food, and as a single man he often consulted a list of unusual restaurants he had discovered around the city. He did not feel it too much to ask of a wife that she cook well. But Marge had cared nothing for food. With another laugh, she'd pointed out that she'd been lunching successfully on grilled cheese sandwiches and Cokes for years and hadn't gained a pound or known a sick day. Even her family, she said with a certain pride, had cared nothing for food. Misguided friends and business acquaintances, in fact, used to send her family small fancy boxes of jams and jellies and cheeses from off there in Wisconsin, and they remained on the pantry shelves until the jam crystalized and the cheeses either dried or rotted. They would have felt that such food as Westbrook liked far too rich for themselves, and thus seemed to set themselves up as Spartan aristocrats, with more important things to do than think of their stomachs. They stuck close to eggs and vegetables and were suspicious of sauces.

So Marge had not learned to cook. Once a week Westbrook was served up with canned baked beans and frankfurts boiled so long they paled and burst their seams. With them she might serve hard little pinkish tomatoes packed four in a box. Sometimes she did not cook at all, but carried home potato salad in a carton and envelopes of sliced chopped meats, mosaics of sliced olives and pieces of macaroni like white worms working their way through the pattern. If memory served, this meat was called Luxury Loaf.

More and more they went out for dinner. She complained of a fatigue — nervous fatigue, she called it. He couldn't imagine why she should be tired, for the apartment was too small to be demanding.

"I'm simply exhausted," she'd say, and at the words her shoulders would sag and she would depart to where she would run water.

All this he might have endured, knowing from talking to other men that the best marriage is no picnic, that disorder and disappointment figure in it. Women were one thing before marriage when they were after a man and another thing when they had got him.

But he would have endured it all, the untidiness, the un-reasonable laughter, her addiction to movie magazines and the to-ings and fro-ings of Jackie Kennedy. And there was her habit of pinching a chocolate to find out beforehand what was inside it. (If its core didn't suit, she replaced it in the box.) She did the dinner dishes with the breakfast dishes. There were the uncovered pots of paints and the brushes with which she falsified her eyes. A device heated up spiked

cylinders like tiny hedgehogs and these she placed in her hair
to alter the shape of it. She owned slippery unguents and
sharp astringents that replaced honest soap and water. A
cinch of straps and buckles for supporting hose she tossed
beside the bed; it resembled a harness used in last-ditch therapy. She refused a third drink at parties but added, "I'll
just drink part of Tom's."

Drink part of Tom's, would she?

Now he remembered her solely for a web of artifice and
not for what he would have wished — for her bearing of his
child. Yes, she was barren, a handsome, empty chalice. For
some time that possibility had been on his mind, that she was
barren. Her face began to look barren. Perhaps she had gone
so long without sex before she married, had married so late
she had simply dried up like a stream. Was that possible?
They had coupled perhaps a hundred and fifty times in three
years, had never used contraceptives. His conversations over
cocktails at home often turned to how much children meant
to him. He had assumed children meant as much to her. And
she was growing older. He introduced into the house foods
said to cause or promote fertility — parsley and bread rich
with wheat germ. He attempted to convince her that everybody needs liver, but although they now agreed on liver in
principle, they did not agree on the length of time necessary
to cook it. She preferred her liver pink inside. Westbrook,
like most Westerners whose lives have been rather close to
beef, preferred his liver well done. Somehow long cooking
removed it a greater distance from the butcher pen.

They were about to eat liver again one winter's evening in
the second year of their marriage; the sleet tapped monot-
onously on the window. He was in the middle of his second

sherry. Dance music was low on the phonograph; thought-less or insensitive, she had chosen an album of music that could only remind him of happier times between them — music from *Gypsy*, a musical they had enjoyed together in New York, and later over German beer and Welsh rabbit bubbling in thick ramekins typical of the Blue Ribbon just around the corner from the theater, they had looked into each other's eyes promising each other many things.

A line from the show, as he remembered it: "You're a man who wants children."

As they sat there with beer and Welsh rabbit, children must have been on her mind, too.

But now as the sleet tapped, Marge was saying, "Do you want me to put your liver on?"

You would think that near the end of two years a woman would know how many drinks a man wants before she puts his liver on, and certainly not in the middle of his second. He got little pleasure from a drink when he knew food was frying away in the next room.

"Are you about ready for your liver?" she asked now.

"Why, I don't know," he said.

"It takes yours longer than mine," she said.

"Well, all right." The music was ruined anyway.

"Fine," she said. Recently (because there were but the two of them), they'd been eating their evening meal on their laps — buffet, she called it. Buffet did not require the setting up of the drop-leaf table, the lighting of candles, and could be eaten with the hands alone, or with one tool at best. Everything about them was going to pieces, sliding this way and that.

He spoke suddenly just before she moved into the small

kitchen. "Do you think," he said, "that you might be sterile?"

She stood there looking at him. "I? Sterile?"

"It's a question that has got to be asked," he said.

Her mouth narrowed. "I've known from the first that you regarded me as a brood mare."

He suspected she had read that line in a novel she had borrowed from the lending library around the corner. "Is there anything unusual," he said, "in a man's hoping his wife will bear children, and is there anything wrong in her knowing of a man's desire?"

"Nothing at all," she said, "but usually a wife expects to be loved as well as used."

That was a hard one to answer. "I've never felt," he said, "that you had any great love for me. I think you were tired of standing behind that counter. If I looked on you as a brood mare, you looked on me as a meal ticket."

"Christ," she said, "what cruelty. What abysmal, pigheaded selfishness, and the thing is, you don't even recognize it."

"Thank you," he said.

"Well," she said, "at least for once you're being honest."

"I grant you," he said, "honesty is no great virtue. It causes nothing but trouble."

"And since honesty has got into the picture," she said, "I'll admit it's often been on my mind to inquire whether or not you were sterile. Or maybe a low sperm count?"

Low sperm count! He was as shocked as if she'd called him a son of a bitch or a queer, or struck him across the mouth. It was distressing to consider her moving about the apartment believing herself tied to a man with a low sperm count.

"I happen to know otherwise," he said.

"Then it seems there are things I still don't know," she said, "in spite of all this honesty."

"It was all in the past. A long, long time ago."

"Nothing is really in the past," she said. "Everything always comes up again in some form or other."

"It appears," he said, "you're also something of a philosopher. Yes, some things in the past count and exist. And it seems only sensible for you to see a doctor."

"I don't quite get the connection," she said, "between your last two thoughts, if thoughts they are. But yes, I'll see a doctor. I'll be delighted to."

He was relieved that his suggestion had not angered her. He rose, went to her, leaned and kissed her. "Good girl," he said.

A week later she returned from the doctor's as elated as if she'd found something pretty on sale. The doctor, she said, had declared she was quite capable of bearing a child. "So now it's up to you to see a doctor. Would you mind getting me a drink?"

Naturally he doubted she was telling the truth. He therefore called the doctor from WBOT.

He found it painful to suggest to the doctor that he didn't believe his wife, but surely doctors were familiar enough with doubts and urgencies to forgive him. A doctor would understand why a woman might lie about her ability to conceive and give birth, for a barren woman might not look on herself as a true woman.

"You can understand my feelings," he told the doctor.

The doctor was rather breezy about it. "Oh, certainly I understand. But there's no doubt about it. None. your wife's in real great shape. Good pelvic spread, good —" Westbrook scarcely heard the list of his wife's worthy measurements and attributes, for you see what that made of him. The doctor continued. "Maybe you'd like to come in for a checkup?"

Westbrook waited a week considering whether he should have his wife see another doctor, and then he made an appointment for himself with quite another doctor. Somehow he couldn't bring himself to face that other one.

Westbrook sat for some time in the waiting room; he could not put his mind to the literature at hand, cheerful articles in *Reader's Digest* and sober ones in *Fortune*. From time to time a telephone rang in an inner office. It annoyed him how the telephone takes precedence over a human being whether in a shop or in a doctor's office. He supposed that was because there was something mysterious about someone on the other end of a phone and nothing at all mysterious about the person who sat before you, once the face had been seen. That, he thought, explained masks — that the mask over the face . . .

A voice was speaking. The nurse. "The doctor," she said, "will see you now."

There are few worse words in the English language.

He explained he knew he was not sterile, and since an ashtray was handy, he lighted a cigarette.

"Then you've been examined before?"

"No. A girl I once knew."

"An accident?"

"Yes."

"Your accidental pregnancies are sometimes the most certain."

"I don't follow."

"It's due to your frame of mind. A man is not ordinarily thinking about pregnancy when he gets a female pregnant accidentally. He's thinking about sex and not pregnancy. Anxiety about pregnancy very often causes sterility. Anxiety that you're going to cause it or anxiety that you're not going to cause it."

"Psychological causes, then."

"And physiological. Somewhere along the line you may well have had a mild case of mumps and attributed the pain to a headache. Do you recall such a time?"

"I'm not certain." In fact he recalled being ill for a week in a camp in the Adirondacks.

"Then we'll examine you."

Westbrook wanted to be certain. If time or anxiety or even some stealthy disease had made him sterile he wanted to know it. It was better to risk the knowledge that he was sterile or possessed of a low sperm count than to never have been certain and go on wondering and to continue to be chained with hope to a woman with whom he was not in love. And it was fairer to her, too. She had not been a bad sort — there had been good times.

Foolishly, it had never occurred to him how potency is ascertained — perhaps some kind of blood test, and he did dislike giving blood. But it was not to be a blood test at all, not at all. Simpler and worse.

"Simply masturbate."

Simply masturbate.

He could not at first put his mind to the task, knowing the nurse who handed him the small glass beaker knew what was going on, knowing the small room in which he stood with the door locked was host to many like him who were called on to complete an act most men had abandoned long ago. But imbued with the morality and fears of Grayling, Montana, land of stern pioneers who had carried their Bibles with them in their saddlebags, he could not rid himself of the idea that masturbation was shameful; in his heart of hearts he still believed it might lead to impotency and even madness. A book he had once come upon by stealth in his father's den, a book carefully placed behind other books, painted a ghastly future for a boy who abused himself.

He succeeded only by summing up before him the face and body of a girl named Maxine Gates. If ever he had loved, it was she he had loved.

He succeeded.

And he left the office a disillusioned man.

He would have preferred an amicable separation, something that would have allowed occasional telephone calls and cards at Christmastime. Otherwise it is always possible that you will meet again someone with whom you have parted on bad terms, and you will have to smile and speak, or pretend blindness or cross to the other side of the street.

"Midnight Line" had just been launched, and luckily that project so occupied him he had little time to consider his sterility. Returning to the apartment just after six one morning, he opened the door and stood inside, knowing at once that something had happened. In two years' time he had become accustomed and even dependent on the sounds a woman makes — her breathing in the bedroom beyond, the rasp of file on fingernail, running water, the twice-flushed toilet, the sip-sip-sip of bedroom slippers on bare floors.

And this morning there was no sound. Nothing.

Silence so authoritative — as if it had a purpose of its own — he found himself tiptoeing to the bedroom in order not to disturb it. Was the realization that her husband was sterile enough to drive a woman to do away with herself? Stranger things have happened, and good God, he didn't really know her. What can you know of a woman in two years? After forty years he scarcely knew himself. And it had always been Marge's custom to greet him with a pot of coffee. It appalled him to think that a lack in him would cause a woman's suicide.

At the open door of the bedroom he stood, shocked.

She had ransacked the room. Yes, ransacked. So there was a violence in her nature he had never encountered before. Angry fires stoked far inside her had blazed up. Ransacked. Drawers pulled out at crazy angles. Everything that had belonged to her she had taken, stuffed away in her two big suitcases. He noted she had taken nothing of his and nothing he had given her. These last articles, as if to draw his close attention to them, she had cast onto the bed — her wedding ring, a wristwatch, a bottle of perfume and a pretty long robe with buttons that had once made her easily accessible when she dallied with him. For good measure, she had torn up the bed — their marriage bed.

To what purpose such violence?

Indeed, a man is better off without such a woman. Not that it was entirely her fault, perhaps. Simply say that he and she were not well matched.

He turned and closed the door behind him, closed that chapter.

Or hoped to. He sat in his chair for a time. In a little while he thought he might make himself a piece of toast and a cup of coffee, first thoroughly rinsing out the pot, a simple operation Marge almost always forgot to do. Yes, and while it was perking he would look up the name of an attorney, a professional man he had not until this moment ever before required. But we do what we must.

And he admitted to himself it was sad to contemplate himself as totally alone. If they had been able to talk, to compromise, to have found happiness as some childless couples do in sharing the love of a dog in common, some nice clean breed.

No, he was alone, now. He was a priest, and his children were those who called and listened to Midnight Line. Fickle children they were, and his only so long as he served them as they would be served. Fragile reeds to lean on, and often he regretted he had not been more provident, had not saved, had nothing of real value except a collection of stamps that had begun as a hobby and now must be looked on as savings.

For he saw now, as his fifty-fifth birthday anniversary approached, that a man is as responsible to his later, older self as he would be to his son — had he one. And he could not but regret sometimes that, in a sense, life had passed him by. Would he not have been happier, a man more vital, had he not willed trouble to pass him by? Would he not then have been worthier of the majesty of death — alone though he be at the end, with no son to part his lips and say, "My father was a man"? A priest only, but a priest, by God, and he let them filter their lives through the comforting fabric of his emptiness.

He himself no longer had a tale to tell.

A few minutes before six on a usual morning the five little red lights before him on the console would have blinked out: the telephones would be dead. With only a few minutes remaining of "Midnight Line," no one called, for who can make himself understood in so short a time?

The problem of those moments of dead air he had solved years before by stirring the air with what became known as Westbrook's theme, an orchestral version of "Goodnight, Sweetheart," played so quietly it might have been the background for a dream. The music meant little to him personally; he had been told it had been the favorite tune of the King of England just prior to the Second World War. He associated it with a lively aunt, a sister of his mother and quite unlike her, who sometimes came to visit with her portable phonograph. The tune was wildly inappropriate if one remembered the words and it happened to follow a call by a man whose wife had just left him after first wiping out their joint bank account, and cruelly appropriate if it followed a call from one whose child was recently dead.

Goodnight, sweetheart,
Till we meet tomorrow . . .

Meet in the divorce court? In heaven? And each new meeting found everyone altered, changed by the previous night and the most recent dream. The human lot. Each human being brought into the world one little brick to erect a structure, a bridge of some kind, perhaps. What the bridge spanned and what lay beyond it were no clearer than the moment when the first lungfish crawled gasping out of the water and began to walk. Religion sought the answer through fasts and penance, through prayers and routine sheddings of blood. Philosophy explained it with talk . . .

The followers of "Midnight Line" accepted this foolish music as his and theirs. It celebrated an emotion most wish to feel and to reciprocate. As the music grew even softer, receding into the distance, disappearing like a slowly fading smile, Westbrook's habit was to murmur, "Goodnight, goodnight, and goodnight — and good morning." His voice rose on the word "morning" as if it were a question, and it lingered in the mind, an unresolved chord that found its home key only the following midnight, when Westbrook spoke once more.

But on this morning of his fifty-fifth birthday anniversary, one little red light still glowed; one telephone was alive somewhere. He waited a few seconds. Whoever was on the line was certainly a first-time caller, for the others respected the little coda of dying music. Was it someone needing help?

Well, he was the one who helped.

So it was not in a spirit of curiosity but of generosity that he took the call, pressed the button that put the voice on the air. His action was part nostalgia, a wish — like traveling to the market for berries — a need to make a gesture recognizing this special day's significance.

"Good morning. You're on 'Midnight Line.' "

It is likely that few heard the voice that answered him. Most would now have turned from their radios, settled down to coffee, gone to the bathroom or turned to a lover. Some had gone out their doors to work; some embraced their loneliness and some resumed the anger.

He listened.

The air was alive with silence, a silence of hollow anticipation like that sensed when the sustaining pedal of a piano is depressed, and no note is struck. Then came the sound of breathing, the breathing close to the telephone that often precedes an obscene call. The tip of Westbrook's finger grew sensitive with an urge to touch the panic button that stopped the tape and silenced the voice before it could go on the air.

Then, the Voice. "Happy birthday, Westbrook," it said. For some reason that simple statement paralyzed his hand. Before he could touch the panic button, the Voice came again. "I know who you are."

The light blinked off.

A moment later, out of habit, he emptied the ashtray of twenty cigarette butts into the basket beside him. He arranged his desk, the pencil here, the tray there. He tore the top page from the notepad, folded it, and tucked it in his breast pocket. On it was written the single note he had made in six hours, the phrase Capital Punishment, for that curious institution had been the chief subject of conversation during the final hour. As his callers talked and talked that night it had occurred to him that so many out there who listened and called had had a more than academic interest in Capital Punishment. The question had likely arisen with brother, son, cousin, friend or even father. Many had more than a cursory interest in Death Row.

He rose. He left the studio and locked the door against the janitor — but not entirely out of habit, for he was conscious of the act. It was important at the moment to do everything exactly as it had always been done, for some mechanical quality in the Voice suggested it had come from a great distance, and had been tempered and dehumanized along the way.

"I know who you are."

III _____

IT HAD BEEN WESTBROOK'S CUSTOM to walk from the hotel where he had his "dinner" to his apartment, a distance of just over a mile. In broad daylight there was small danger of being detained and mugged, and in walking he had time to observe and keep in touch with the city. Walking at an even pace, it took twelve minutes unless he was held up by lights. He liked to think of himself as a man who walked a mile each day, who had the right to expect the health that comes from regular walking.

As a boy he had seen advertisements in *American Boy* for a device called a pedometer that measured the distance one walked. It had resembled an Ingersoll watch, nickel-plated, according to the text. It had something to do with the motion of the body and the length of stride. His allowance, a dollar a week and handed over to him privately by his mother, precluded his owning a pedometer. His mother realized a boy had to have something — especially a Westbrook, in that

town. But as a Westbrook it was unthinkable that he augment his allowance by delivering papers, mowing lawns or
distributing fliers for the Rex Theater. Such chores were for
boys who lived down on Kentucky Avenue where the sidewalks gave way to paths, or across the Union Pacific railroad
tracks, and what they earned was not spent on pedometers or
bicycles, but on food and clothing.

Westbrook spent his weekly dollar wisely. From the back
pages of *American Boy* he regularly ordered a few postage
stamps; he recalled the nervous anticipation that preceded
the arrival of the "approvals," beautiful pieces of the stamp-
maker's art that conjured up romance and distance and dynasties, bits of pretty paper celebrating revolutions, fallen
heads and republics, tickets to a world beyond Grayling,
Montana.

I know who you are.

Frank waited at the curb at the front entrance of the
Tower in the black limousine. Perhaps Frank had chosen
black as appropriate for possible funeral parties. "Won't need
you this morning, Frank," Westbrook said.

Frank had already hopped down from the front seat and
prepared to hold open the door. "Then you don't want to
take a chance on berries?"

"Berries? Oh yes, berries. Not this morning. I'll walk
home."

He did not stop at the hotel to eat his "dinner."

He had meant to spend a few hours with his stamp collection — what to add, what to set aside, what to think of trading on Tremont Street, where his face was familiar.

Where Pollinger the Jew knew in one sense "who he was." Unlike many whose enthusiasms are violent but brief, Westbrook had persevered at his stamp collecting; he had not left behind in attic or clothes closet — as many had — a partially completed Scott stamp album to later remind him — should he come across it — of youthful whimsy. And deep inside him was a need to own what other people wanted and couldn't have because he already had it. Pollinger on Tremont Street had valued his collection at above twenty thousand dollars, but there was no question of sale. Of Pollinger he had wanted only a professional opinion, as some women inquire of their jewelers if the rings they wear are worth what they hope, that they might continue to carry their heads high. What was his collection worth now? Collections were regularly destroyed by fire, were lost when moves were made, torn up by children, chewed by rodents, lost in the trash. Collections were stolen by thieves who had an eye for more than portable silver and television sets; collections fell into the hands of knowledgeable fences who demanded high prices to compensate for the chances they took. The remaining collections, like his, ever increased in value.

But it was not for its intrinsic value alone that he cherished his stamps and not merely the owning of something other people couldn't have, but because of its association with that time in late puberty when a birthday was a welcome occasion, a step closer to the unspeakable gifts said to wait just beyond the threshold of maturity — one's own money, one's own house, the use of one's own woman, and getting out of Grayling, Montana.

For one thing, he was a boy who wanted out of Grayling.

But who in God's name can say who anyone is, since one doesn't even know himself who he is, since one is different at different times, one thing then and another now, a different person to different people, this in this situation and that in that.

He had expected to experience a sense of safety in returning to his lofty apartment and locking the door behind him, for there in that place he could be "himself," the room reflecting as it did "himself." He had chosen and bought the furniture and had arranged it, substantial pieces, some of them expensive, like the partners' desk and the Chinese screen of teak, brass and jade. Some personal things, like the rusty tin basin that had been his grandfather's. He had chosen the Buffet prints on the walls precisely because they were pointedly devoid of all human presence — he had quite enough to do with human presence when he was on the air. And it was his peculiar personality that had prompted the two birthday gifts on the partners' desk — the cologne and the initialed cuff links — a sense of who he was.

Yes, it was possible that the givers of these gifts had complained of Westbrook to some male friend or brother who took it upon himself to attempt to disturb Westbrook with a crank call. But he could conceive of no circumstance, no gathering, no cocktail party or lunch that was a proper setting for either one of those women to say, "I want to tell you about Westbrook. He is, in fact, a son of a bitch." But if either woman had felt hurt by him, why had she sent a gift?

He had done no more than break off a relationship. Each

was better off without him. There is no room in a priest's life for a woman, and no room in hers for him.

Any friend or brother would naturally know "who he was" since he was known in thirty-eight states. Or did the statement mean "I know what you are"? What kind of person you are? But no brother or friend could expect a man to marry a woman half his age. And the older woman, the cuff-link woman, had proven herself untrustworthy as a wife by her drinking, and if Westbrook knew she drank, it was certain a great many other people would, and could discount whatever it was she had to say. On all sides you hear it said that there is nothing, absolutely nothing, worse than being saddled with an alcoholic partner.

It was hardly conceivable that it was a friend or brother of either woman when you considered the distance that surrounded the Voice, the sound of distance and the crackling that accompanied the call, a crackling possibly due to faulty connections but a sound that reminded Westbrook of telephone wires running high over wilderness or prairie.

His family was dead — died out; the big old house — the Westbrook "mansion" — was sold. He was the end of the line. He had no family to wish him happy birthday. Only Maxine, of all the people he'd known in the past, would have any interest in "who he was." The Voice was certainly not Maxine's. The Voice was distinctly masculine, if somewhat mechanical, like a robot's. He had heard there is a device that can be slipped into the mouth that alters the voice — a false tongue, perhaps, a false palate.

Had Maxine a brother or cousin? Had she been close to some other man even when she was supposedly "his"? The circumstances of Maxine's life, her traveling salesman father, the curious hodgepodge of objects in the apartment did suggest a family larger than just the two of them. Inherited things. Had there been photographs of relatives?

Maxine's father would surely be dead by now, or so old his voice would not have approximated the timbre and strength of the Voice.

A friend? Possibly even Maxine's husband. There was no reason to believe she had not married after his departure. Girls who had done far worse than Maxine got married. Things are mercifully forgotten. One of his own acquaintances had — by her own admission — had an illegitimate child. Some twenty-five years before, when Westbrook had left Grayling, Montana, people were already beginning to condone actions and to overlook transgressions they would never have overlooked when he was a child, actions and trangressions his mother would never have overlooked.

Westbrook's family had been the oldest in town. Their old house with the mansard roof he himself had heard called "the old Westbrook mansion." Not a mansion by Eastern standards, but a mansion when you considered the difficulty in the far-off days when it was built of getting all that yellow brick out there on what was then an empty vast prairie that stretched up the foothills to the mountains. The railroad had not then come within fifty miles of Grayling. The courthouse and the jail attached was constructed of the same imported brick. Now, the courthouse had a stubby tower with a clock in each of the four sides that struck the hour and the half-hour — struck the still air as a stone strikes water, throwing circle after circle of sound. Westbrook remembered sitting up late studying for high school examinations — hearing it strike once for twelve-thirty, once for one, and once again for one-thirty. This experience, this space of an hour that marked the first hour of morning not quite morning — for it trailed just behind the curious importance of midnight — this experience he had named the Three Ones. It was an hour when he felt most himself — who he was — as others feel most themselves during the holidays, or out hunting, or under the spell of burning leaves. Naming the hour had given it a shape, faceted like a jewel; it had a power and meaning of its own, like the charms gypsies are said to wear against their naked skin. To this day, hearing the faint sound of twelve-thirty or one or one-thirty struck in some distant suburb of Boston, Westbrook seemed to wrestle again with the formula for sulfuric acid or a problem involving gases or levers. His marks in high school had been important — perhaps because he had not been a popular boy, good marks instead of friends sustained his ego. And he persisted in the lonely business of collecting stamps when other boys had taken to beer drinking and driving their girls in their fathers' Hudsons and Oaklands and parking among the cottonwood trees out near Mountain View Cemetery.

He seldom got a chance to drive his father's Chevrolet.

So he had not graduated with memories of football games and dances and beer and sex in the back seat. His memories were rather of a handful of A's on a report card and the faces and gestures of a few teachers, and of a Miss Violet Eastman who had said his voice had the power to attract. He would have liked now to be in touch with Miss Eastman. If she were still living, she would be proud of him, or proud of herself in having been proven correct in her judgment.

Shut away in his room in the old Westbrook "mansion" he had wondered how the clock sounded to those beneath in the attached jail — the petty thieves, the vagrants who drifted into Grayling on the freights hoping for work on some neighboring ranch or farm; the local drunks some found amusing, the quarrelsome rabble that hung around the Pheasant Pool Hall or Skeet's Bar.

In that town you went down to the station to watch the Union Pacific pull in, snorting and hissing, perhaps to assure yourself that something was possible, something was better to the east or west. It was of some assurance simply to know that a vehicle of escape existed. You watched the station agent, Old Pete, who walked with a limp from some earlier entanglement with a horse, haul out the express wagon and line it up alongside the baggage car. Sometimes he loaded on it cartons of sour-smelling, peeping baby chicks, sometimes a coffin containing what remained of someone whose beginnings in Grayling, Montana, had at last overcome his hatred of them.

And in that town you had at least once gone behind the courthouse where that face of the clock confronted a vacant field where dogs gathered in the spring and sniffed at each other. From that point you watched the barred windows, hoping to see a face, the face of someone who was not free, as you were. A boy Westbrook knew had once accompanied his father into one of the cells. The father had gone there to bail out a hired man. The boy had described the cages of iron latticework, the filthy toilet and washbowl, the cast-iron army cot and torn gray blanket. Someone had been sick in the corridor, and even for fall, it was cold.

It had been some years since the jail had been the scene of an execution. That grim function was now attended to at the State Penitentiary to the north and east, where the proper facility, the gallows, was instantly available in a special yard with a high fence around it, lest somebody see who had not been invited to see. But told over and over again in the Pheasant Pool Hall and in Skeet's Bar was the story of the last local execution. The convict, whose name was Jake, had shot another man in a quarrel over the possession of a woman in that part of town called the Cabbage Patch. There paths wandered between the sagebrush and ryegrass and connected a scattering of log cabins and tarpaper shacks left over from the very beginnings of the town, and there hired hands and cowboys, too old to work, suffering from terminal illness "breathed their last."

Asked to make a last request, Jake did. Jake said Yes, he did indeed have a last request. The sheriff assumed this last request would have something to do with food — what else would do Jake any earthly good in so short a space of time? Something almost impossible like strawberries out of season, or fried oysters which, like lobster tails and fried halibut, were greatly fancied around Grayling, Montana.

Jake told the sheriff he wanted a woman during his last hour.

Because the mystique of granting a last request was so deep-rooted, because those who live cannot help but feel obligated to those who are about to die, a local whore had been approached on the matter. Until that moment, Kate

Kelly had had no special dignity in her profession; she was not known to have a special knowledge of foreplay or of the dark arts of perversion. No, she was but another of dozens in the seven cribs in Grayling, another pretty girl who had escaped farm chores and a nagging mother. But from that moment on, Kate Kelly was a celebrity, her name more widely known in the state than the most important families in the town. And she had a nose for the right thing. Kate had not charged the county a cent for her services. Who could not help but be impressed by her generosity and the fact that she possessed a quality that could stiffen even a condemned man's prick?

Was the story true?

The town abounded with stories and legends. What were the true circumstances behind the suicide by hanging of a young doctor in the neighboring town of Beech? Had it to do with his humiliation by a local rancher? Who had really won the famous race from that same settlement to Grayling, between quite another doctor in a Cadillac and a well-liked bootlegger in a Hudson Super Six? They had averaged eighty miles an hour on a dirt road.

Was it true that a headless, armless and legless human torso turned up in a gravel pit outside of town? One of the legs, they said, was later washed up on a sandbar in the river. It had been identified as a man's leg. Then why had it been so carefully shaven? The stories could not be proven or disproven — not so much because they had receded so far into the past but because they had been so often and so positively stated as fact.

Westbrook remembered Kate Kelly as an old, painted

woman known for good works of a vague nature, some kindness to the poor, footing the bill for a drifter's last operation in the local hospital — the Hale Memorial. A gift that made possible a new roof for the Catholic church. A madam for many years, by then, she ran the Crystal Rooms and held gaudy court with her girls in the early hours of the morning in the Sugar Bowl Café in booths with green baize curtains sometimes pulled and sometimes not. She was said to be rich. She was said to spend the winter months in California, or was it Florida? She had married and had a daughter quite unaware of her mother's profession. Or she had not married and had a son somewhere. She bought her clothes in Chicago. She had been backed in her original enterprise by Mr. Green who owned the department store advertised in the *Examiner* as The Store Beautiful. There, in the shoe department, you could stand in front of an instrument and look down and see the ghostly X rays of your feet, each tiny bone identifiable.

Westbrook had never been to the Crystal Rooms. His knowledge of these rooms was secondhand. He had done no more than pore over *The Diary of a French Stenographer* and handle a blurred photograph of a man naked except for his socks and the Paris garters that supported them in the act of mounting a woman who had decided on shoes, as well. Westbrook's fantasies he resolved in private and alone. Never had he climbed the rickety back stairs of the Crystal Rooms to "get his ashes hauled," as they said in Grayling, but the boys on the football team had, and on the night before their graduation they had trooped up there to celebrate their manhood. They spoke of a young whore who had had little slits cut in her dress so her nipples peeked through, just so.

"For you boys," she'd said.

They spoke of mirrors alongside the bed.

Now in their gray caps and gowns they clowned to show they did not think that they thought that anyone thought that they thought they were educated, and they sported their new wristwatches, their Hamiltons and Elgins and Howards — the customary graduation gifts in Grayling, Montana, reminders of the value of promptness, the inevitable flight of time, and of those who loved them and had above seventy-five dollars to show it. Where would next year find them — and the next? Who were they, where were they going?

And who was Westbrook?

He was a graduate who had no wristwatch.

As one who had had long experience with obscene and sick calls, Westbrook was certain that the first call of the Voice was like the first-dropped of a pair of shoes in a room overhead — sooner or later he would hear the thud of its mate; rather, in this instance, there would be two more calls — the first call the first leg of a tripod, and then two more calls. The first call, having announced it was known who he was, would be followed by a second telling him *what* he was, and then a third call making a threat of some kind repeated maybe week after week until the Voice . . .

A Mr. D. called from Oil City, Pennsylvania. Mr. D. was forty. Just more than twenty years before he had been on the second string of the high school basketball team. His wife who was not his wife then was going out with a player on the first string but something happened, he couldn't imagine what, she was so pretty, but she turned to him who had always loved her, and they got married.

She had ambition for herself and for him, and he answered the first of many advertisements in the papers over the years, to be a salesman. She said anybody with a smile like his ought to sell good because that's what they wanted. He knew he was not very high-powered, but he believed her; she was so sure of herself it might rub off, some of it. Back then she cared a lot for the looks of her hair piled all high that a friend she had who was a man hairdresser did, and so at night he had to be careful of her. But twenty years ago a little girl was born to them. He was on the road so much, had to be, selling, and being true in strange towns. But it looked like all he had those years was his smile. He seemed always trying to sell the wrong things. First it was handkerchiefs when everybody used Kleenex and then men's hats, and finally ladies' stationery.

Suddenly he knew his wife didn't like him anymore; she told him she wanted more for their daughter than he could do, so they left him when he was off selling and he came home to find a note. All he had left of them were two pictures he had paid for in frames on the wall and he thought someday when he looked up there they would realize how hard he had tried and they would come back. She said he couldn't cut the mustard.

They came back while he was gone. They broke into the house because they didn't have a key and all they took were the two pictures on the wall, not even a note. He guessed his smile was the wrong kind, or you needed more than a smile.

Westbrook told Mr. D. that the day would come when he would be glad to have got rid of them both — that all a man can do is try, and if they didn't see what the essence of a real man is, they didn't deserve him and to keep smiling. Someday somebody would smile back at him.

But Westbrook's advice was perfunctory. His mind was not on the small tragedy of Mr. D. in Oil City, but on the Voice. The hours, the days slipped by. By the end of the week his memory of the sound of the Voice was as vague as a last wisp of smoke, and his memory of the memory was fast disappearing as mist over water vanishes with the rising of the sun. So there you were: the voice was nothing but a crank caller, never to be heard from again.

In a way, he was grateful to the Voice. It set him to thinking, to examining his past, and once he'd done that, he would cast it aside forever. One thing he knew, one thing we all know, is that what he was then was not at all what he was now, and that is a comfort, maybe the only comfort, of growing older. Maybe that fact compensates for the failing eye and the sagging muscles, and that when one gets suddenly to one's feet one must consider which leg is best used first.

A stranger to Boston, but recently come there from the tiny local station in the boondocks of Connecticut, Westbrook had asked the Old Man what a newcomer ought to see.

"See?" the Old Man had asked. "Oh, I see. See." Although the Old Man had spent most of his life in Boston, his people were not natives. What his father's father had been he didn't know. Unmarried and childless, the Old Man had little interest in family, in traditions or in the past. Radio was his life, as it had become Westbrook's, and it had fulfilled him as it had fulfilled Westbrook — until just recently. Once, the Old Man said, he had found himself on Atlantic Avenue and had walked a little farther and examined Tea Wharf. He'd sat for some fifteen minutes, he said, only to find out later that he'd been sitting on the wrong wharf — not only on the wrong wharf but in the wrong part of the city. "I never had much sense of history, I guess. But *see*? I suppose the Custom House Tower."

Westbrook went up in the tower, the last few floors in a second caged elevator that held but two people. Iron bars prevented troubled souls, unable to come to terms with a new day that promised no more than the preceding day, from hurling themselves off. Westbrook pressed against the bars and looked out at the harbor. Beyond was Portugal.

He wandered along Long Wharf, through the long drafty shed like a covered bridge, and wondered about the lost Tea Wharf. What he imagined was like an engraving in his American History book in Grayling, Montana. Miss Snodgrass had once remarked that he alone of her students wore a necktie. Her hooked nose had insured her virginity.

A tame sea gull stood on one leg and questioned him. "Putt-putt?" Others wheeled and mewed above a battered trawler. A cat chewed on a fish head.

He lunched at a counter near Faneuil Hall, rubbed elbows with wholesale grocers and butchers from the market; one had not troubled to remove his bloody apron, a reminder that meat has a violent past.

One Sunday afternoon in early fall he haunted the historic gloom of Louisburg Square where two statues stared across a tiny fenced-in garden, Columbus and Demosthenes, immi-

grant Italian and persuasive Greek. The big brick houses of
the Brahmans on each side were silent; the window glass
looked blind. No one came and no one went.

He asked a dozen natives the way to the house of Paul
Revere. An Irish cop directed him to it. It stood so close to
the sidewalk that pedestrians jostled him, their eyes inquiring why he stood there. Revere the artisan, the silversmith,
had felt himself so equal to the merchant princes he dared
build his small house on the same street with them. That was
a simpler civilization, when clever hands and a sharp mind
were the equal of money. It was a society still in flux. Who
was to say, in America, who was the aristocrat—the rich man,
the artisan or the intellectual? As late as the Copleys, as late
as the Emersons, Alcotts and Thoreaus, the question was
moot. But it was money that triumphed in the end, for
money is universally desirable, and money can conceivably be
acquired by anybody, not like creativity and intellect, which
depend on an arrangement of genes, not merely on the gift of
cupidity.

Westbrook was one of a dozen pilgrims who Thanksgiving
afternoon stood silent before Plymouth Rock. The past, in
the East —"back East" they called it in Grayling, Montana —
the past was vast and yawning; Time was lost beyond the
horizon of the sea, or narrowed like a railroad track seen from
the observation car and disappeared into infinity. What was
antique in Grayling, Montana, was scarcely outmoded in
Massachusetts.

But no Brewster or Bradford or Cabot ever looked on his
beginnings with a deeper sense of tradition, so biblical a

reverence for family and holy responsibility than Tom West-brook. Who was he? That's who he was. A lonely boy, he attached himself to the Westbrook tradition and the West-brook past when the Westbrooks had amounted to some-thing. In that past he had a sense of pride, of order and identity that others found in the possession of a skill, or in being the center of a group of friends. That was the core of his dream — to make the Westbrooks important again.

As a boy he had wandered the single sagebrushed street of a ghost town, false-fronted buildings, broken windows, a town abandoned almost overnight when the miners got wind of another and richer strike fifty miles over the mountains. Only Westbrook's great-grandfather had remained, with his wife and twenty-year-old son.

The old man had known something of the beds of streams and rock formations. He used his brain as well as his brawn. He used a book as well as pick and shovel and sluice box. He knew there was more to living than a full belly and fast women. He understood the value of patience — like West-brook after him. He knew that impatience is a costly vice.

There followed two terrible winters, living on venison and jackrabbits and hard little potatoes they'd grown in the brief summertime. Sickness. The twenty-year-old son lay close to death. They prayed — people prayed, then. Westbrook had the old man's buckskin-covered Bible.

The second spring, when the water ran again and bluebells nodded among the sagebrush, the old man squatted again on the bank of the stream, panning for gold. He thought he'd found a new lead. Things pointed that way. Just back up there —

In the middle of a summer's day he walked into the cabin. They say he removed his hat, poured himself a cup of coffee, and he sat down.

"Well," he said, "I found it."

Once each summer Westbrook and his mother drove in the Chevrolet to the ghost town. It had to be a Sunday. Only on that day was the car available to them. Other days Westbrook's father needed the car to drive himself the few blocks down South Pacific Street to the insurance office, or for his questionable "out of town" trips. Westbrook's father did not accompany them on their annual pilgrimage; it was significant that he remained behind, resting from the demands of his insurance business and allowing his wife — no Westbrook at all — to carry on a tradition that had been founded by old Westbrook himself threescore years before. It was not Westbrook's father but his mother who had taken Westbrook to the capitol in Helena to see for himself the photograph of the old man and the portrait of his grandfather the judge that hung in the courtroom to the east of the rotunda. It was he, the judge, who had almost died. But for Westbrook's mother, Westbrook might never have known of his great-grandfather's "papers" — deeds and agreements and the diary in faded spidery script he had kept over the years when Montana was still a territory.

"And that's your heritage," his mother had said, and then solemnly in the summer heat they had gone downtown in Helena and eaten ice cream. To this day the taste and temperature of ice cream, like Proust's madeleines, summoned up their wandering through the gloomy halls of the capitol, the museum in the basement where were displayed Indian artifacts, arrowheads, sharpened stones for scraping coyote hides, rawhide saddlebags embroidered with dyed porcupine quills. The bones of a notorious criminal who robbed stage coaches of gold dust and during one terrible winter ate the tenderer portions of his frozen comrade were there under glass, and the twisted foot of another criminal, whose name had been Club-Foot George, testified to the wages of sin.

Preparations for the annual trip to the ghost town were solemn. Westbrook's mother but little understood automobiles. The Chevrolet must first go into the garage for inspection. His mother understood there was danger in overcharging the battery, and this could be avoided only by turning on the headlights as they drove in the daylight. As a consequence, the battery had once gone dead, which his mother put down to not having turned the lights on soon enough. Westbrook's task was to wash the car and to clean out the inside with a whiskbroom. Once, cleaning out the inside, he had come upon an article that explained the nature of his father's "out of town" trips. He had not known what the thing was, at twelve years old. Since that time he had come across several of them — all quite as used — just inside Mountain View Cemetery where boys drove their girls. The object explained his mother's so often "lying down" in the middle of the afternoon. It explained her desperate attempts to please her husband with special dishes to surprise him.

"Oh, your father does love a good steak." As if his loving a good steak set him apart, made quite a man of him. Hour after hour, when he was away, she leaned over her darning ball repairing the damage done by her husband's searching toenails.

The article found in the Chevrolet sealed Westbrook's pity for his mother and confirmed his suspicions of his father, suspicions that had first been aroused by his finding behind books in his father's den a letter from a woman signed "Fritzi" and known to Westbrook to be a Mrs. Hale. Is this what a man is? Westbrook had asked himself. Or is this what my father is?

The food he and his mother carried on their trip to the ghost town was traditional — a can of Van Camps pork and beans, bacon, and potatoes for slicing thin and frying in bacon grease, such food as the first Westbrook might have eaten. Westbrook laid the fire near the original Westbrook cabin, tumbling now into ruin, sinking into the welcoming earth. The door that once swung on leather hinges now lay flat. The powdery manure on the sod floor brought to mind the stray horses that crowded in to escape horseflies in summer and the howling wind in winter.

Westbrook's father had let the land the cabin stood on go — let it go for a few dollars in taxes. He had absolutely no sentiment about it. Now, in a sense, Westbrook and his mother were trespassing on their own past. But then — did it really matter who owned Plymouth Rock?

The gold old Westbrook had discovered was no bonanza, but it was a good beginning. Another man might have weighed out his gold on his pocket scales and hiked on to another camp.

Not old Westbrook. He had patience.

He bought cheap land from the government, ten thousand acres of meadowland on both sides of the river to the south of the settlement that became Grayling. Then patiently he waited for the railroad he knew would come and make the land valuable.

He ordered bricks to be freighted in and oversaw the construction of the Westbrook "mansion." Its rooms included two indoor toilets; its chandeliers were clusters of tulip-shaped globes fed by acetylene. At the bottom of the stairs he installed a tall mahogany clock that told not only the time but also the phases of the moon, a heavenly body said to cause madness; the meat of pigs butchered at the wrong quarter was unhealthful; under the moon's influence, women grew sickly.

He sent his sickly son, almost thirty now, to Stanford where he took a degree, married and sired a son, Westbrook's father. The old man indulged the sickly son, set him up in Helena where he read law and went into politics. The old man kept clippings of his son's progress and the dinner parties his wife gave. There was little room in such a social and political life for the little boy, Westbrook's father. That little boy lived with his grandfather in the Westbrook "mansion" and had rocking horses and hoops and pony carts. Yes, the old man spoiled him.

The old man lived on, known for his white shirts and polished boots. He lived to see Montana become a state and his sickly son, a judge.

It might have been different had any later Westbrook cared for the land, their inheritance and their trust. But the judge was improvident; he liked high living. Just as the judge's father was known for polished boots and white shirts, so the judge was known for his stable of Hambletonians. His guests in the capital city of Helena included the rascally Copper Kings who needed a friendly judge. There were rumors of scandal, of votes bought, witnesses bribed, cases fixed; but copper money cured that and nothing was proved about the judge. Montanans looked on such shenanigans as somewhat dashing.

But bit by bit the Westbrook land fell into the hands of people named Bart and Hale. What investments the old man had made were in silver mines; he was all but wiped out in the panic of '93 that left ghost towns everywhere. With what remained of his money, his grandson, Westbrook's father, rented an office in Grayling, bought some file cabinets and a typewriter, hired a woman to add up figures and went into the insurance business. He was a tall, long-legged, loose-limbed handsome fellow with a face shaped like a fox's. Although he had not been on a horse in years, he wore hand-made cowboy boots with colored inlays he designed himself, sometimes butterflies and sometimes roses. He wore a big black Stetson, creased just so; he thought this costume good for his business, and dressed like this a good twenty years before even shoe clerks dressed like cowboys. He could be seen almost any afternoon in Skeet's Bar playing rummy. He told a good joke.

The tall clock at the bottom of the stairs had stopped a long time ago.

"Sometimes I wish we could get it fixed," Westbrook's mother said.

"Oh for God's sake will you stop your nagging, Ruth," Westbrook's father said. "Nobody within a thousand miles could fix that clock."

What had they all got out of it — the Civil War captain turned gold miner, the sickly judge, Westbrook's father in his high heels — Westbrook himself?

Old Westbrook's wife had got a purple taffeta gown and diamond earrings, the only objects of value that came eventually to Westbrook's mother who sold one of them to install a furnace and the other to buy one of the Chevrolets. The sickly judge had had brief splendor — perhaps the high point was a trip to New York in the private railroad car of a Copper King; he had had his portrait painted. Westbrook's father had got a failing insurance business. Old Westbrook himself had got the solid gold watch he'd always wanted.

And Westbrook? The watch, eventually, and ambition and a name. Such was his inheritance.

And it was all hollow because he had no one to leave it to.

In Grayling, it was not usual for high school graduates to go on to college. Grayling had inherited a Puritan ethic that maintained reading, writing and arithmetic were skills enough for a man to make his way; further study was presumptuous. What more did a man need to run a ranch, what more to sell sacks of feed, what more to distribute Ford cars about the country? Many a tale was told of college-educated people who were worth far less than some who had never ventured beyond grade school. But each year, two or three who presumably thought themselves superior went on to the state university where the females hoped to become Kappas and the males, Sigma Chis, and so live for four years in big houses with white pillars out front. These, as their high school graduation approached, found themselves apart — the dentist's son, the banker's daughter. Once a boy went East to Harvard and became a doctor. He never returned.

And it was a rare day when any graduate of Grayling High School enrolled in the local normal school, a two-year affair housed in a single red-brick gothic structure of towers and spires and strange windows on the edge of town near the Hale Memorial Hospital. Once there had been great hopes for the institution. Pictures of the groundbreaking ceremonies were on file in the *Examiner* office. The governor had come down from Helena. He spoke, and later on shook hands with people. The normal school was to be a four-year college. Failing that, it now trained young women and a very few young men who could not hope to be more than teachers. Teachers were not highly thought of in Grayling; women not attractive enough to marry became teachers; men not aggressive enough to succeed in business or having no prospect of inheriting land became teachers. Both groups were unfulfilled. It was no secret that a teacher of French who wore high heels had seduced the eighteen-year-old quarterback in the furnace room; the janitor exposed them. The nature of the boy's character is clear: he went on to make the winning touchdown that made Grayling High School the state champion.

A male teacher managed to marry one of his own students; he went out of town to do it.

No, the normal school was not a step up. It was a last-ditch try.

Westbrook — as a Westbrook and because his marks were good — had believed money would be available for the state university in Missoula. He had sent for a catalogue. Lying on his stomach on the bed he heard the courthouse clock strike; he searched in the catalogue for a direction; somewhere hidden in the schedules and course descriptions must be the map of things to come. What potential did he have that might be trained and finally tuned? That might be sold?

His voice.

He circled Speech in the catalogue, and he circled Public Speaking. As once he had looked up the word "whore," he now looked up the word "forensic." The course called Speech was aimed at making a student best present himself. Speech was a valuable aid to those who wanted to go into teaching or into sales. It was basic for those who contemplated going into the medium of broadcasting.

Contemplated.

Medium.

Broadcasting.

". . . you have an attractive voice."

Miss L. called to say that the restaurant she frequented (because it lay close to her work) had refused to sell her a child's portion of hamburger. It had been her custom to order the Big Four Burger, so called because with the shredded meat arrived potato chips, coleslaw and pickle. The bread above and below the meat was not counted.

She had never been able to use more than half the generous helping of meat and the coleslaw she ordinarily pushed aside with her fork, adding to the waste. She had welcomed the appearance on the menu of a child's portion which better suited her stomach. Of her it had often been remarked that she "ate like a bird."

"But that's the child's menu," the waitress said.

Miss L. said she knew that.

"It's not the adult menu," the waitress said.

Miss L. said she knew it wasn't, and went on to indicate something of the small bore of her stomach. "The larger portion is simply wasted on me."

The waitress suggested a doggy bag.

Miss L. said she possessed no dog, and that the food remaining after she had finished with it was hardly worth the trouble to take home.

"But if there's so little left," the waitress said, "why don't you want the larger portion?"

Miss L. explained that as a child she had been taught to eat everything on her plate. It was a principle with her. And she did not intend to walk out of that restaurant carrying a doggy bag. She would like to speak with the manager.

The waitress said the manager was with the dentist; the noon hour was the only time the dentist could fit him in, and to see the manager would do no good because other adults had attempted to order from the children's menu, and if they all did that, how was the restaurant to make a profit?

"Do you mean to tell me," Miss L. asked, "that the restaurant makes no profit on the child's portion?"

Not so much profit, the waitress imagined.

Then why not serve a small amount on the adult portion? "There wouldn't be so much waste and you could hold back the pickle."

"But that would be the child's portion," the waitress said. "And you couldn't have it."

Westbrook knew his father was a spendthrift, that he could expect no help from that direction. What surprised him was that his mother had made no plans for the emergency. It was her habit to hold back little moneys from household funds for objects she believed she needed, a new dress, a hat, but she went out so seldom that what she needed was not much. Since she knew that eventually the question of college would come up, why had she not put aside some each year in savings? But no. The house needed repairing. The roof leaked. She touched her hair. "The normal school is perfectly good."

Especially until he knew exactly what he wanted to do.

He had no more been able to say he wanted to be a radio announcer than he could have said he wanted to be a dancer.

Perfectly good. Perfectly nothing.

At the normal school there was no school of Speech. His father advised bookkeeping and accounting, not with a view to teaching it. "You might want to take over my business someday."

Some business, someday.

That would be when his father was entombed in Mountain View Cemetery attired in his Masonic apron that was somewhat larger than required to cover his private parts that were not at all private, as Tom Westbrook knew.

But what else was available in Grayling? And if something better existed to the east or west — as the arrival and departure of the evening train hinted — how, with no money, did you get away? Now, enrolled in the normal school, the call of the train whistle was sharper than ever. The slow-paced striking of the courthouse clock insisted that few escaped its tolling.

As the end of his second year at the normal school closed, his father remarked that the tall woman with the green celluloid eyeshade who added up figures was thinking of retiring. Westbrook might well inherit her green shade and high stool.

But that was when he met Maxine Gates.

Drifters were scorned in Grayling, Montana. Having no hindering, worldly anchors, drifters washed up the world over, got into trouble or caused trouble. The daily papers confirmed the fact that drifters were responsible for the bulk of the crime and unrest of the country. People from California. Drifters were not only those footloose workers who lounged around the Pheasant Pool Hall but traveling salesmen as well, those fellows in snappy suits who operated out of the Andrews Hotel and were seen night after night in roadhouses. More than one divorce in Grayling was laid at their feet. Certain women find drifters appealing.

If salesmen had had any feeling for wife and children they would have chosen a more sedentary occupation, one that permitted the putting down of roots; it is not likely that anybody living in an apartment is going to put down roots:

the soil is too shallow; apartment people will not accept the reasonable responsibility of a mortgage.

The Matador Apartments had a poor reputation. The very name had a foreign odor and suggested untidy goings-on. It was the only apartment building in town. Its only permanent residents were Miss Innes the librarian and her old father who fell and broke his hips again and again, always the hips. Miss Innes and her old father understood African violets long before anybody else did, and they kept cats. Few other residents remained longer than a few months; their departures were often nocturnal and frequently preceded by unspeakable violence and appeals to the police. The dark halls were redolent of frying food, steaks and chops that require neither thought nor much preparation. Some dwellers there attempted to mask the odors of food and cats with incense, but such smells are better stopped at the source, and who can smell incense without suspecting women dressed in far too little and lounging around and waiting?

The father of Maxine Gates appeared suddenly in Grayling and operated out of the Matador Apartments selling electric generators to ranchers and farmers a hundred miles in all directions. In the Matador he did little more than hang up his hat. His wife was a photograph in a silver frame on the rented bureau, if it was his wife: it is understood that there are relationships outside marriage. He and Maxine had brought little of themselves to the place but two easy chairs slipcovered in faded, flowered cretonne and a thready Navajo rug shrunken out of shape by careless washings.

Maxine! It was a name almost as strange as the names the

Mormons fitted to their children, the Mormons who were already moving into the town. The Mormons called their daughters Darlene, La Verne and Valoise and their sons Leroy — fancy names to add glitter to a hard-working, businesslike people. If Maxine's father's name had been Max, the name Maxine would have made more sense.

Her hair was red. For that reason alone Westbrook's mother might have called her cheap. Red hair is so often purchased. But her hair was honestly red, all of it. And she had such a smile. Her clothes fit closely and were constructed of materials perhaps better saved for formal occasions. Her shoes were not bought with walking in mind, and she kicked them off and sat with one foot under her. He found that charming, and her habit of running the last few steps as she approached him. But even then, Westbrook sensed some lack in her. Maybe the vanished mother? Possibly she dressed as she thought her mother might have dressed. Some of her clothes may have been her mother's, made over. A want of self-confidence in Maxine moved her to anticipate every wish of her father's and — later — of Westbrook's. Westbrook distrusted generosity.

"Watch out for overgenerous people," his mother once told him.

Maxine Gates was ready to part with whatever she had of value, money, things, and herself.

Herself she gave first.

Like many another, he had used his draft notice as a lever, an argument for sexual accommodation. Perhaps not so bald as that, but he had brought his notice with him on their third meeting at her place in the Matador, had unfolded it and handed it over hoping it might alert her to his probable departure and possible death. He himself was not worried. The war was as good as over. His eyes were poor, and the local draft board was notoriously lenient. Few in that ranch and farm country took much stock in Europe and the Pacific.

He had brought a pint of gin, not so much as a gift but as evidence that he required cheering up. Their first meetings were talk only. He spoke of his ambition to study Speech, to go into broadcasting, and at his disappointment at not getting to the university.

"Then I wouldn't have known you," she said, and that was the second meeting. She spoke of Chicago and of St. Louis and Omaha; he gathered that all cities had a Matador. Had she mentioned a brother, cousin or close friend? He couldn't remember.

Would she like a drink?

"No, but you go ahead. I'll fix it. I fix my father's. He's got some mix."

He would have respected her more if she had submitted to him only after she'd had a drink or two. The effect of the liquor would have excused her. He was astonished at how quickly she responded to him. Although he had had no previous sexual encounter, he suspected this was not her first. He had expected her to be ashamed.

But no. "I love you," she had said. "I wouldn't have let you if I didn't love you."

Did she mean there was such a thing as love at first sight? And it was he who was ashamed. Half dressed, he felt exposed as before a stranger; he turned away to pull on his pants. When she came back from the bathroom, the sound of the flushed toilet a recent memory, the cheapness of the apartment closed in, the flaking paint on the window sashes, the door scarred with gouges with a knife wielded by someone who had desperately once wanted out; the chandelier wanted two light bulbs.

And there he met her father. Although it was only the middle of the afternoon, the man was in pajamas; he might either have just got up or was just going to bed. He had been on the road all week, he said. He was catching up on his sleep, he said.

"How are you, kid," he'd said, said it in so offhand a way that Westbrook felt the man had said those words to many other young men in Chicago or Omaha. "Maxine, honey, bring your old man a beer, will you? And bring your friend here one."

And then as if he'd known Westbrook all his life and saw no need to play host, he sat down before the radio and listened to a ball game.

How are you, kid. A familiarity that smacked of vaudeville and circus types. John Gates.

. . . kid.

Was there something in that voice that resembled the Voice?

Maxine had a quick eye. She had noticed almost at once that he had no wristwatch.

Embarrassed, he had said he had never wanted one, that in Grayling you only had to keep an ear open to the courthouse clock to know what time it was. And you were not out of sight of one of its four faces in any part of town. And he rushed on to tell her about his great-grandfather's gold watch that wound with a key, and how that would one day be his. Bringing up this symbol of his lineage was probably pretty big guns to face the daughter of a man who might have difficulty accounting even for his own father, let alone great-grandfather.

"Oh," she said. "An old watch like that is a nice souvenir but I bet it doesn't keep good time." With their gypsy background it was not likely either she or her father would understand it was more than a souvenir, that such a watch kept not only time but a tradition.

She was a neat, quick typist and wrote business letters for her father, for which he paid her. She clerked in The Store Beautiful Fridays and Saturdays when the rich ranchers came to town with their wives to shop and sit in the green leather chairs in the lobby of the Andrews Hotel.

During the years of the First World War the soaring prices for beef and wool left the ranchers around Grayling with bank accounts beyond their dreams and they began their building of their new houses on the ranches and their houses in town and now their women required something more stylish than that found in the Sears, Roebuck catalogue and they wanted somewhere to go to be seen in that which they were now more stylish. This accounted for The Store Beautiful on the one hand and the Andrews Hotel on the other. The Andrews Hotel — or as it was printed on the stationery available in the drawer of the desk in each room THE HOTEL ANDREWS — had replaced the old Melton Hotel across the Union Pacific tracks as the best hotel in town. It was, indeed, the only other hotel, but it doomed the Melton side of the tracks as the wrong side, although both hotels were in plain sight of each other. The old Melton still accommodated drummers like the father of Maxine Gates and dryland farmers who had not shared in the boom and must spend a night in town after a painful session at the bank. The old Melton did not replace the coiled ropes inside the windows of the upper floors with metal fire escapes and the cook in the kitchen still came out and talked to the guests.

Who Harry Andrews was, where he had come from and where he had got the money to build his hotel was a mystery. He had appeared, bought land on the corner, built the hotel and there he was and there it was. His family, too, was mysterious. Surely they had once been associated with the theater. The two Andrews daughters were almost identical twins, Faye and Fern: they brought to mind the Gish sisters; their hair was not so much red as pink; they were at once active and fragile and partial to garments of crepe de chine and chiffon and surprising tufts of feather or fur. Their luggage was often seen on the baggage truck at the station where GRAYLING was spelled out in neat whitewashed rocks on the lawn. It was said marriages and divorces were in the background. The brother clearly resembled the young Douglas Fairbanks. The Mother resembled the daughters and would appear suddenly in the lobby, smiling and breathless, and vanish up in the elevator leaving behind a whiff of perfume and the memory of heels much too high for a woman her age.

They lived upstairs in a "suite," perhaps in crazy elegance, for their meals were sent up on covered trays from the restaurant below; the florist delivered flowers. The mother or the daughters or possibly the son made serious music on a piano. One of the girls sang. *The Life of a Rose* comes to mind. Her voice was clear in the halls.

What Harry Andrews had created and at the right time was a Peacock Alley. For the big cars, the Packards and the Lincolns, were parked out front on Fridays and Saturdays, the drivers and passengers relaxed in those big green leather chairs or walking in the lobby over a floor constructed of tiny white octagonal tiles like those in the public toilets beyond. They spoke with old Harry Andrews and with young Harry. The men spoke of thousands of acres, thousands of head of cattle and sheep, the white-faced Hereford, the roan or red Shorthorn, the black Angus, the black-faced Hampshire sheep and the Rambouillet. They talked of conditions up Black Canyon and of the flow of water in Grasshopper Creek. Often they retreated into the past. Chuckling to alert a listener to the humor of a story, they recalled old Cruikshank who in the early days ate badger meat and used the tallow to oil his saddle and of old Jerry Burk who on his wedding night sobered up to find himself tied to a stall in his own barn.

But the Westbrook Chevrolet was not parked out front. The Westbrook Chevrolet was parked before Skeet's Bar.

The Andrews Hotel explained Westbrook's later affection for the Hotel Pierre in New York and his "dinners" at the Ritz in Boston. The old Chevrolet explained his Jaguar, and Skeet's Bar explained his parking it at fashionable curbs.

The watch Maxine bought for him was the first inkling that he'd grown into a man who attracts gifts from women, and he had refused it.

"Honest, I can't." An expensive watch and he was tempted.

"But don't you see it's because I love you?"

So he took the watch. He took it because it was a very fine watch.

Then John Gates was asking personal questions. "What did you like to do when you were a little kid?"

Mumblety-peg. Kick-the-can on long summer evenings until it got too dark to see and the bats were abroad.

It was clear Maxine's father hoped to establish a childhood similar to Westbrook's.

"How long have you people lived here in Grayling?"

Westbrook told him.

"Then you'd be what they call pioneers."

Yes.

The father with a glass of beer. "What are your plans for yourself, son?"

IV

MR. N.'S VOICE was breathy and sly. "Westbrook? Say, I've been doing crazy things," he said. "I've been dressing up and going out in the alleys behind expensive restaurants where they throw their garbage and digging in and eating it where people can see. And I'll tell you what I hope, Westbrook. I hope the police or somebody gets me and puts my picture in the paper and my mother sees it, because, Christ, I hate her."

Westbrook could not look back on Grayling, Montana, without a desire to "get even." It is the desire to "get even" that leads to murder. Murder may be an end in itself — a means of removing the offender. If Society is the offender, the murder may be only in passing.

And the desire to "get even" is the drive that makes a man a success. Behind his headlong drive is some snub or insult. Sometimes the precise offense is small, in itself, in hindsight.

Sometimes the precise offense is forgotten, and there remains in the heart only a corrosive residue, like lye.

"Just you wait until I'm rich."

Or famous.

Just you wait.

The Old Families who parked their big cars in front of the Andrews hotel all had a pretty good record of marrying each other. Love as a motive for physical union was not so strong as the desire to bring together two parcels of land, or to wed two bank accounts. It is not to be wondered that husbands strayed — some a few blocks to the Crystal Rooms over the City Drug Store, some to Salt Lake City where they set up their loves in obscure hotels.

Some wives disappeared with salesmen. One chose a truck driver and later waited on her former friends and allies when they came to eat lobster tails at the Sugar Bowl Café. Alcohol did it.

"Wasn't it awful about Helen Chapman?"

Mrs. Chapman had danced nude on a table in the Andrews Hotel dining room after hours. The walls were then pretty with artificial grapevines and clusters of the fruit in glass.

We all know a family who walks in light when the rest of us walk in darkness, or simply walks. Everybody wants to know that family, and he who dies carries home a bit of the glitter. Sometimes that family is richer than other families, and sometimes not, but always that family has style; often the style centers around a woman. In that family even tragedy has style, and who better faces tragedy, when it comes?

It is galling when our own family might have been the

equal of that family, and galling that that family is not even aware of us and of our envy.

For Westbrook, that family was the Hales.

Westbrook might have dated Betty Hale in high school; later, he might conceivably have married her. Such a plan was certainly on his mother's mind.

"I saw Mrs. Hale today." His mother, peeling off her gloves without which a woman was no lady. "Talked with her on the street."

Westbrook heard her with embarrassment. Her social meetings with Mrs. Ed Hale were in the dusty, dark halls of the DAR up over the hardware store and never at the Hale house in town unless at a political rally where any Republican was suffered. Mrs. Hale and his mother had little but the DAR in common. For the last repose of DAR members a pleasant section of Mountain View Cemetery had been set aside so that DAR bones, even in death, might be exclusive, and perhaps there his mother and Mrs. Hale might at last become equals. That may have been in his mother's mind when sometimes she fell silent at the table and lifted her chin. At such moments he remembered she was once pretty.

But never stylish. What she stood for — Victorian morals, a simple dress, good posture and the Westbrook family — had once been valid; but with the loss of the Westbrook land and money, her standards were but a shabby front like the Westbrook "mansion." She made gifts of homemade fudge at Christmas. She plumped up sateen pillows on the sofa; she prepared tomato aspic molds; she cleaned unused rooms; kept the doors closed to save heat. They had a "nice little

roast." If shrewdly carved it lasted two meals — and maybe
leftovers for sandwiches. She restrained her flesh with corsets
and hummed hymn tunes. Westbrook doubted Mrs. Hale did
either.

For Mrs. Hale was stylish — "smart," a word that embraced
a world far beyond Grayling. She wore pumps with the high-
est heels; her clothes came from Marhsall Field's in Chicago.
She was not seen pawing over cloth in The Store Beautiful.

Secure as the daughter of an Old Family married to an Old
Family, she invited to her house anyone who amused her —
newcomers, car salesmen and a dentist who had recently appeared and now maintained the Hale teeth. She turned up at
roadhouses along the way to Butte — the Red Rooster and
the Green Lantern — with blackjack tables in the back room.
Squinting against smoke from the cigarette she held in her
lips, her rings flashing, she played a good game. With her she
had her furs and sometimes her hard-drinking husband, and
sometimes not. In her easy, confident drawl, a reminder that
her family had southern connections, she made friends with
bartenders and waitresses who wisely did not press the relationship. She was close to her cooks and maids — called hired
girls in that country.

". . . and Violet — I swear that's her name — and Violet
said to me, 'Jesus Christ, Mrs. Hale, I can't get my hands on
that God-damned chicken!' " She gave her cast-off clothing
to her help, sometimes casting it off after a single wearing.
She and her friends after an all-night party sometimes repaired to the Sugar Bowl Café when the dawn advanced over
the Rocky Mountains and ate plain fare, pancakes and sau-

sages, and watched the off-duty whores and their supporting pimps.

All this Westbrook's mother knew, if not that Mrs. Hale had slept with her husband.

And yet, "I saw Mrs. Hale on the street. With Betty."

". . . with Betty."

Montana aristocracy was local. No one town was so much more important than another that Old Families there could expect to be deferred to. Shortly before the turn of the century, it appeared that Butte might become the New York or Boston of Montana, for in Butte lived the fabled Copper Kings who imported French châteaux piece by piece and reassembled them on the barren gray hills where grass sickened and died from the deadly fumes from nearby smelters.

Local aristocrats were proud of their peculiar beginnings — what tribe of Indians had frightened their grandmothers, up what gulch Grandfather had discovered gold or bought his first land. Private stories of hardship, fires and sickness and sudden death. It was important when Grandfather had arrived in Montana. A sheep rancher whose grandfather had arrived in 1860 was superior to a cattleman who arrived later. You had to be rich indeed if Grandfather had arrived after 1870, for by then the railroads were running and everybody came in.

The local families grouped themselves around the richest among them. Rich meant your land was worth half a million. Such a family was easy with more than one bathroom. Bathrooms had a peculiar cachet, for the oldest members of the Old Families remembered — some of them fondly — treking to the outhouse in the middle of wild blizzards that swept down the valley. Later on they installed plumbing in an unused bedroom, but the outhouses remained for hired hands and cowboys who never, except perhaps in town on a spree, had flushed a toilet.

Ed Hale was one of those who are said to be sons of bitches except when drunk and by drunk they meant laughing and joking and pinching female parts and driving off into the river. Drunk, Ed Hale committed practical jokes with pails of water, lengths of rope, insects and reptiles. Men were left confused; women, in tears. Shortly before one of his wife's bridge luncheons he had smeared honey on the toilet seats.

So sometimes Mrs. Hale turned up solitary in her jewels and furs at the Green Lantern and murmured to Tennessee, the bartender.

But there was the big white house in town with fluted pillars for the winter months so Betty might attend the Grayling schools, and the even larger house on the ranch and all those acres and well-bred horses and white-faced cattle.

Laying down a bridge hand, Mrs. Ed Hale sometimes had to laugh. "I don't know what I'm going to do with Ed," she'd say. "Gone now in Helena two weeks and nary a postcard!"

Nary. Helena.

If there was a focal point to Montana society, it was Helena, the capital city. Most Old Families had sent a representative there. Ed Hale himself was more politician than rancher. It was said of him who wore suits like a businessman that he had never so much as stepped inside a bunkhouse or so much as sat on a horse. He had never been so happy, it was said by those who wished him happy, as when he sat in the legislature. The hotel was a good one; the Montana Club was a good spot for dinner, buffalo steaks cut from the choicest portions of that doomed beast. In the bar, under one of several oil paintings by Charles M. Russell of cowboys and Indians in their several moods, Ed Hale had once declared himself "the Prince of Grass Valley" and displayed his princely character by tossing handfuls of silver dollars about the room. Now, no silver bell has a prettier sound than silver dollars flung down on hardwood. At once the most unlikely people crawled about the floor. Westerners understand boasting and the tall tale; Westerners admire openhandedness; that incident had little to do with Ed's not being returned to the legislature, but his feelings were hurt. He continued to favor Helena, had so many friends, picked up so many tabs, told so many stories.

And among his friends was the governor himself.

". . . and word gets around fast in prison," said Mr. C. J. who had paid his debt to society, manslaughter, and now drove truck for some understanding people, God bless them.

Word got around fast when a new prisoner was brought in, and faster if he were young and good-looking. Oh, then the fellows took their time shaving and patting on the Old Spice, but Moose Nelson got first pick and he had a tattoo he showed.

Pretty Italian kid up for armed robbery for the first time, stood there scared. Moose had got to him in the toilet. Said he was some chicken.

". . . and the kid tossed in the gasoline and threw in a

lighted match. Then the keys running and Moose Nelson screaming in his locked cell. Mr. C. J. guessed they fainted before they died. There ought to be something different than sex. Mr. C. J. still couldn't stomach the smell of roasting pork.

A toilet was the scene of Westbrook's humiliation.

Mrs. Hale laid down another hand of bridge. "Ed's gone and invited the governor down to the ranch for the weekend," she said. "I'm going to give the old boy pot roast."

Old boy. Pot roast!

"The old dear," she went on, "has to put up with so much bad fancy food he likes a change."

Who but Mrs. Hale would know of the governor's desire for pot roast — and wasn't it good to know the governor so had his feet on the ground that he required it?

"We're not going to do much about them," she murmured. "They need a rest."

They?

The governor's lady, of course, and the governor's daughter.

"Not doing anything about them" meant the nearest Hale neighbors would be asked in, two families whose land abutted the Hale acres, and this did not include neighbors who were neighbors of the Hales when they were in town. So nobody's feelings could be hurt — either your land abutted the Hale land or it did not, and the guests would not be so numerous as to disturb the governor's need for rest.

Few had seen this governor, the capital was at such a distance. They had seen pictures of many governors. A handful had seen a governor on the platform of an observation car.

And now a governor would be walking the Hale property, commenting on the Hale sweet peas, moving out at mid-morning to the fields to see the white-faced cattle standing around, drinking from the Hale tumblers and relieving himself in a Hale bathroom.

Pot roast!

Pot roast might calm a man distracted with stately cares, but the governor's daughter was another kettle of fish.

She was in no need of rest

Far from it. Betty Hale was planning a party at Shoshone Park, so named for those Indians who had once owned that shady area before the whites banished them to the hot, barren flats of southern Idaho. Shoshone Park was a country club for the public. There was talk of introducing facilities for playing golf, a pastime no longer, like the wearing of a wristwatch, considered effeminate. Anyone could join the club. Few did, for it was secure in the hands of the Old Families except for the Friday night dances; you paid a dollar for a snippet of colored ribbon to pin to your lapel to prove you had paid.

The music was by the Owens-Jeffers Orchestra — piano, banjo, sax, cornet, drums and violin — organized by Frank Owens and Bill Jeffers of The Men's Store (Arrow shirts, Florsheim shoes and Hart, Schaffner & Marx suits). There, being measured for his first suit, Westbrook first understood "what side he dressed on" meant on which side of his inseam he sheltered his penis.

Owens and Jeffers wore the identifying striped blazers of red and white of twenty years before when they'd formed the orchestra at the university. Now, balding and sweating they tackled music of a newer day — "The Music Goes Round and Round," "The Peanut Vendor," a Latin American trifle born of the Good Neighbor policy. But however jazzy their blazers, they were more comfortable with slower tempos that did not test their middle-aged hearts — tunes celebrating domestic waterways, the Missouri, the Wabash, the Ohio.

> *Moonlight on the river Colorado —*
> *How I wish that I were there with you.*

The Hales might well have brought in music from the outside, but that was the Hales for you — loyal to Grayling when the cards were down.

"We old people," Mrs. Hale remarked, "intend to keep out of the young things' way." Typical of her to speak of herself and the governor as Old People. Young things! "Betty's making the plans, God help her." And Mrs. Hale shook her head acknowledging the social burdens of the young.

Betty Hale.

Thirty years later, she still entered Westbrook's dreams. Whom had she married? Had she remained in Grayling? Had she children? Did they resemble her? Her beauty left him speechless and awkward. She had not troubled her straight chestnut hair with pincurlers or subjected it to punishing machines; she simply washed it and it glistened. She was not caught up in the foolish fads that disturbed lesser girls — baggy angora sweaters, jodhpurs or riding boots. She understood a tanned skin and white frocks. The word "creole" fitted her. Yes, she walked in light.

News that she would give a party for the governor's daughter polarized the senior class; like a wall of stone it separated the sheep from the goats.

Her close friends were the sons and daughters of the Old Families with a few leaders thrown in — the captain of the football team, a big virile young man who was desired by a Midwest university for his muscles and speed at moving over the ground. And the president of the class, and a boy who was bound to be valedictorian although his father was the janitor: in the past quite unlikely people in Grayling had later on made names for themselves in far places. You never can tell. One was in the movies; his shadows were seen in the Rex Theater. He had changed his name, but they do that because their real names aren't right. Another went off and wrote books. You could tell a lot of people in his books.

A few goats, too stupid to realize they could never be sheep, smiled and spoke to Betty Hale, but their case was hopeless, and wisely they retired to their side of the wall. Possibly they were glad they had so early in life faced and failed a crisis that was bound to loom sometime. A good-hearted blond girl who recited dirty limericks in which Wheeling rhymed with ceiling had never hoped from the start; nor had a vague, dreamy girl who pronounced "scepter" "skepter" in the phrase "mercy's scepter's sway." She turned up some years later as merchandise in the Crystal Rooms. One wonders if she ever looked back on Shakespeare.

Westbrook?

"You'll have to trot yourself down to The Men's Store and

get yourself white flannels," his mother said. "You'll need them anyway for graduation."

It would have been kinder if Betty Hale had summoned guests by word of mouth. But she did not. She sent invitations. And it would have been kinder if she had mailed them all at once. That she did not was a source of cruel hope to certain sheep-goats. Teachers complained of a lack of attention and of horseplay in the toilets.

But on a Friday all had been delivered. The sheep abandoned the school at the passing bell to prepare themselves for the evening's party. Ahead stretched a delightful avenue of bathing, pressing and combing; the boys must wash their fathers' cars.

Westbrook remained behind at school. He sat in one of the toilets which had no lock, invisible except for his feet and six inches of leg. Someone, maybe a male teacher, entered the room and relieved himself into one of the procelain stalls, and sighed. As mortals who suffer illness and contemplate death we are offered small compensations: to empty one's swelling bladder is as pleasurable as slaking thirst.

Westbrook, on the toilet, pulled up his feet.

Whoever it was departed. The articulated brass arm that closed the door sighed and Westbrook heard the towering silence of the high school.

Outside a half-dozen goats formed a circle and played catch. Their shouts were as sharp as the barks of the mongrel dogs that flirted among them, wild with the game.

Westbrook was one of them. He did not join them.

I know who you are.

He was a boy who knew the Westbrooks no longer counted in Grayling, Montana.

It had been only ten days since the Voice spoke. As Westbrook let himself into his apartment he felt again his humiliation at the hands of the Hales. Until the Voice spoke, he had thought the Hales behind him forever — but no. He had transported them East — and given them the name of Edwards. For when he pushed Sewall Edwards and opposed him, he was punishing the Hales whose place in Grayling he resented as he resented Edwards's place in Boston. Edwards and his son, like the Hales, walked in a special light.

Maxine's father with a beer in hand. "What are your plans for yourself, son?"

"I'm not sure," Westbrook said. His plans certainly did not include marriage.

"Oh, sure," her father said. "Fellows aren't sure until they settle down."

Settle down.

But Westbrook had laid his cards on the table. Just as Maxine and her father had laid their cards on the table in admitting to the gypsy, hand-to-mouth existence, talk of other rooms and cities, he had laid his cards on the table early in the game when he told her his future lay beyond Grayling, Montana. Such vague plans could not include her. He had told them of the Westbrook family. They had seen the old Westbrook "mansion" and it had impressed them. To a family with such roots, marriage was serious.

Foolish investments in silver mines and Westbrook's father's proven inability to make anything of the Circle W Insurance Company and his trips out of town had damaged the Westbrook name; but whispers destroyed a family named Rayburn.

The porch of the Victorian Rayburn house was supported by thin pillars turned on a lathe; they resembled piled-up spools. The house had long needed painting and shoring up. The yard was gone to meadow; cats stalked birds and field mice. Wild bushes pressed against the windows. By the time Westbrook knew the Rayburns, they were already ruined, their children fled to cities and out of the shadow of the old people's disgrace.

At fourteen Westbrook knew the magic of words — connotations, denotations and overtones. He believed he knew what "prostitution" meant. He had looked a long time at the word "whore," a subtly moving word. He knew what "exegesis" meant and "idiosyncrasy."

Through the Rayburns — because of them — he learned the word "abortionist." He had heard the word whispered regarding them. He looked it up.

". . . commits an abortion."

Commits.

For an abortionist is what Dr. Rayburn was — if he was now permitted a doctor's title. Westbrook was not certain whether Rayburn had been convicted and had served time at the penitentiary or had only lost his license to practice. It was hard to imagine Rayburn in a cell in prison garb.

Doctors drove Franklins. Rayburn's was an old horse-collar model, so called because of the shape of the false radiator —

false because Franklins were air-cooled and did not freeze in the winter, that season when doctors are required to halt the racking cough and attend the broken bones. The dark green paint had turned to chalk. When other men were busy doing what they did, Rayburn walked slowly down the path through the high green grass, timothy seeded by birds from nearby hayfields. His hat would be straight on his head. He was bearded like Charles Dickens. Having reached the old car, he paused and looked back at the house, should anyone there wave to halt his departure. Then slowly he climbed into the high front seat, started the engine, and drove off. The effect was like the dignified departure of a huge baby carriage.

He'd return, hat still straight on his head, perhaps a paper bag in his hand.

Westbook had once been inside the house. Mrs. Rayburn had telephoned to ask if his mother could spare butter.

Turning from the telephone, his mother had said, "Funny. Why didn't she just come over?"

Westbrook could have told her why Mrs. Rayburn didn't just come over. She didn't require butter. What she wanted was human contact, and felt she no longer had the right to make a direct approach to it but must make it obliquely through the impersonal service of a telephone that presented her voice but not herself.

"You run over with it," his mother said. He had not realized his mother was not so certain of her own position that she could enter the house of two old people whom society had damned.

Mrs. Rayburn had huge thighs and tiny feet and a face so

sweet it recalled a girl's. She embarrassed him with thanks. "Oh, this is so nice of you and so nice of your mother." She clasped her delicate little hands under her vast waist. "And so now you sit right there and I'm going to bring you a nice piece of cake and a glass of milk." She assumed as women do that boys were but empty stomachs on legs. He sat on the edge of a worn plush-covered Morris chair in the house of an abortionist, a house of dark paneling, curlicues, drop-lights that had once consumed gas, turkey-red carpeting worn thin from aimless traffic. A dusty red swag of faded velour, parted in the middle, drooped like wings over the dining room door. Beyond was a huge print of a painting of a woman holding a child.

The house smelled of meat and cabbage, cheap simple foods that gave little trouble, of cloth boiling in solutions of Fels Naphtha, and of soiled garments waiting in wicker hampers. It smelled of human sickness and simple cures, sulfur, menthol and oil of cloves.

And now a shadow was at the front door against the long oval of frosted glass. The abortionist entered, and stood cranelike first on one leg and then on the other, removing his rubbers. "Well," he said, when he had gotten himself straightened out and on both legs again.

"See who's come to call," Mrs. Rayburn said, so light a voice from so heavy a body.

"I brought over butter," Westbrook murmured.

"So it was butter, was it," the abortionist said in a faint, friendly voice. "And I see by the *Examiner* that the high school band continues to give a good account of itself."

"Yes, sir. I guess they're pretty good."

"My husband when younger," Mrs. Rayburn said, "played the violin beautifully."

"Oh pshaw, Phyllis," the abortionist said.

It embarrassed Westbrook that the abortionist felt free to expose his wife's given name. He felt the man begin to draw him into their circle.

"Well, you did. Credit where credit is due. Oh, I'd give my right hand to play an instrument."

The abortionist winked at Westbrook and chuckled. "Phyllis, if you gave your right hand, you wouldn't be able to play your instrument."

"Oh my goodness," Mrs. Rayburn said. "You say such things."

The abortionist spoke again. "Do you play an instrument, young man?"

"No sir," Westbrook said. He could not imagine music in that room. That was a room that heard little plans.

. . . think I'll go upstairs now.

Little puzzlements.

. . . can't think what became of it.

Small hopes.

. . . turn out for the best.

"Well, no matter if you don't play music," the abortionist said. "I see you appreciate it. Phyllis, give the young man another slice of that good cake of yours."

Westbrook's mother had begun to shell peas, a frequent summer chore. She had just begun to shell them because they still hit the metal floor of the pot, a nice mess of peas. Then she fixed him with a look at once intimate and conspiratory.

She started to speak, thought better of it, and then did speak. "What did it look like over there?"

"It was all right," Westbrook said. "They were all right."

"All right, were they?"

"The doctor plays the violin."

"Plays the violin, does he?"

"There's a great big picture of a lady with a little baby."

"With a little baby, is she?"

Years later, Westbrook realized the picture was the Sistine Madonna.

The word Maxine Gates spoke was like a blow to the stomach. That word was "pregnant."

Stunned — he was stunned. The walls closed in, the walls of the seedy Matador Apartments, and that door with the scars on it. That she might get pregnant had not recently occurred to him. Why should it? They had copulated three or four times a week for five months and nothing had gone wrong. She had learned, he supposed, to "take care of herself" in Chicago or St. Louis.

Pregnant!

He opened his mouth. "What are you going to do?"

"Why, nothing. I love you."

His mouth made no sound.

She touched him. "Don't you see? I love you." And then, "And you said you loved me."

Had he? Yes, but only out of passion. For the effect of the word "love," like certain profanities, was an effective whip and heightened the last enthralling throes. I love you, I love you, I *love* you.

His tongue was quite paralyzed. He took a bottle of her father's beer from the refrigerator. When he had money he put beer in there himself. Prying off the cap, he felt she had suddenly become a dangerous stranger.

And so she was. He had never allowed himself to know her. Knowledge of a person traps you. And now she had trapped him.

"What happened?" he asked.

"I guess things don't always work."

He could have shaken her. Not work? Yes, he had heard it said that even a condom wasn't always safe.

In the beginning, he had often been on the point of buying condoms, but in the drugstore in town he was known, and one of them in there was a woman, and likely to wait on you. Things got back to people.

"I'll think of something," he said.

And she began her weeping. He held her, hating to. Sobbing, she said and said and said his name. He could have shaken her, feeling the unreasonable anger one does at stepping on a kitten.

He spoke against her neck. "Does your father know?"

Oh, that close, despairing odor of tears! "Of course not, Tom."

"What do you mean, 'of course not'?"

"I'd tell you first, wouldn't I? It's not my father's business."

Not her father's business? Now he saw. She wished him to know first because she held him responsible, as if he'd committed a crime. It may have been in her mind that *he* tell her father, as in the old days you asked a father for his daughter. Maybe she felt things had got to that point. Well, he was not afraid of her father. There was no question of her father's "thrashing" him, a word his own father used in connection with a person's being thoroughly punished by a larger person. The father could only punish Westbrook with words and with his eyes — or threat of the law.

"I'll think of something."

On that line, he left the apartment. He had never been more anxious to leave a place, and he clutched to himself the desperate if brief hope that what had happened in that room had happened in that room only and outside that room what had happened had not happened.

Pregnant! There is no more shocking word.

Westbrook often thought how curious it was that after making love he was so indifferent to a human body. That mindless drive, of course, was Nature's way of propagating herself. After orgasm, nothing remained but a sense of the tawdry. And now the shabbiness of what he had done — they had done — had come home to roost. No question now of being indifferent to that human body upstairs cloaked in the close smell of tears. That human body had become a millstone, a dead weight. But, like his shadow, inescapable.

"I'll think of something." She obviously took those words to mean he would look for a job. But what jobs there were — even teaching jobs — went to returning servicemen. Going to work for his father would trap him, end his plans before they began. Sitting on a high stool adding up figures could do nothing for the name of Westbrook around which his plans revolved.

He wished Maxine Gates did not exist. She could not have imagined how hard it was for him to touch her when she wept and cried that she loved him. Love? He knew nothing of love.

"I'll think of something."

Folklore said if a pregnant woman rode horseback hard and long she would "come around." And such might have been a solution, had he been a young rancher or even a farmer, one of those misplaced Austrians or Czechs whose fathers had trusted the handbills distributed by the railroads and now scratched out a living on the flats beyond the town, dependent on rains that seldom came. But, solitary and friendless as he was, he had no access to a horse.

And he had heard it said if a woman will drink a pint of raw gin and take a hot bath, and soak there . . .

His back to the wall, he was ready to try anything.

In the State Liquor Store he bought a pint of Dixie Belle.

He took it to Maxine Gates the following afternoon. Her father was off on a sales trip, hoping to distribute generators to the east. Her father wasn't expected back for a week; his movements were predictable — he called Maxine every night when he was away, and brought her little things. Westbrook had never heard the man's telephone voice.

He set the Dixie Belle on the table beside the very bed where the trouble had started. It was an irony that he had once before brought Dixie Belle up there when he got into trouble in the first place, and now Dixie Belle must get him out of trouble. What hopes people do have of gin.

And now she asked, "What's that for?"

Hating her voice, and how she looked at him, he explained.

"I never heard of that," she said.

Sensing she was about to drag her feet — her tone of voice — he longed to shout at her, shout her down. Hadn't heard of that solution? He doubted that.

"And Tom," she'd said. "I don't mind. We'd be having a baby anyway sometime."

Baby. "We're not ready. I'm not ready." God in heaven — couldn't she realize he was hardly twenty years old? "I haven't even got a job."

"But my father —"

Not Your father, but My father. Had she perhaps heard that his father could not afford to support a jobless son? If she had, it was true. Had she heard that his father would prefer not to support him even if he could? That was true, too. Or did she think so little of herself she believed his father would not support him because of her and her pregnancy?

"That wouldn't work," he said.

"But you think *that* will work." The gin. Her mouth trembled. He brought a tumbler from the cramped little kitchen and filled it. "Wait here," he said. Yes, he himself started the water running in the tub, cupping his hand around the flow of it to test the temperature. Had to be hot. Hot as she could stand it, people said.

He said, "Gulp it down."

He shuddered to watch her. She gagged and gagged, her eyes rolled back in her head, but she got it down. She gagged on the second glass. He helped her undress, hating the sight of her naked flesh. He led her to the tub.

She cried out.

"It's supposed to be hot, damn it," he said, and ran a little cold water. "Now try."

At last she could stand it. He wanted to push her. He left her to soak. He sat on the bed and then abruptly rose and sat in her father's chair. He wanted no more of that bed. Twenty minutes seemed a reasonable time for the gin to "work." He kept his eyes on his watch and then on the alarm clock on the table that crowded the room with its inane ticking, repeating Max-ine-Max-ine-Max-ine. He hated cheap alarm clocks, hated the people who bought them, what alarm clocks represented: be here, be there, hurry-hurry-hurry, you're fired, fired, fired.

Weak from the hot water, drunk with tall gins, she stood unsteady while he dried her.

"Oh, Tom, please . . ."

Please what?

He stood behind her, held her up and guided her, his hands under her arms.

She fell as if stunned to the bed and he pulled at her and arranged her. He pulled the bedclothes up. He remained there until he knew she was asleep. To her deaf ears he said, "I'll call you in the morning."

Whenever he thought of her, whenever she popped into his mind, he saw her naked, stumbling, and then asleep at five in the afternoon.

V

WHEN WESTBROOK ATTACKED the abortion laws on "Midnight Line" he hoped to destroy them that other people in a mess might legally approach a doctor.

He had no patience with hypocrisy and jeered at the Catholic contention that abortion was murder. He felt those who supported abortion laws wished but to populate the earth with more Catholics to support more pale celibate neurotics and elect more corrupt Irish and Italian politicians who themselves would breed more and more of themselves.

He was delighted with the weight of the mail that applauded his move and he dismissed as hogwash the letters of protest, most of them from clergymen who, refused the exercise of their private parts except to empty their bladders, would never experience the shock of the word "pregnant."

"I'll think of something." That meant he must get hold of a doctor to fix things up.

Dear good God, if old Rayburn were alive. The old man might have helped him because he had brought butter and listened to talk of fiddles. Westbrook had heard that some women did abortions. And some way to get money, because people wanted money. He'd heard two hundred dollars was the sum.

Oh pshaw, Phyllis.

He would have to find somebody in Butte, somewhere big enough for anonymity. But distance complicates things, and telephone calls, and letters, and then the damned money.

His mind began a mouselike darting and flirting around touching this and that object he owned of value. His mind touched his stamps. For more than ten years he had put a dollar a week into stamps, which were now worth maybe five hundred dollars. But to realize the value you had to approach professionals, and there was no time for that, the professionals being in Chicago and New York and Boston. His stamps weren't worth a dime in Grayling, Montana.

He must think.

So he walked down to the end of the town to the pawnshop not far from the Cabbage Patch where the stores and bars deteriorated in construction and reputation. There the pavement turned to dirt. There in the pawnshop the cowboys hocked their saddles and fancy belts with silver buckles they'd won in rodeos. There people parted with their rings and cameras. Among the abandoned Masonic and Elk material displayed in the window — barred like a prison against the desperate who might break in to claim their property — was perhaps something of his father's. Westbrook had never been inside. The son of the watchful old man in there had been just ahead of Westbrook in high school. The son was studying law back East. There was good money in trading on other people's misfortunes. And then you sent your son back East.

Westbrook handed over his wristwatch, his face hot with the shame of the pauper. He was appalled at how little the thing would bring. He knew what Maxine Gate had paid for it, or said she did. Had she lied to impress him? His hand itched to snatch it back. But he left it there for twenty dollars.

Sons and daughters steal from their parents; some steal to prove they have the right to; some to punish their parents; some steal to satisfy the criminal inside. Some steal out of need.

His mother had a little cache of money. Some of this she put aside from household money. She had attempted to increase her cache selling fudge to friends. She had joined Fireside Industries. They sent her a sign to tack up just outside the front door that said FIRESIDE INDUSTRIES in Old English script and they supplied the materials for making things to sell, paints to decorate china plates and designs to follow to make that possible for someone who is not much gifted. Music boxes to sew into the stomachs of dolls, lengths of linen from which threads could be drawn to make geometric designs in place mats and handkerchiefs.

It hadn't worked out. And the sign out front gave strangers the right to enter and look around the mansion and to report that all was genteel and threadbare.

Her little cache she kept in two- and five-dollar bills inside a heart-shaped red satin candy box; the fabric was rotting, warp and woof had fallen apart. It was tucked under hand-embroidered underthings; it had been long since she had had any reason to appear "feminine" when slightly clad. To those soft garments clung the odor of violets, injured innocence and lingering hope. His mother had never ventured beyond floral fragrances into the dark realms of musk. And it was the scent of violets and the past it evoked that caused Westbrook to leave the twenty-seven dollars intact and not his fear of discovery, for had she questioned him he would readily have admitted he had removed the money; he knew she would not press him, knowing why he had removed it was not fit for her ears. Oh, the past was many things, and it was his mother — pretty and young, then. He recalled her comforting voice long after he had forgotten the cut or insult that had brought him running to her.

So he must turn to his father. What an irony that at last he must count on rather than deplore his father's acquaintance with immorality.

His father had been napping in his "den" — that retreat of the aging male animal; it smelled of stale tobacco smoke and the subtle emanations cast off by the slumbering male body. His father was under a fake Indian blanket he had won at the fair and fully clothed except for his fancy boots which he had set up side by side. They alone were alert: his father grunted and mildly pawed the air, a sound and a gesture meant to cover the embarrassment of a grown man discovered sleeping before the proper time and in a makeshift place.

"Come in?" his father said.

Westbrook couldn't recall being in the room alone with his

father before. Alone in the room he could imagine it a museum of Westbrook memorabilia and not a human dwelling place. "Anything on your mind, son?"

Anything on his mind!

"I'm afraid I'm in trouble."

"Yes," his father said, rising, "people get into trouble. You can't live without trouble."

Westbrook hoped his father was not now going to philosophize.

"There's no one I can come to but you," Westbrook said.

"Yes. I used to go to my father."

"It's about a girl."

"You've got a girl in trouble."

How like his father to jump to that conclusion.

"Yes."

His father fumbled into his fancy boots, moved slowly to the humidor, removed the top. "Cigar, son?" The offer struck Westbrook as curiously obtuse, since the offer of a cigar is a ceremony that follows the birth of a child.

"No thanks," Westbrook said.

"That's right, you don't smoke."

Of course he didn't. Couldn't afford to. And his father might have known young men no longer smoked cigars.

"So I think I'm in trouble."

His father cut off the tip of a cigar with his pocketknife, a bone-handled Case such as ranchers carry to skin and to castrate. It was all of a piece with the California pants and the Blucher boots and the old Circle W branding iron leaning in the corner. "Do you love her, Tom?"

"No."

"Does she love you?"

"No."

"You're sure of that?"

"Absolutely."

"If she loved you, I figure she'd have a right to marry you and give the little child a name and then you could both do what you wanted after that."

"She doesn't love me." He hated love.

"Then I can't let you both ruin your lives."

Westbrook kept silent.

"So I'll look into things," his father said. "Try to find somebody. And the girl will need money for . . ." And now his father was kneeling before the old Westbrook safe of funereal black, its cold efficiency tempered by the long-ago application of a painted rose that flaked away. "How much do you suppose is — for it?"

Frightening that his father should be ignorant of the cost of what he supposed every grown man knew.

"I've heard two hundred."

His father fiddled with the dial; the difficult combination sanctified the money behind it. And his father counted out old bills. Westbrook's hands flinched at their texture, limp from passing so many times from anxious hand to eager hand for goods and services. "Thanks. And someday —"

"Forget it."

But Westbrook was not let off so easily. "Remember that snapshot? Remember, Tom?" To one side of the old Westbrook house over in Helena was a dim picture of a man and a little boy holding a fish. "Remember?"

"What's this for?" Maxine said of the money.

Did she think for God's sake it was for a honeymoon? He didn't say "abortion." He said "get things fixed up." And then he saw her eyes

"I don't want to get things fixed up."

So all along she had planned to get him.

So he spoke right out. He said what a woman means by love and what a man means is often different. To a man it is often sex. Sex alone can come to nothing, he said.

He said they had nothing in common. She must see that ambition and achievement and family were more important to a man than sex.

Oh, he said he was bound to disappoint as a husband since what she wanted, marriage, and settling down before he'd even got started, was out of the question. Yes, out. He laid up words as a mason lays up bricks. He spoke again of his great-grandfather's beginnings, the old man's dream. A man must be true to his inheritance and take up the burden of those who have failed.

And that is where she laughed. Laughed, and she said a rotten word.

He took a breath and went right on. "I know," he said. "I have an obligation to you, and so I got the money for you." He would take her in his father's car to the person who would fix her up. His father was inquiring. He talked and he talked like a sleep-talker. He stared just over her head at the wall beyond and talked and talked, laying up words.

It was her voice that woke him to the moment.

"You coward," she said. "It's murder, and I'll go alone."

Sticks and stones
May break my bones . . .

A coward? Was that "who he was"? But that was so long ago. We are not what we were. Everyone has a right to expect forgiveness — if there were anything to forgive. Her anger would have subsided as the years went by. She would have married, moved into a house, made friends, met the mailman at the door, gone back in and made herself a cup of tea in a sunny kitchen. That's what happens.

It was insane that the Voice should borrow her old anger, harbor it, cherish it, make a career of it and stalk a man who had done his level best to be of use to other people. The Voice was sick — sick as a priest knows so many to be sick. Such are better off out of the way, shut up in an institution.

And again he let himself into the glassed-in cubicle and prepared for "Midnight Line."

That morning the conversation was of birds.

As summer faded and winter loomed, Mrs. A. longed again to greet her little chickadees. Each winter they flew to her in Wellesley, and there they found crumbs aplenty. The same pair cheered her each year — but maybe not, for she understood a bird's life is a short one; then again, maybe in a mysterious way the location of her property was passed on from old birds to young birds when the old birds felt the end was near and Wellesley beyond their powers. But the birds looked the same, and to each new pair, if that's what it was, she gave the timeless name: Mr. and Mrs. Chickadee. Mr. and

Mrs. Chickadee with their peepings and hoppings and aerial insouciance made winter a delight.

Mrs. B. had now returned from Cape Cod where she visited delightful friends with a cottage quite near a well-known artist who was sometimes seen painting; he wandered the beaches in shorts and a funny straw hat; he sat on a verandah looking out to sea, and always alone. Mrs. B.'s friends, friendly people, were bent on crossing over to his territory and calling him to a weenie roast, for even famous people suffer loneliness, since many pepple hesitate to approach them, but not Mrs. B.'s friends. Mrs. B. could watch gulls forever, how they wheeled in the sky on silent wings. As a child she had marveled how easily they sat upon the water — it seemed they had something to teach us. She had clipped from the *Monitor* a poem entitled "Gulls." It was now before her. Did Westbrook mind if she read it? It was so short?

He did not mind.

I have a need of gulls . . .

But now the tone grew darker. A man knew an old couple who had harbored a parrot named Kooka for many years. They had bought the fowl at a reputable shop when parrots were in greater vogue. Childless, they had become emotionally attached to it, and would entrust its care to no one else. Their movements, unless they carried the bird with them, were circumscribed.

Last year it bit the old man as he was fondling it; he died of psittacosis. Torn between her devotion to her husband and duty to the parrot whom they had shared, she kept it long enough for it to bite her to death. Impersonal authorities destroyed it. There seemed to be some lesson here.

Yes, and at the airport a jet sucked up clouds of starlings on takeoff and crashed.

A black-backed gull flew into South Boston and attacked a little puppy. Alone in the world except for the little puppy, a woman had fought the gull off with her purse. Gulls are bigger than you think. They have ugly, cold eyes.

It was all familiar madness as six o'clock approached and the last minutes were at hand. One by one they turned from their phones, washed their hands, opened a beer, crumpled a letter. One by one the lights winked out; Westbrook reached for the cartridge that bore the strains of "Goodnight, Sweetheart."

One light remained.

He took it off the air. He heard the distance.

Off in the void a mouth opened and a tongue moved.

"Maxine died."

VI _____

HE CLEARED HIS DESK of notes, shut a drawer on them, emptied the ashtray into the wastebasket. He closed the door of the glassed-in cubicle and locked it behind him.

He passed under the portrait of the Old Man and passed beside the three now-full-blown roses soon to be replaced by three more scarcely past their bud.

He did not stop for his "dinner" at the hotel but walked directly to his apartment, entered, closed the door, locked it behind him and then locked a second lock he'd had a man install when local muggings pressed closer.

Then he washed his hands.

He was born knowing the meaning behind words as some are born with perfect pitch, those with ears so keen they know what tone rings out when a wooden table is struck.

When he was six he and a little girl walked through grass beside a stream; there they found a decomposing muskrat.

The body was huge with bloat. They had stopped short before this mystery of death.

Then the little girl said, "Pee-yoo!"

He had turned to look at her, instantly recognizing she was not drawing attention to the festering rodent but to herself and her sensitivity. Had she been truly sensitive, she would have remained silent and let him, a male, speak the word.

He remembered the little girl's piglike broad nose, and then her thumb and index finger pinching it against the stench.

Maxine died.

A stone dropped in water.

A door closed.

But not slammed. The slammed door would have been "Maxine is dead." Not, "Maxine died."

"Maxine is dead" would have meant the Voice believed Westbrook had plans or thoughts concerning Maxine, that Maxine remained a pivotal figure. "Maxine is dead" would frustrate thoughts and plans. And the phrase put the death in the very recent past. Yesterday. A week ago.

But "Maxine died" meant a door was closed years ago.

"Why hadn't the Voice spoken sooner then? Because the Voice couldn't reach him. The Voice had searched and searched, listened and listened — doubted, and then at last was sure.

I know who you are.

Like an outlaw, like an animal, he'd been the object of a long search.

But the end was not physical harm, nor even confrontation,

for then the Voice would have called from a point nearer Boston — there was distance in the Voice. The Voice meant only to trouble him with the fact that Maxine was dead.

No, *died. Died* said, ". . . as a result."

Result of what?

He knew from his experience with would-be suicides that you can trace telephone calls. Once the conditions had to be ideal. The caller had to be kept on the telephone, cajoled, flirted with, while on a second telephone you called the police who contacted the telephone company who went to work with electronic devices, beep-beeps and flashing lights, and there you were. Recently the process had become more sophisticated. After filling out forms you could have the telephone company attach a device to your telephone that would keep a caller's line open even after he hung up, but the police must be convinced that the call was a threat to life, obscene, or a routine annoyance call — the call, and then the heavy breathing.

The Voice had made no threat. The telephone company and the police would not be used simply to satisfy curiosity. And this new device would zero in only on calls within the area of the central office. A caller from long distance need not worry about his call being traced. The device would keep the trunk line open when he hung up, but a trunk line services thousands of square miles and a hundred thousand telephones.

The sanitarium for abortions had a nasty reputation, not because the facilities there were inadequate or unsanitary but because what went on there was illegal. His father had talked to him about it, and had seemed satisfied all was well. Now, all over Montana outcroppings of boiling water had mystified the Indians and given birth to legends about angry gods and afforded precarious livings to those who gathered the water into concrete pools and claimed for it medicinal properties. Crippled old people and the young with ugly skin will try anything, but the waters at Jordan Hot Springs were merely a front.

There went the girls who had got themselves into trouble. And prostitutes went there, for they were fertile and sometimes careless with someone they may have loved.

Just as one stops at a diner known to be preferred by truck drivers who, having few comforts, must search out good food, so one would choose a sanitarium that enjoyed whores' custom. Whores have the money, can go anywhere, know the risks involved and where the risks are fewer.

No. He was certain nothing ugly had happened there. And he had been willing to go with her. Hadn't cared who might recognize him there, by that time.

It was she who had prevented him. And used the word "murder."

Yes, you are the less for the death of someone who was close; for like your own hand or lips she responded to you, and you to her. And death, any death, prompts you who lingers behind to wonder if the old have anything to tell the young.

Backward, turn backward. Make me a boy again, just for tonight. What do you say to the boy?

Say, But youth is ephemeral, gone in the space of a winter's afternoon; like poles outside the windows of a hurtling train the years flash by and back over the horizon. Elusive as the rainbow, the years irretrievable as yesterday fall as secretly and swiftly as the leaves and vanish on the wind as you catch your breath.

Let nothing shadow your brief, bright years. Know that much you thought mattered does not. Snubs. Insults. Whether your wallet was stuffed with bills or empty. Whether you were the first or the last to be asked to dance, or your dress the prettiest. What anyone thought. Hurt feelings. For one day in all amazement you will say, "How could that have grieved me? How could that have shamed me?"

Say, Almost everything passes and only what does not is worth your while. Music? Perhaps. Books? But surely love, and children.

It might have been.

Had he even an inkling of his talent then, he would have married her. What did it matter that she was not Betty Hale. It might have been he who had led her into a house where sun lay flat on the kitchen floor. And how she had run to him those last few steps and stood on tiptoe to be kissed. And he would not now be the last of the Westbrooks, the end of the line with nothing but a good salary, a handful of postage stamps and a little fame.

He looked back with nostalgia to the day when he first realized he could afford to keep a hundred dollars in his wallet. Since then he had become so secure he had reduced that sum to seventy-five dollars, but carrying money still prompted a sensation of security and power. That power he had tested on several occasions.

Eating his "dinner" at the Ritz Westbrook, when he had

owned a car, never worried about parking tickets; the attendant in the Ritz parking lot had an understanding with the police. In the meantime as he "dined" he watched car after car belonging to the unimportant ingloriously hauled off upended to the public garages where they were impounded. It is a shock indeed to see an empty space where only moments before your transportation had been. Shock, then dismay, and then rage — but there's nothing for it but to taxi to the public garage and hand over fifteen dollars to repossess your property.

"I'm Tom Westbrook" had a dozen times caused a ticket to be torn up, but once that had cost him his autograph.

The yellow painted curb in front of the old gray stone church on Bowdoin Street was generally respected. Westbrook assumed the space was reserved for a hearse and the attending flower car bearing blooms which, heaped on the grave, would hide this newest wound in the earth and last until it had scarred over a little. However, the space would have accommodated three hearses and a flower car, a circumstance not likely to arise. Further, from what Westbrook knew of the neighborhood it was not likely any of the local dead would be honored by so many flowers that it took a special machine to carry them. Up and down the street poverty was in the doorways and in the garbage cans. A sign beside the door of the church purported that the church was Episcopal, but the old fellow inside seemed to consider himself a priest instead of a minister — that is what his clothes said — black pants with a black robe buttoned by many little buttons down the front. In this outfit he sometimes swept the steps and the sidewalk, now and again stopping to upend the broom and inspect the straw. Westbrook would probably have had no contact with this thin old priest except that for some years the Old Man had lived across the street near the top of the Hill at the old Bellevue Hotel, and there Westbrook went Sunday afternoons for beer and pretzels in the pub — one week the Old Man treated and the next Westbrook treated — and then they went upstairs in the ancient elevator and played checkers, at which the Old Man was very good indeed.

Except for the checkerboard, for piles of no longer published magazines leaning in the corner — *Literary Digest, Collier's* and *Liberty* — and the Old Man's first microphone on the writing desk, circa 1924 when Westbrook was nine years old in Grayling, Montana, the high-ceilinged dark old living room was impersonally furnished in hotel Victorian.

It had not seemed unreasonable when there was no other parking space to pull up to the yellow painted curb before the gray stone church. Several spring Sundays for as long as four hours, Westbrook parked there with never a sign of the thin old priest. However, one summer afternoon just as he prepared to cross Bowdoin Street back to his Jaguar, the old fellow came out, down the steps and began a close inspection of the car. Westbrook slipped inside the coffee shop of the Earl Hotel just across, ordered coffee, and watched out the window. What was the old fellow up to?

Twice the priest circled the car, but didn't seem interested in the license plate he might have phoned in to the police. He touched the leather upholstery, looked in at the dashboard, glanced up, and then tried the gearshift. However he had rejected the flesh and the devil, he had apparently not rejected the internal combustion engine. And then he did a most unpriestly thing: he kicked the front tire.

Not many weeks later, Westbrook was just about to fold himself into the Jaguar when the door at the top of the church steps opened and the old priest hurried down and faced Westbrook — and smiled.

"I have a parishioner inside," he said. "I'm afraid she's in trouble again."

Westbrook stood speechless. The word "again" somehow involved him in the woman's plight. How on earth was he to react to this statement? And around him the city of Boston went on. A lean dog glanced from side to side loping along the gutter. A helicopter chugged airily in from the airport and hovered over a building. A young woman quarreled with a child who held a balloon; the traffic surged up Bowdoin Street and turned right at the top near the State House where no one was allowed to park but the governor, the legislators — and Westbrook.

"I'm afraid she needs seventy-five dollars this time."

Westbrook stared, aware that he was face to face with an appalling innocent who believed anyone in trouble could look to a stranger for help. He found himself reaching for his wallet.

The old priest cleaned him out, right down to the last bill.

Recently he had eaten alone at the Ritz Bar. Across Arlington Street in the Garden the swanboats drifted on the pond carrying little children on a magic voyage.

It had been long since he'd eaten at such an hour, years

since he'd been awake at that time, for the strain of playing priest to so vast and demanding a congregation required plenty of sleep.

Near the window, at a table for two, two smart-looking women fondled dark glasses meant from time to time to save their eyes from daylight, to supply an air of mystery or to render themselves fairly unrecognizable to those who might otherwise know them. They sipped whiskey sours. One spoke easily but slightingly of Chicago. Her presence in that vast town had been recently required because of the sudden death of her husband's old aunt. Her husband had been tied up, so the burden had fallen on her; she had had to leave the Cape even as the summer began. The hotel where people stayed in Chicago had gone downhill. Should she ever again be required in Chicago, she would put up at the Blackstone.

Her companion leaned forward. "The Blackstone!"

"I'm afraid so," the woman said. They hesitated between the Chicken Salad Ritz and the cold sliced beef. Either was a nice change from the searing heat outside.

But they had not yet purged their brains. Gingerly they probed a tragedy that had visited one of their own class — the father of a badly retarded infant. The father's gentle education and formidable amateur skills before the mast had not precluded a homely knowledge of electricity, that silver is an exquisite conductor and so is a diaper soaked with urine. He had attached the handles of the silver serving tray to an extension cord, set the little child down on it, and all was over.

"Did you know him?"

"I knew *of* him."

"How awful for *her*."

"Yes. She was just ahead of me at Miss Pride's."

On a banquette that half-encircled a table sat two men his age. They were done with eating. What tools they had used to feed themselves were now properly on their empty plates, their neatly positioned silver signaling no more food, an open invitation to the waiter to carry off their leavings. Their napkins were rumpled little tents. The one had asked the other to lunch there. They were not close friends but recent business acquaintances, a way of saying each sold something. Since they lunched at the Ritz, what they sold would be heavy machinery or insurance in excess of a hundred thousand. The cigarette lighter one of them touched as if he found wisdom there was emblazoned with a device that would turn out to be his company's insignia, some drop forge and tool works.

Not close friends, or the one would not have volunteered information that the other, as a close friend, would already have known.

"My son is at Harvard. He's twenty-two."

Pride in every word, and Westbrook understood the ultimate end of the drop forge and tool works, but there was more pride in "He's twenty-two" than "He is at Harvard."

At twenty-two the future master of the tool works had survived measles, whooping cough and a dozen indifferent teachers; he had learned to drive and to dive and to play squash. He had sidestepped drugs and alcohol — two topics popular on "Midnight Line" — and he had come to terms with sex. Now he stood broad-shouldered and clear-eyed, his father's immortality.

"He is twenty-two." The words made Westbrook feel inferior to the man who uttered them; for a man who has not or cannot have issue is simply less a man. He wished he had some means, some graceful way to introduce himself to the speaker, to say, "I am Tom Westbrook. I am heard in thirty-eight states. I am a power. I will be remembered."

He raised his chin. *It might have been.*

When the dream is shattered, what then? We plod on like stoics, grudgingly hopeful that perhaps endurance is an end in itself or will lead to some reward. Maybe someday it would be said of him, "He was a man."

The Westbrook "mansion" was gone, its space occupied by a supermarket. His father had moved into a "nice little place." He had not expected his mother to go before his father. She went suddenly and at a critical time for Westbrook. The man Edwards had just been brought in over everybody's head as manager and it would not have done for Westbrook to absent himself just then. His father understood. His father had lasted two years longer and had made all his own arrangements so there was no need to travel out to Grayling, especially since his father had had himself cremated. One cannot feel the same obligation to a box of ashes that one feels toward a human body. . . . *in Mountain View Cemetery.*

From his window upstairs in the old house he had often watched the hearse and the trailing sedans wind up the bare side of the hill to the spot where almost everybody in Grayling ended. The cemetery was so near the town anyone wishing to could glance down at the north face of the courthouse clock and see what time it was. Heizey Frolicker drove the hearse, he who so resembled Teddy Roosevelt, the glasses, the flashing smile, the hand suddenly shot out in greeting. The hearse moved faster in the wintertime. Stray horses knocked over the fruit jars of flowers; frost felled the tombstones. How remote death was, then.

Maxine's father, returning from his territory, would toss his hat at the chair. "Hello, beautiful. How you been?"

Oh, Christ. But now it was done with. The Voice had closed the door at the end of a long, long corridor. And in memory of her he had attacked the abortion laws — that first test of his power. He might have lost his job. Instead, he became invulnerable. In memory of her, in atonement, he had given himself to others.

Then how account for this uneasiness when the next and the next sessions of "Midnight Line" passed and the Voice was silent? This perverse longing to hear the Voice just once again? This reluctance to believe the last door was closed?

It may have tried to get through and failed because of jammed telephone lines. Regular callers sometimes complained they had to wait a month. But some flat, robot quality in the Voice suggested a stalking patience. Maybe even now the Voice waited in some room. Westbrook saw a shabby raincoat, a faintly lighted pay phone just off a highway.

If Maxine's father were still living, the man would be more than seventy.

VII

DARKNESS CONDONES the bizarre.

The early hours of "Midnight Line" were a crazy quilt of mad trivia about dogs, maimed cats and bloodstained upholstery.

Mrs. B. no longer counted on human beings. Couldn't count on them as friends. She had so turned in on herself she now trusted only her dog who along with her was listening to the program. He cocked his little head. She said if her dog could speak, it would. Whatever she ate, she shared with her dog. If she made meat loaf, she made enough for two.

Then suddenly she laughed. She said her dog had buck teeth.

Now a woman called to share her recipe for meat loaf. Her husband said her meat loaf was the best he'd eaten, and as a traveling man he had sampled much meat loaf. A lot of onions and no other seasonings than salt and pepper and handle the meat tenderly. When her husband got after a meat loaf of hers none remained for dogs, and she had never heard of dogs with buck teeth. Was it a fox terrier, like in His Master's Voice that used to be? What had become of bulldogs and fox terriers and you know how dogs got to look like who owned them. She had an aunt who had one and did.

An attorney announced himself. His voice was high-pitched and edgy, no voice to make a good impression on a jury. His lack of a mate and small quarters made it virtually impossible (he said) for him to keep a cat he had found under his car in the Navy Yard where he had gone to confer with a client. The cat's tail had been cut off at the base of the spine so recently it still bled and no one at the yard knew what to do about the cat, so it bled on his hands and on his pants and he used paper towels he carried in his car for his windshield when it needed it.

He had no knowledge of a nearby vet, had never owned an animal, couldn't take the responsibility, and couldn't think because the cat was clawing him not realizing he was trying to help so he wrapped the cat in paper towels to keep some blood off the upholstery and took it to his apartment where it was now, with him.

Westbrook gave him the name of an animal hospital and thanked him for his call.

You saw so few cats in the city and so many dogs, yet the shelves of stores were heavy with food for cats, with preparations for their health and trinkets for their amusement and occupation and sacks of material into which they might shit.

Now came a spate of calls with advice for Mr. J. the attorney.

A woman urged him to carry the ruined animal to a refuge

across the river in Cambridge. A woman had left behind a half-million dollars and the cats accepted there were not put to death but in pleasant surroundings they were allowed a natural death like anybody.

What cats were accepted at so grand an establishment? The ones they had room for.

Mrs. S. felt sorry for the cats whose applications were rejected. She had had an experience similar to Mr. J.'s, not with cats, but she had gotten blood all over her upholstery which was of a faun color — you know, light — and the trick was to get right after the blood before it "set."

A caller wondered if Mr. J. had found the other end of the cat's tail, if he had looked for it.

Miss R. was a bore. Westbrook would recognize her on the street, tall, thin and flat-chested, her long arms spattered with pale freckles. She was forty but a terrible mindless innocence kept her deceptively young and busy with the silly concerns of youth. She most certainly had before her notes to prompt her speeches. She was accident-prone. The oven door opened and tripped her. Hot fat leaped from her pans and seared her. Cuts and bruises were an old story and her weak ankles twisted on the safest of floors. She fell asleep in the sun and her fair skin blistered under the cruel rays. Hospitalized, she found that her insurance had lapsed. She was mystified by the loss of money she had hidden from herself. Like Christ himself, she suffered and spoke for all once a week.

She reported the earliest of birds; each spring she gathered into her arms the first pussy willows and she called them pussies, her little pussies. Deep in the summer she could not endure the agony of cloth next to her skin; she wandered nude about her rooms. Friendless but for Westbrook, she drove alone in a machine bequeathed her by her father, who had wanted a boy, to a marsh she had known as a child and there she plucked the cattail. Returned home, she arranged them in appropriately tall vases and prolonged their lives by spraying them with lacquer.

Westbrook was adept at shutting people off. Patiently, patiently he waited until a garrulous caller had carelessly made a point.

"So be it," he would say. "And thank you for your call." The caller's sense of being abandoned was alleviated by his gentle voice and thanks.

Miss R. was another matter. She never made a point without adding the word "and." Her monologues were excruciating rosaries hung on that handy conjunction.

"But I'm not finished, Tom."

She was tyrannical, a trait common among the truly stupid.

And now she was reporting that two squirrels had since early spring dwelt beyond her bedroom window.

"A male squirrel and his little mate was with him."

Westbrook's voice was edged. "I think maybe we've had it with the male squirrel and his little mate. You made that clear last month."

And that was the end of Miss R.

Because the third of the little red lights before him had glowed steadily for some thirty minutes.

And there it was.

"Westbrook?"

He took the Voice off the air. He heard a close rustling—rubberized raincoat? Telephone rubbed on stubble of beard?

"Maxine died in childbirth. She . . ."

Westbrook's profile had the sharp, deaf-mute expression of

a newly prepared corpse. Two minutes ticked by—dead air—
time enough for a drowning man to relive his life.

But now at his right hand the little lights ordered him
back to his priesthood.

There is no such time as the present; as the word is spoken
it slips into the past or glides into the future. Because the
present does not exist it is pointless to consider it. Past and
future are a different matter. Having no past to turn to,
Maxine's father sought answers in the future. Westbrook
remembered him sitting at the table looking for answers in a
game of solitaire.

"Maxine, honey, get your old dad a beer?"

Her father had looked so like a boy. And beer beside him,
he played the game in silence, laid out the cards so carefully,
touching his lips with his tongue, and the outcome meant
something more than a brief triumph over some recent reversal. What did he see in those cards?

Having no future, he turned over the cards of the past.

The state institutions in Montana were supported by the
public and the public was free to inspect them. The buildings of the sanitarium were off to the right on a hill as you
drove north from Grayling to Butte. There the tubercular
sat on porches hacking and spitting. Beyond them were
empty fields.

The turreted stone prison in Deer Lodge had a store outside the gate where tourists might buy the handiwork of
prisoners, watchchains of braided horsehair, furniture for
dollhouses, footstools and chopping blocks. Guards with

rifles stalked the catwalks. Murderers knew their end—hanging by the neck until dead as the judge insisted—and at last they knew the very day. But not the hour. They would know that later and suddenly, with footsteps at the end of the corridor.

Seniors in Grayling High School who elected sociology took a trip in the spring. They traveled to the State Insane Asylum in Warm Springs.

"He's in Warm Springs" or "She's in Warm Springs" was said of mad old sheepherders who had seen one too many sheep or of cooks who saw no end to cooking and suspected rays were being beamed on them by sworn enemies.

Many elected sociology. Mr. Ogren was unmarried and he was jolly and drove his own car and filled its space with those who needed it.

Tables at Warm Springs were set apart for visitors, but it was nicer to carry lunches and to eat under the trees in the pretty park. So the girls packed fried chicken and potato salad (kept cold to protect against death by botulism) and Mr. Ogren brought along oranges and bananas from the Safeway and he laughed.

A disagreeable odor lurked in the main building. Sour mops and madness. Old people sat on benches, some cooing and fondling dolls. A boy Westbrook's age had long used the same bed. He laughed under the covers and his name was Clyde.

One room they did not enter.

And the Orphans' Home.
Through the mails to those it was hoped were tender-

hearted came red cardboard hearts the size of a silver dollar with strings attached to tie to a coat-button, if you would.

HAVE A HEART AND HELP A CHILD.

The stern brick buildings not yellow like the courthouse from whose tower the Three Ones tolled but red brick and the buildings were forbidding in their simplicity. No gothic towers like those that set apart the normal school. No turrets like the state prison's; for the eldest orphans were only fifteen with no experience yet in theft, rape and murder.

Out front was a broad, close-cropped lawn where the orphans were forbidden to play. In the center of all that forbidden green an American flag on a tall white pole waved and testified to a dutiful government.

The playground was to one side, half an acre of serviceable cinders enclosed by a hurricane fence that sloped inward that frisky orphans might not shinny over and escape what was in store for them.

Orphans? Westbrook had never known one. They were the bastard sons and daughters of waitresses and ranch cooks who had grasped a moment of rapture with drifting cowboys and hayhands. Or their parents had been consumed by flames in a shack in the Cabbage Patch. At sixteen they were turned out to work on ranches. Some had learned how to grind valves, clean the jets of carburetors, to advance and retard the spark.

The girls — what is there for an orphan girl?

In high school everybody was a De Molay except for a few Jews, Roman Catholics and dryland farmboys who couldn't afford the dollar. Neither were the order's mysteries open to the blacks, but no one had ever seen a black in Grayling except in the movies where they sang and danced and shuffled around and made people laugh and everybody felt better.

As a De Molay you took the first step to Masonry, a step to dark secrets and the right to dress up in robes and things. Westbrook was a poor De Molay. He was not elected to even the meanest office but had once been a substitute for an officer with mumps as Outer Sentinel and for two hours he sat in the vestibule where people left their damp coats and he watched a gilded wicker basket of dusty crepe-paper roses the Order of Eastern Star had left out there as the last stop before the dump. His brush with the society left him with an impression of sleazy purple plush, peeling gilt and throne-like stools.

The sociology class sallied out in the spring to inspect the mad in Warm Springs; so the De Molays moved across the state to a town chosen as ripe for the Conclave, a gathering of brothers. Meetings were scheduled and dinners and dances and speeches prepared by hearty Masons, their spiritual fathers. Townspeople opened their homes to strangers. Quite plain daughters with damaged skin and sweaty palms might expect blind dates with boys who had damaged skin and sweaty palms as well. The closing ceremony of the Conclave preceding the benediction pronounced by a Protestant clergyman was the singing by massed De Molays of the song "Mother," the words written large on a huge blackboard on the stage to prompt the ignorant. The final phrase of each verse was ". . . my best girl," and it was sung to the tune of "Old Black Joe."

Westbrook was overlooked when cars were dragooned and seats assigned for the drive to Bozeman. Recently he had learned to drive the old Chevrolet, but not so he could ride around town, a sport his mother called "joyriding." ("I saw them all out there joyriding.") Joyriding led to drinking and sex and fatal crashes in Railroad Canyon; the Highway Department set up tall thin white crosses where bodies were found, as a warning. No, his driving was for family convenience. ("If your father got sick, you'd have to drive.") A little accident at the First National Bank made his mother abandon her driving forever. She had been questioned by Skinny Nelson, the sheriff. The time had passed for driving and bearing children and bolting the Methodist Church for the Episcopal. She classed cars as "open" cars and "closed" cars. She was proud that the Chevrolet was "closed."

That he drive the ninety miles to Bozeman for the Conclave was closely considered by his father whose boots were not made for walking.

"No room in the other cars," Westbrook lied. He lied because his father liked his having friends. "Ike Nelson and Steve Barret want to go with me."

"All right then, son."

"Drive slowly," his mother said. "Then if anything happens or something drops off you can stop in time."

He drove off in the direction of the Nelson house, the lunch she had packed beside him. There were brownies in it.

An hour later he passed the Orphans' Home.

He had never before been so far from Grayling. He wondered what on earth had prompted his parents to let him go.

He cared nothing for the Conclave — only wanted to get away. His mother had slipped him fifteen dollars from her cache, urging him to hire a room at the Baxter Hotel, but he intended to sleep in the car covered over with the gray lap-robe. He was going to get whiskey and he was going to find a girl.

He found the girl at the opening dance, a function housed in a big shed of new lumber close by the Madison River whose surface reflected the light of the western stars. Teen-agers loped and hopped around. Many drank, for drinking begins early in the state of Montana. Each delegate had a badge of white cardboard that revealed his name and home-town. Some wore Turkish-inspired fezzes at a jaunty angle; the Near East is somehow significant in Masonic ritual, something about Saracens or somebody; and strange hats lend insouciance to even the doltish.

The girl sat on a folding chair against the bare wall. She smiled so quickly and went so willingly to the old Chevrolet parked among the trees. Halfway there he was first attacked by a frightful illness called the Swoops when the earth sud-denly slides away and your brain is awash with nausea. In the near distance the orchestra played "You're Driving Me Crazy" and he was drunk, so awful drunk, and would she like a little drink?

Oh, yes, just a teensy-weensy one, though, and her name was Alyce and how to spell it. She hated the other way. It was too ordinary. And her father was with some men in Spokane. Did he know about the Hotel Davenport in Spokane? With birds in the lobby? She was pale and thin, thin hands, thin feet; her dress of kelly-green crepe de chine was outlined at the V-neck with coarse, gilt braid like that on sofas. "Oh listen," she said, "this is so crazy."

The Swoops attacked again in the back of the old car. He had to get sex before he got sicker. He wanted to know he could. Then he'd be like everybody, he wanted to be like everybody and be a little boy again and cry if he wanted to. "I'm a Westbrook," he said, close to tears.

"Silly! What's a Westbrook, anyway! Oh, this is just crazy. We oughta go back." But he was arranging her on the mohair cushion and she was allowing him what his mother called intimacies.

"Wait a sec," she whispered. "All right. Now."

Her breasts were dull as a dollop of dough, but still he knelt on the floor feeling around. And then the Swoops struck hard and he vomited.

Some on her.

She sat up and slapped him hard. "You nut," she said. "You crazy boob."

He slept covered over with the soiled velour robe, his knees pulled up to his belly, fending off the spring chill.

But it was heat that woke him, the sun beating straight down on the metal roof of the old car. The windows were rolled up; the heat expanded the gas of his recent vomit. Gasping he crawled out of the car and carried the offensive gray velour robe ahead of him, holding it gingerly as he might carry off the lifeless body of a diseased animal. He brought it to the banks of the Madison River. He floated it, and with a stick flicked off bits of the lunch his mother had packed for him, loathe to have physical contact with what had so recently been a part of him, his sustenance. No part of it was the brownies; those he had disposed of the afternoon before. Beyond him, in the middle of the slow-moving river, the root of a tree resembling an enormous gray molar had been washed up on a sandbar.

And that was the Conclave.

But in the years that followed he chiefly remembered, as if it had a special but puzzling significance, his passing the Orphans' Home the previous day. Beside the home, quite near the highway, inside the hurricane fence, the children had chosen up sides and screamed as they fought for possession of territory like dogs in a pound.

At some distance from them, in the corner nearest the highway, one child had stood alone, staring out through the mesh at the old Chevrolet.

Never later had he been able to account for what he had done. He had slowed the old car to a crawl, and then waved to the child who, for a moment, simply stared, but then waved back a slow angular wave. At that wave, Westbrook had pulled the car over to the shoulder of the highway where the tumbleweeds were already getting a hold in the poor earth. He stopped, picked up the lunch beside him and got out.

He walked over to the child, feeling that eyes watched him from the upper windows of the brick buildings and that what he was doing might be prohibited by rules tacked up on a bulletin board inside.

The mesh of the fence was too small to receive the

newspaper-wrapped lunch as it was. He unwrapped it — and recognized a truth: that it is right to give an orphan brownies but not a ham sandwich; the one expressed affection; the other, pity. And nobody wants pity, especially one who has a right to it. So he poked the brownies through the mesh one by one and without a word the little boy accepted them.

Had he, at that moment he stopped the Chevrolet, an inkling of the simple future? Past and future — was Time all of a piece, and did it move back as well as forward, ebb as well as flow? Such would explain why artists passed over in their own time come into their own years later and why Tutankhamen's tomb lay hidden until the day when archeology was prepared to preserve the treasures inside.

At sixteen he faced an awkward piece of his future.

For in those minutes of dead air on "Midnight Line" when the Voice like an old wax record was speaking, he clearly saw Maxine's father sitting at that table laying out the cards, seeking an answer in an ace or a jack of diamonds.

Must he put the little boy in the Orphans' Home?

". . . in childbirth. She had a little boy."

VIII

WESTBROOK USUALLY SLEPT well from nine in the morning — just after the second half of *The Today Show* — until three in the afternoon in a double bed, a fourposter of dark mahogany, carved pineapples crowning each post. The primitive ropes that had once supported the horsehair mattress he had replaced with slats, and the mattress with box springs and a Beauty Rest. If the calls had been tiring and he had been required to play more than a host, he sometimes had to unwind before retiring. A little nervous, he would take a glass of warm milk before he slept.

But the Voice laid bare a weakness he had not suspected — a cranky bladder. He had taken his milk and had climbed into bed and then he was up and in the bathroom before his blue toilet, his mind crying "Urinate!" and his bladder crying "Not yet!"

The little boy would be thirty-five years old.

A baby had become a child and then a boy and then a man, and this man had nothing in common with Tom

Westbrook — nothing but blood. In that man was a cluster of chromosomes identical with his own. And Westbrook stood before a mirror to see a man who suddenly had a son. He was not now a priest but a father with real and not fancied responsibilities. A door had swung open. He was not the end of the line.

Responsible, he made two practical moves. He wrote to the clerk of court in Grayling, Montana, for a voting list. He wrote to Mountain Bell Telephone for a Grayling directory. It was reasonable to think his son's name, either Westbrook or Gates, might appear there — unless the boy had been given to an orphan asylum. Then, God only knew what name the boy might have. He was appalled at the formless enormity of what lay ahead. Should these moves not work, he must turn to a professional.

Mr. F. had long been a controversial caller on "Midnight Line." He called on Fridays quite early in the program and Westbrook let others speak directly with Mr. F., who believed himself gifted with extrasensory perception.

Should so shadowy a power exist, it mocked privacy and rendered useless the dimmed light and the barred door. He who practiced it need not guess what went on in the bedroom nor what words moved over the telephone wires suggesting trysts and mischief. He *knew*.

Mr. F.'s claim to this intelligence inflamed Mr. H., who remembered bread at five cents a loaf and who challenged Mr. F. and demanded that if Mr. F. did indeed have such powers, why didn't he tell the police what had become of the Brink's robbery money? Mr. H. referred to a holdup in which robbers carried off millions of dollars in a Brink's truck. Lacking sufficient bags they had had to leave behind two million dollars, an awesome quantity of precious paper. Why did not Mr. F. reveal the lair of the Boston Strangler who still walked abroad?

Mr. F. in his tiring nasal voice had explained again and again to Mr. H. that all powers are not granted even to those who have ESP, but that did not satisfy Mr. H., who accused Mr. F. of being a common fraud. Was Mr. F. prepared to tell Mr. H. what he, Mr. H., had in his hand at that moment?

"What you have in your hand?" Mr. F. asked. "You have your telephone in your hand," and in thirty-eight states there was good-natured laughter. In thirty-eight states they wished Mr. F. well; it is heartening to believe that someone can see around corners. If magic is abroad, some dark day we ourselves might dare call on it.

Mr. F. had in the past guessed correctly that a woman had recently gone into Philadelphia where she had visited her sister, older than she, who had married a policeman. By the policeman she — the sister — had had no children, and so they owned and loved a dog. Mr. F. identified the dog as "smallish" which it was indeed, but failed to name its race.

With astonishing accuracy he had described the room where a former showgirl sat, even to the blue cretonne curtains and low, white coffee table on which was a pack of Kent cigarettes.

"And you got something loose, something loose on," said Mr. F., "and I see a glass in your hand." All true.

Westbrook's own remarkable ability to piece together lives from odds and ends did not come from seeing around corners but from his well-tuned ear, his familiarity with common patterns of life and his sharp attention to trivia. He knew that one fact leads to another, and that the consequences of a single act fan out. Having heard and attended to Mr. F., he knew Mr. F. as he was, a bachelor neither homosexual nor heterosexual — simply sexless — and that his freedom from sexual appetites granted him a certain poise. His voice pegged him as of the Irish persuasion, and his insertion of the letter "y" between the first and second letters of the word "salad" placed him south of Boston. He lived with his mother, a widow cruelly torn between wishing he would marry and fear that he would; for a wife would carry him off and she would be left to her dark little duplex and memories and a statue of the Infant of Prague wrapped in cellophane against the grime of the city.

Mr. F.'s cronies were quite like him. They were thirty-nine or forty "years of age," worked in the post office, wore suits the jackets of which they removed when sorting mail. They were fans of baseball but did not play. They bowled once a week and had a few beers and talked about what transpired in the mailroom. Mr. F. and his cronies were modest, loathe to expose their naked feet and never their private parts. They wore pajamas and slept late on weekends. They good-naturedly put off doing little jobs around the house their mothers suggested. As men, they defended their right not to wet their hands in dishwater or to carry brown paper bags in public. As they aged they looked more and more like women and more and more resembled their sister, the nun. None had read a book since high school and each was uneasy with those who did, but all had owned a dog at whose death they had removed themselves to the bathroom to weep.

Westbrook knew the Mr. F.'s of this world.

He knew something more of his son than simply that he was thirty-five.

He knew they had allowed the destructible fetus to grow into a human being, and to be born. And being born, he knew it must now have a name. Maxine, pregnant, and her father would have settled on a name. John? Certainly not Tom.

Westbrook shook his head, appalled at the mistakes men make in youth, and he was penitent, as men are, after the fact.

The little boy was half an orphan and could turn to no one but a peripatetic grandfather who must occasionally drop in somewhere — the Orphans' Home? Maybe on holidays? — for John Gates had been a kind man. Thanksgiving? Christmas? (Paper wreathes pasted to the windows that looked out on the highway.) But birthdays would be sad occasions, maybe deliberately uncelebrated: birthdays in this case were anniversaries of death as well as life. And after so many birthdays the question would loom, Who is my father?

The kind thing is that the little boy was told his father was dead. That would account for much. The father, then, had died before the little boy's birth. It was likely that John Gates had awarded the mythical father a set of credentials, that his looks had been described (narrow feet, cleft chin), that he had been accorded small human traits, quick laughter, skill with firearms or a carpenter's tools, a love of Nature, a knowledge of the songs of birds. Since John Gates had not been imaginative he might simply have described some friend of his as the little boy's father, and that description the little boy took to bed with him.

But someone knew the truth, and he was the Voice. And vindictive: the Voice would now remain silent a few days — to try him, to tease him, to trouble him. But the vindictive do not let well enough alone. As the pervert must expose himself once again, the Voice must speak again, and again. One day the Voice would say one word too much. A slip of the tongue and Westbrook would know where his son was. There are detective agencies. The Voice didn't reckon with Westbrook. Patience was a Westbrook trait. The first Westbrook had suffered failure and cold and hunger beside Jeff Davis Creek until he found his gold; this Westbrook would sit it out on "Midnight Line" until he found his son.

Eventually we come to accept things we once swore we could not accept — the drunken wife, the drugged child, homosexuality, constant pain, poverty and shame. We once thought we could never again hold up our heads if we lost a job — for losing a job means that somebody holds over us an obscene power and we are less than a man. We accept horror so long as we are allowed to live. Why should we want to live? Because tomorrow may change everything. Something may come up. Somebody may speak. Our eyes may meet sympathetic eyes. Suicide is no good, for that is death — never again would we see the drift of clouds or unlock the secret of a new leaf by crushing it and holding it to our nose. Never again to feel a handful of sand or know a child's delight in a flower. But these are large things.

We accept tiny things, the annoying drip of water, a friend's dentures soaking in a glass. Constant itching. Westbrook accepted the fact that his life now centered around the Voice. You never warm to the banal words of love songs until you love, nor know what a father feels until you have a son.

As he suspected, the Voice was silent for a time. It was not until the end of September that the Voice spoke again — just fifteen words. While he was wrestling with the problem of those words a molar on the left side of his mouth began to die and the pain was frightful.

His dentist was said to be the best in the business, a small, dark, intense man whose clients were the best in their business. These men could be seen getting in and out of Dr. La Rosa's chair with what aplomb remained to them. Westbrook had not considered Italians as dentists — on the whole the educated among them prefer gentler pursuits that might allow them to be loved rather than admired and feared, but this man had planned and constructed the partial plate of the Protestant Episcopal Bishop of Massachusetts as well as shoring up the mouths of the Roman clergy. Good as he was, he took telephone calls from his broker while patients' mouths were paralyzed or stuffed with tools; and if by chance you admitted to a layman's interest in dentistry, cursory as that was, he was quick at your side with a clear plastic box of teeth so deformed they might have been those of monsters. But his equipment was the newest, his drills all but inaudible and his graceful assistant, smelling of Arpège, lent a pretty note to a grisly business. She was happy to play diverting melodies for music lovers who happened in the office through speakers the doctor had concealed in the walls.

After remarking on the weather, Dr. La Rosa leaned close and whispered, "Do I give you injections?" as if you and he were already a part of a conspiracy. So soft a voice could only be answered with a similar whisper or simply a movement of the head. If he gave you injections, he cupped the vicious little syringe in his hand so it was quite out of sight when he pressed it home.

To distract the mind and lead it into happier channels, the doctor had introduced magazines into the waiting room. Most had been chosen for the brevity of their articles, that they might be finished in the short time you waited before being summoned beyond — *Reader's Digests* with instructions on how to be happy and to live longer, *Field and Streams* for the killers among his clientele; *Harper's Bazaar* for fashionable ladies with rotting teeth; *Forbes* for those who cannot long be without thoughts of money. And, of course, *Sports Illustrated*. Westbrook had already read the current *Reader's Digest*; *Forbes* did not interest him as he supposed it should. Nor, for that matter, did *Sports Illustrated*. Like many who, in youth, were poor at sports, Westbrook was later contemptuous of those who either excelled at them or watched them. Occasionally someone unfamiliar with the format of "Midnight Line" stumbled on to ask, "What do you think of the Colts?"

Think of the Colts? What could you think of them? Big, dimwitted young men who kicked and chased and carried around an inflated leather bladder while thousands equally dimwitted cheered them on. What did he think of the Colts? And since the Vatican Council had pulled the rug out from under the Roman church and the Protestant sects had ruined themselves by taking no stand on anything at all, religion was no longer an opiate of the people. Sex and sports remained as opiates. So long as the rabble could ejaculate and cheer touchdowns, the prospect of revolution was remote.

Los Angeles defeated Cleveland.

The Yankees shut out the Red Sox four to zip.

It was San Francisco over Cleveland.

It was, was it?

Trounced, edged, routed, mawled, squeaked by, smashed, battered, downed — words that evoked the violence their stupid hearts required.

Their very names were childish — Bears, Giants, Pirates. Such might have been the names of grammar school gangs with passwords and hidden cigarettes and treehouses where they could get away from the grown-ups and masturbate over girly magazines. Their minds had remained the minds of tots, but now they played ball and had the right to marry and to breed.

He picked up *Sports Illustrated* to lose himself in the inanities of what they called the World of Sports, not to banish the thought of the patient who had preceded him and now sat silent clutching at the arms of the chair, but to escape pain and his growing anxiety over his son.

The article he read was in thoroughly bad taste and concerned a ballplayer whose name was a household word in those households whose members were moved to care how fast people ran or how high they jumped. The young man's little-boy grin had sold millions of cardboard boxes of a breakfast cereal that snapped to attention at the addition of milk.

His contract was worth a hundred thousand a year. His private life was blameless. No stories circulated concerning his sex life. Pictures of his women did not appear in *Playboy*. No one hinted that he had equity in several shady, lucrative night spots. Fathers held him up as an example to sons; to daughters as a model husband. It was thought he hunted and fished a good deal when he could "get away." He got plenty of sleep in a bed quite his own.

And who do you think was in the background?

Mom, that's who.

He and Mom had had nothing, nothing but pride and love for each other. Mom set to, and began to bake bread, and she sold it, and she prayed to her God. Her son's picture was ever before her on the piano in the house he eventually bought her, and where he repaired for Thanksgiving and for Christmas. Her picture he carried in his wallet. He was a good sport about appearing at Rotary. In the old days while Mom baked away and prayed, he delivered papers and clerked in the A&P. But he had found time for football practice.

No, it is not to be wondered that he received an athletic scholarship to college, and that he did not abuse it as many do, for his marks were consistently well above what was required. Frankly, Mom had wept when she saw him off on the bus, but her baking and praying days were about over. She might have dried her tears, but who was to say they were not for joy?

For now here she was with her boy in a color picture in *Sports Illustrated* wearing a simple navy blue outfit; her hair, organized now by a permanent, was of a lighter blue, and in her eyes was still something spunky. If necessary she would turn her hand to bread again. Why, to see those two in color was to believe again in the America we have lost and in Old Dog Tray. Mom and her boy and their dream come true.

"A sympathetic reporter stepped forward to question her, asked if she still baked her own bread, and she smiled. 'Once in a while, just to keep my hand in.' she quipped."

"Davis's father had pulled up stakes shortly after the boy's birth. Davis was asked, 'Is your father still living?'

" 'That depends,' Davis said. 'He sent me a wristwatch when I graduated high school but I sent it back to him.' "

What concentrated hatred must have moved Davis's fingers in doing up that small package. And now Davis was rich and lean and hard.

The article in *Sports Illustrated* struck cruelly close. Westbrook wished it had struck even closer. He would gladly have been hated in exchange for his son's success. He was simply hated, had nothing in exchange. Certainly the Voice hated him. Not many hours before the Voice had spoken again.

His son was not rich and lean and hard.

"*They live in a trailer. He don't see good and now he's broke his glasses.*"

IX _____

TRAILER COURTS ARE LAID OUT tic-tac-toe and Pine Street intersects Elm. There are gathered the temporary and the terminal; coffins and basinettes are equally considered. A young couple not yet with sufficient funds for a little house with a breezeway settle for a trailer and they are going to fix it up cute, real cute; when the time comes they can sell it to an old couple who for the second time in their lives must repair the hideous vandalism of children. The old people have sold their immovable real estate where as they said they'd just been rattling around since the kids had grown up and never came to visit anymore because Ed liked California and it was so far; he sent dates and almonds from out there. There were all those stairs and the storm windows to get up, and they'd always liked the idea of a trailer. The idea made many old people feel wickedly footloose. This was kind of a last fling! But they got no farther than this trailer court where there are a lot of rules. They had thought óne day they might just pull up stakes like a couple of crazy kids and go to Florida but now they feared to cut the umbilical cord that nourished them with electricity and telephone service and carried away their sewage. They found they now led a life quite as sedentary and circumscribed as the old one, not at all the life you'd expect of those whose homes were on wheels.

A family in a court distinguished itself with a pink or a blue or a white or even a purple trailer of a shade bizarre enough to delight a French Canadian; some made themselves special in setting up outside a folding chair of aluminum tubing and plastic webbing; there one might sit and look across the street at people sitting in their chairs. Some elected plastic birdbaths pressed to resemble stone. No birds came but sometimes the water reflected passing clouds, such clouds as they remembered.

The children didn't come because there was no room now.

When Westbrook heard "childbirth" in the phrase "died in childbirth" he assumed the Voice was educated because that is an educated word. It followed that his son was somehow educated, having the Voice for friend and champion, and if educated, with a stable income and very likely in some such trailer court, part of a recognized, even interesting American community. It was a wonder someone had not written a book about life in a trailer court.

Thirty-five was not too old for a young man to still be living there.

But the words "he's broke his glasses" and "don't see good" shattered that comforting image. The use of "child-birth" was a conscious elegance picked up on television or in a paperback and used as other simple people say "at this point in time" rather than "now." The Voice had hesitated to say, "She died having a little baby," the normal speech of the Voice — he was sure of that — for that sentence was far too graphic for one as sensitive and kind as the Voice. For the Voice was sensitive and kind as well as vindictive. For that Westbrook was grateful.

"In a trailer" sketched out a far different life than "in a trailer court." At worst, his son was living in a Cabbage Patch where the seats of wrecked cars serve as furniture, shacks go up in flames and violence is commonplace. At best his son was parked in some kind person's backyard, and safe only so long as he had that person's goodwill. It is truly horrible to be dependent on someone's sufferance; it leads to self-doubt and can permanently alter a personality.

The backyard was a last resort, and the boy was probably behind in his payments on the trailer. If he could not afford forty or fifty dollars for glasses it was not likely he could keep up, and without glasses he could hardly be expected to work at whatever he worked at. From time to time Westbrook now removed his own glasses to experience the sickening sensation of a world out of focus. Anybody truly dependent on glasses knows the defensive insecurity that hides behind poor sight. He had heard that complete blindness strengthens the other senses — especially that of touch — but it was his experience that partial blindness overburdened the other senses and resulted in nausea.

But Westbrook's glasses were not "broke." In a single gesture he could assume them and become whole.

Thank God the boy was not alone. "They live in a trailer" said that at least two lived there. If the boy shared the trailer with another man, the Voice would not have used the cohesive "they," knowing the man would be of no interest to Westbrook — unless the Voice meant to suggest homosexuality and that was impossible because to the class from which the Voice came sexual deviation as a subject of conversation was taboo.

There was, then, a wife — even a child. My God, what was he getting into! Himself a grandfather! And the use of the vague "they" hinted the Voice had chosen carefully what it wished to reveal. "He's broke his glasses" meant hardship, not enough food, an appeal for a loan, a refusal, the loss of a job. And the Voice interceding for the boy argued that the Voice itself would see that the glasses were replaced. But having found out who Westbrook was the Voice must guess — however uneducated and unused to talkmasters on talk shows — that Westbrook had a substantial income — if modest savings. Then why in God's name didn't the Voice give him address or box number where he might send a check?

Cruelty?

The sane among us act in patterns of time; we consult watches, calendars and almanacs and offer them as gifts to help friends organize a little better. We learn early that promptness is a virtue; prompt people prosper. Our first report cards have little spaces on them for marking down times "tardy."

We fret if our bowels fail to move once a day.

Parents require a letter once a week; silence means trouble or the loss of love.

"It's been over a week since I heard from you. Is anything wrong?"

To accommodate classes in French and chemistry and the times when the local Internal Revenue Service is available to "help" with your tax the week is arranged in alternate days — Monday, Wednesday and Friday on the one hand; Tuesday, Thursday and Saturday on the other. Sunday stands isolated, a hiatus into which unpleasant reflections creep, a day steeped in guilt at having abandoned God and lost one's innocence. Some escape by fleeing into the country with sufficient food; some into neighborhood bars where pinball machines help one forget; others entertain friends with speech or cocktail or themselves lose consciousness. Once a month the moon waxes and wanes and once a month women under fifty move distrait through their rooms, snap at their husbands or sigh against the cushions.

Certain families, perhaps like birds, take a solid pride in arriving at a vacation spot on the first of July for more than thirty years, and in some areas along the coast this awesome dependability is admired as much as money. The yearly advent of Christmas, like devastating floods and wars, once more draws divers people close; we allow strangers to enter an intersection first and we slide the sugar bowl down the counter to them.

Each seven years we reproduce ourselves. Each fifty years wrinkled old people hold hands for a snapshot. Each seventy years the fortunate may view Halley's comet. Each hundred

years the end of the world is trumpeted. Time, time, time —
it is man's prime time the employers buy; a man is left with
his awkward hours, and these he uses to commute, has an
hour to feed himself, three hours to sit before the shadows on
television and ten minutes a week for copulation. The rich
buy time, time to be themselves, but so often the rich are too
stupid to furnish time with taste; with but few exceptions are
the rich gifted. Their answer is that they don't need to be.

From the first time the Voice spoke until the last, Westbrook could discern no commitment to any pattern of time.
It spoke seven times over a period of three months but neither weekly nor monthly nor every ten days nor on Saturdays
only. It spoke as haphazardly as tragedy strikes.

Now a Mr. G. was on the line.

It was characteristic of many of Westbrook's following that
they could not solve their problems and turned to him who
could. He kept beside him a ledger listing the telephone
numbers of helpful organizations, boards, agencies, priests,
ministers, rabbis, doctors and hospitals. He knew what mor-
tuaries burned or embalmed most reasonably and where cut
flowers were cheap.

And once he had welcomed the Mr. G.'s and the Mrs. P.'s,
welcomed their dependence on him for the sense of worth it
accorded him as a priest and as a recognition that he was
indeed a man who could cope with life, and for the power it
gave him over Edwards, Upstairs.

His strength had once been his patience and his detachment — two quite rare qualities. But now he found himself
irritated at their punctuating every other sentence with the

word "Right?" and the phrase "Know what I mean?" They called to ask for a cheap lawyer, whom to approach about lost welfare checks, whom to call for a tank of oxygen, what to do when the landlord knocks and threatens, what were the symptoms of leprosy, and if the moon was a planet.

A young man breathed a few seconds into the telephone. Then he condemned young women for wearing miniskirts and going topless.

"It gets too much for a fellow," he breathed. "Know what I mean? You're walking along like and you see them like that all topless like that and they shouldn't to a man. They get fellows all bothered, right?" Westbrook saw the breathing young man lying naked with the phone and a copy of a pornographic magazine open to a photograph of a woman riding a man, an ugly little tableau that required speech to bring it to life.

Mrs. M. was black or a Southerner, or both. Her voice was thick with liquor and she was weeping. Her telephone picked up small bumping noises. She said she loved a man so much it made her sick.

Westbrook told her many would think her lucky.

But the trouble was, she said, the man wouldn't do what she wanted him to.

In the background was a man's voice, and Westbrook saw them half naked, pawing at each other, falling back on the rumpled bed slopping drinks. A radio made faint music.

He asked how old Mrs. M.'s man was.

"He is fifty-five years of age."

Westbrook said some men that age are impotent.

What did that mean?

It meant her man couldn't do what she wanted him to do.

She said the man wanted to talk over the telephone.

The man did and, yes, he was drunk. He was Mr. F. and he loved the woman as much as she loved him but he couldn't do it.

"Throw away that bottle," Westbrook said. "And then you can do it."

With this drivel they jammed the telephones.

Those who inherit riches can afford what others cannot.

They can afford to be stupid.

For they can expect their money to attract anxious, sometimes amusing sycophants who will fetch ashtrays and light cigarettes and overlook stings and insults meant to remind them of their place so long as a little gilt rubs off and they are tossed scraps. But some rich, distrustful of those who would light their cigarettes and play bartender, seek out themselves and show a solid front. So did the last dinosaurs, lumbering perilously close to the bottomless pitch pits, turn to face the enemy.

The horse, long a fashionable beast in England, is sometimes required by these American rich; and though it must little concern them, horse droppings are an admirable fertilizer if not the equal of the neater leavings of the gullible, unfashionable sheep. The view from the back of a horse is a novel one and the movement of horses, especially at the trot, alerts the dozing liver.

These rich command the seacoast and occupy it in the summertime except where testy fishermen, never having had enough money to realize its importance, refuse to sell, and there where demagogues have seized the dunes and turned them over to the public. But from the coast yawls at a thousand dollars a foot fan out over the waters and offer their spinnakers to the obliging winds.

Some trumpet their money by putting vast distances between where they were and where they will be, and for as long as possible.

"Where are they going this time?" and "How long will they be gone?"

Some may cruise around the world for one hundred and ten thousand dollars, but less comfortable quarters are available on the same liner for an attractive sixty-eight thousand. Passing through waters and moving over the earth, these lucky travelers will encounter commodities quite unknown at home. Strange customs are observed — the wearing of jewels in the nose, the systematic lengthening of the neck from childhood with ever-increasing numbers of brass hoops, the decoration of the skin with hot irons and little knives, deforming of the lips — all in the name of love and beauty. Farther afield exotic animals pause at the waterhole, some with long necks, some with spotted or impervious hides, and some with fanciful horns.

But sometimes these rich, twisting in their beds, are visited by thought; they become uneasy about the worth of money and their relation to it, for they are no more than parasites on society like the hired fools who suck on them. How must they justify the space they occupy? For they have created nothing, made nothing with their hands, taught nothing, healed nobody. Well, publishers will print the jottings of those among them who are notorious as well as rich and fix them forever between hard covers, and other publishers, for a fee, will print the scribbles of the merely rich. Perhaps the answer is to clerk in a thrift shop where discarded ball gowns and waffle irons are within reach of the needy. Go into politics. Become a Catholic or otherwise go down among the poor.

What a pity that the mates of the rich often stray like the mates of those with more modest moneys, and what a blessing that they have the means to hire detectives to trace the movements of the guilty one and know in what hotel and at what time and under what name she gives herself to the scoundrel. The modestly endowed must learn to live with doubt or to resign their positions and themselves become detectives. If not, to turn to battery or murder or suicide. It is the rich who can afford to *know*. The rich can research the past, locate a friend or an abandoned child.

But he had his stamps.

He imagined a trailer, spotlighted as if by the moon.

The baby would have been born in March when an entire fall and most of a winter had gone by. The leaves had fallen; the mountains were veiled with the smoke from distant forest fires. Cowboys trailed herds of cattle into little settlements, loaded them on the cars, got drunk across the road and rode off. The stubble in the fields glowed with frost when the sun rose. And at last the snow fell, and fell over Grayling, Montana, and the wind howled high above the striking of the courthouse clock.

Couldn't sleep. He hadn't taken more than aspirin in his life and that for toothaches. No doctor had ever come to the

Westbrook "mansion." He'd had childhood diseases but they passed without incident. His mother had drawn the blinds in his room when he'd had measles because his eyes were bad. Blindness. He was wearing glasses at twelve.

His mother "napping" in her room, but no pills. A cloth over eyes and forehead wet with witch hazel. The scent of violets and witch hazel, gentility and frayed nerves. She was terrified of pills. Attached to sleeping pills the word "overdose."

Yes, Miss Snodgrass. Algebra. The product of the means equals the product of the extremes — the single Unknown. Was it because Miss Snodgrass was so ugly? And kind of the principal to hire her. .

Now, Nytol. Sominex, and then something stronger.

All right. He hadn't really expected to find the name Westbrook or Gates in the Grayling directory, nor on the voting list. Had seemed such a good idea at the time. It was a move. But who, owning nothing, would long remain in Grayling?

The early hours of "Midnight Line" on October 25 were turbulent. Westbrook read the news at two. Nixon continued his egregious operations, applauded by the ignorant and the corrupt. Two men dangled from ropes against the face of a bald mountain in a national park. Helicopters hovered, pilots calling down encouragement. Three children were thrown from a roller coaster. A minister in Alabama announced he would walk on water, beginning the following Sunday.

Mr. T. called to say he'd read of a young man who hurtled

on a motorcycle through Chicago nude except for crash helmet and low sneakers. "He claims he's some sort of god," Mr. T. said.

Mrs. L. was blind. She had willed her corpse to Harvard as cheaper than a funeral. Her body was rendered singular by so many ailments it was a dozen case histories in one. She said Harvard had a bargain.

Death moved Mr. Q., a first-time caller, to ask why not anesthetize criminals before they killed them? Wasn't it the state's purpose to remove a criminal from society? Then why be cruel? What had the state to gain in making even a criminal know the horror of walking to his own execution? Sometimes Mr. Q. wondered what executioners thought about in the middle of the night. "They could put a little something in the criminal's food. Then they could carry him on a stretcher to the place, and do it."

A woman said thieves stole flags from veterans' graves. She blamed the hippies, right? They let their hair grow and threw barbers out of work — right? A barber who was good to her in troubled times was on welfare.

Westbrook cut their tales short, waiting for the Voice.

Charlotte called. Towards him she had a most proprietary attitude. And true, years before, she had been one of the first callers on "Midnight Line." She called on Fridays, and he saw her comfortable in her chair. She was intelligent; she spoke of civil rights and bad housing and of going to the help of the helpless. A good woman, she was humorless like most truly good people. Her slow-paced, positive voice revealed her as one who never forgot to shut a drawer or to pull the plugs from electrical devices. She would remember birthdays and expect others to do the same. He sensed she could be an implacable enemy if one had failed her. For her life had not always been serene. She had had a driving lust for food, for candy bars, and especially the Milky Way. At sight of such her hands trembled — or had. She ate and ate until her feet bulged up out of her shoes and her dresses were not so much garments as decorated tents. At three hundred pounds she threatened all but the most formidable furniture, an object of dread or pity; she had known she was a large woman: mirror and scales confirmed the fact. But alas, we can know without knowing, and all was brought home one afternoon when she lowered herself off a bus and behind her the ugly phrase "mountain of a woman" followed her like a stench.

Later, when she had ceased weeping, she mounted the scales and looked at her bloated body in a glass, and she took stock of herself. She declared herself a slob. "A mountainous woman" she told herself, bewitched by the paradox that cruelty may really be kindness.

Now she discovered within herself a strength; inside she heard the voice of a slim woman crying out for release from that tub of flesh.

"I honestly seemed to be two persons," she had reported.

Through sheer will and the memory of her hateful bulk, she lost a hundred and fifty pounds and exercised faithfully to tauten the sagging skin. Like the arrested alcoholic who looks fondly on another's highball, her hands still trembled for a Milky Way — the rich chocolate coating, the firm nougat nestled within, so satisfying to the tongue, so pleasant to the teeth, and best of all the firm stratum of caramel.

Now that was behind her. What remained of her fatness

was her unflappable placidity. Her victory was complete —
but uniquely unsatisfying; her conquest of herself had left her
unappeased. So she turned outwards. She gathered about her
half a dozen huge women and waltzed them off into the woods
to a house fitted with cruel machines, sauna baths and devices
to force the sap from root vegetables. There she shamed,
cajoled, praised and starved them, and at some profit.

Now she was speaking in her flat, kind voice. "Tom, I
want to tell you something. We're old friends, right? Shall I
speak up?"

"Speak up, Charlotte."

"Tom — your show isn't so good now. You're not patient.
You — "

But had she called to alert him to the return of Christ
Jesus he would have paid her no more heed.

Ten minutes before the Voice had called.

The trailer was gone. The "trailer man" had come and
hauled it off. In some backyard beside a highway, a space was
empty. And so was Westbrook's heart.

On Tremont Street near Boylston stood a defunct hotel of
brown sandstone; token balconies on the upper floors fa-
vored this window and skipped the next; some guests taken
by claustrophobia might once have raised the sash and
stepped out, hoping to recover and to look down. Behind the
windows of the abandoned shops on the street floor the signs
offering the premises for hire had faded and twisted, and yet
the Old Man had said the place was once one of the best
hotels in town, and had himself celebrated the Armistice
there.

"Hinky, dinky, *parlez-vous*," the Old Man had said dryly. "Trees grow taller. Trees grow taller, hotels get shabbier, and we get older." Used newspapers caught in little cyclones born of the wind sweeping down Boylston had lodged before a glass door; beyond it was a small stage on the far wall and an upright piano with the front removed. There comics had talked and gestured, their acts getting ever seedier as the hotel languished and becoming ever more scatalogical. The chairs had long been turned upside down and placed on the lips of the tables to discourage further trade. And six feet beyond the flyspecked door was a woman's high-heeled shoe abandoned in anger or passion, a last statement, a souvenir of one last fling. Now the hotel was host not even to showgirls, the adulterous, or the salesmen who supplied Daddy and Jack's Joke Shop.

The sickness that had brought about the hotel's demise had spread like the plague across the street to an office building of a similar stone.

The elevator shaft in the lobby was of fancy iron grillwork like huge lace; through it the public might observe the mechanics involved. Standing close, he who would be carried aloft could see the elevator rising or descending, preceding or trailing looping cables; a giant birdcage, the elevator shuddered as it paused before each floor. The door of the car was opened by a trained old man who wore a flaccid white glove on his working hand, against calluses and blisters. The nervous, especially women who expected sooner or later to be trapped by fires in some high hotel, buried in the subway or caught forever between floors, used the well-worn marble stairway.

The building was a last haven of teachers' agencies who supplied applicants for an underworld of private schools, companies that sold gummed labels to those who could not or would not write their name and address, devices that sucked in air and guaranteed better gas mileage, aids to enlarge the female breast and to melt the buttocks.

But the detective agency could afford a secretary, an efficient gray-haired woman with proud breasts and an unlined face; whatever material had crossed her desk had neither embittered nor aged her unduly. She sat before a new, expensive typewriter that printed letters by means of a sophisticated golf ball that leaped at the paper. Her scent was expensive, and Westbrook judged this office was not on its last legs.

"You have an appointment?"

It was a rebuke. She very well knew he had no appointment since it was she who would have set one up.

"No. I want to ask a few questions."

She rose.

"Send him in," came a voice from the room beyond. "Send him right in."

In that room a dozen file cabinets stood side by side, all of golden oak, a wood serviceable, ugly and ancient, a wood reminiscent of the turn of the century — serviceable, ugly, ancient years. It was the wood of authority, chosen for the principal's office, the desk at the police station, the superior bench in a courtroom, there where tyrants presided. He might have expected to see a bust of Washington or an American flag. He saw instead, displayed on the wall like a diploma, an enlarged signed photograph of J. Edgar Hoover, the jaw brutal, the nose smashed, the eyes humanoid — a composite of the mug shots of criminals the man himself sent out to be tacked up in public places, criminals who were scarcely more lawless in carrying out their peculiar tasks than he.

". . . should be considered dangerous."

The man who displayed Hoover stood beside his golden oak desk, bald except for a faint gray fringe, but Westbrook knew him to be no more than fifty, a man to whom the appearance of youth was of small consequence — not for him the silly exercises before the mirror. He smoked a cigar. Now, the smell of cigars is the smell of authority, Mosler safes, roast beef at noon, locks and keys and an Old Testament God, a cigar smoker Himself. Before such a man the cigarette smoker who inhales killing fumes feels self-indulgent, disorganized and childish.

For childish Westbrook felt in having determined to take a page from "Midnight Line" and become anonymous, to become "Mr. Forbes" and let "Mr. Forbes" tell a shameful tale, the abandoning of a girl and subsequent searching for her son.

But "Mr. Forbes" was at once shot down.

"I'm Coombs," the bald man said. "I recognized you out there, Mr. Westbrook. They say we've all got a double in looks, but I doubt there's another voice like yours."

What a fool, to think he'd not be recognized by a man who had tickled the fancy of J. Edgar Hoover. "It's flattering to be recognized," Westbrook said.

"You do a great job," Coombs said. "They need you out there. Blow off steam. Politicians must follow you closely. And the psychological thing. The piece in the AMA *Journal.*

They need their hands held. A crazy bunch. If people weren't all crazy you and I would be out of a job. You could write a book."

Westbrook saw an opening to yet be anonymous, and he rushed to it, and he let Coombs see him incredulous. "Funny you should say that. I am about to write a book, but I need facts. And I expect to make it worth your while."

"Forget that. In your position, you might help me someday."

"Well, then. This part of the book concerns a man, a Mr. X. A listener."

And he told the story that ended with a faceless one in a trailer.

And then he waited, as Coombs used his cigar.

"There's a record of all deaths," Coombs said, "in every state capital. Fifty letters would get your first evidence, unless the girl's father left the country.

"And births are recorded and filed in the same place. Your Mr. X would know the approximate date of death, and whatever she called herself in the hospital, her father's true name would be there. There's your second piece of evidence, and likely we'd have the baby's surname then. And somebody, maybe not the father, did the recording, the recording of the baby's birth, and we know his or her name — foster parent, adoptive parent, orphans' asylum. We can follow the boy through the next sixteen years. School records. Maybe truancy records.

"So he's sixteen, now, and the going gets harder because of no pattern of college in the family — didn't you say that? He gets a job. Let's hope he stays in the same town, with the same people, but with a pattern of wandering — didn't you say that? — and needing to be an individual — pretty common among those born out of wedlock or in funny circumstances — he leaves that town. Hope he doesn't change his name.

"We knock on doors, find friends. Acquaintances. Voting records, but few drifters vote. That twenty years from age sixteen, that's the tough nut to crack, that's why we're in business.

"Sometimes it's easier, sometimes harder, but here's a little mock-up of one situation. Farther back you go, the more it costs; the scent gets faint; footprints melt. The fewer clues you've got, the more it costs. Mr. X hasn't many clues. I'd tell your Mr. X to get ahold of a few more clues. Save him a bundle."

Westbrook crossed his legs, as a composed man might. "But suppose Mr. X found no more clues?"

"Well, it would cost a bundle. And with no assurance he'd find the boy. As head of a reputable agency, I'd think twice about taking on a case like this."

"What would it cost — if you did take it?"

"Assume it takes a year — twenty thousand dollars. Of course, if Mr. X were free to get out there and do it himself — most of it's only using common sense and the available agencies. . . ."

But Westbrook, as Mr. X, was not free; because of his dwindling, hostile audience he now felt himself dependent for his salary on Edwards, Upstairs, who waited in the wings, could pull the strings and call the tune. Had Edwards noticed?

X

OFF IN THE MOUNTAINS of New Mexico, up a draw choked with sagebrush and the bleached bones of animals hurled down by flash floods, an outcropping of white chalk resembles a cathedral seen by moonlight.

Nearby is a Retreat House for special priests. They have been spirited there by black-gowned authorities before the secular arm throws them into jail or the madhouse. The house is seldom spoken of, for it is not wise to advertise that priests resemble laymen in finding their vows too much for them. When younger, they had hoped to escape themselves and find simple solace in good deeds and a loyal congregation.

But one day they yearn again for a flesh to touch, and one day turn to drink to evade the dismal future or they fall into madness.

Call the Bishop.

In the Retreat House the remote hiss and murmur of the

Mass is sometimes silenced by screams and curses directed at the God they'd served to give them back some him or her who might have made them whole.

Westbrook the failing priest, condemned by Charlotte and others, could not find his son and so justify his failure, could not touch him.

We scorn the miser who counts his money for we know that is all he has. But money makes those who are trash sought after, if only for their money. That this is true is known by simply raising the eyes.

The prudent among us like to believe that what we own has increased in value. Too bad that what a thing is worth and what we can get for it are two quite different things. In sober fact what a thing is worth is what we can get for it, and what we can get for it depends on how much we need to sell it. The noses of businessmen are as sensitive as pigs' noses; they smell desperation as others smell sweat.

Apart from his ability as a talkmaster, his patience and convincing concern, his often accurate construction of strangers' lives from random voices, snips of fact and a sound choice of alternatives, Westbrook had had no expertise except his collecting of stamps — labels, as philatelists call them: those bent on forming cults or cliques or clubs or religions lend strange names to familiar objects. In financial circles you do not buy stocks; you "take a position." The dead and known dying on the battlefields of Viet Nam are not casualties but a "body count." Red coats are pink coats in horsey circles. The drivers of sports cars call American automobiles

"Detroit iron." In the Christian religion, God becomes three people, one party a holy ghost. So it seems the undistinguished must create for themselves a special world, join clubs named after beasts and birds, impose on themselves weird duties, must perform strange rites and talk in tongues.

Westbrook knew what a "gumpap" was, and an "albino." He knew that the first stamp was called a One Penny Black and bore the youthful profile of Victoria, that it was printed in "fast" and not "fugitive" ink and that rascals and scalawags easily erased the cancellation and used it again. So it was withdrawn and now was worth thousands.

Pollinger on Tremont Street had one. How he had envied Pollinger that stamp!

His collecting of stamps had been as furtive and personal as masturbation. He had chosen to examine and to arrange them in his room in the Westbrook "mansion" when the house was asleep and the Three Ones told the hours. His hands touched them under the light of a goosenecked lamp at an hour when the whores from the Crystal Rooms had turned their last tricks and gathered with their johns for clubhouse sandwiches behind the green baize curtains in the booths of the Sugar Bowl Café, when the telegrapher in his green eyeshade hunched over the key and tapped out warnings of open switches and runaway cars, when a light still burned in a rented room in the Episcopal rectory across from the Hale Memorial Hospital. There Miss Snodgrass who taught algebra — and very well, too — grieved because she had almost no nose, and what nose she had was hooked.

His stamps were a secret strength, coiled and waiting, God knew for what, in those days. But the thought of them had let him hold up his head in the corridors of Grayling High School. Those who passed him there or paused to drink at the bubbler near a window that looked out on the American flag flying from a tall thin pole didn't know the difference between a "bogus" and a "forgery," a watermark from a surcharge.

He had been faithful to his collection as a continuing thread in his life; he had not been beguiled, like some, by triangular stamps or those from exotic principalities He had collected only British stamps, and it had been his dream one day to own a One Penny Black. A foolish dream, but who does not have a foolish dream and who is the worse for one? And now he was going to Pollinger, who was a Jew.

On both coasts the Jews are condemned for holding positions that rightly belong to Christians — especially to Christians of the Protestant persuasion — or would, except for the Jews' superior brains. Likewise, the Jews are the best critics, the most able performers, the funniest comics and the best interpreters. Alas, it is only the fine arts the Christians can call their own. In the wild flights of the imagination, thank God, most Jews but dabble.

As a Westerner he knew little of Jews. He had not tilted with them in the marketplace nor with them competed for a speaking part. Some of his competitors, if he can be said to have had competitors, were Jews, but they had changed their names to hide the fact for the air swarms with anti-Semites who believe they have the last word when they accuse a man of Jewishness.

In the West it is the Mormons who cause the trouble.

The beginnings of the Mormon church are of passing interest. As Westbrook understood it, an angel named Moroni spoke to a Mr. Joseph Smith of Palmyra, New York, concerning several tablets of solid gold Mr. Smith would find if he searched a nearby hillside. Mr. Smith did indeed find them — the original plates of the Book of Mormon, which revealed God's word. The angel, however, had neglected to tell Mr. Smith that the writing on the plates was in "reformed" Egyptian, a language quite unfamiliar to Mr. Smith. The angel suggested that Mr. Smith poke around and he would find a pair of magic spectacles which, when assumed, would allow him to translate the plates into English. And so they did. The curious thing was that the English turned out to be Elizabethan English and not the humdrum English of nineteenth-century Palmyra.

It is the habit of Mormons to move into shabby towns passed over by progress, avoided by railroads and haunted by dreams of rosier days. But with the advent of the Mormons come clean streets and trees and gardens and well-tended lawns. Around the towns these people plant thriving crops, and before you know it they own the Ford garage and are elected to the legislature. Yes, it was Mormon faces on election posters in the pool halls where the Mormons seldom gathered to play shithouse, going there only to select hired hands. Mormons had gotten into Grayling, Montana, had painted houses and built a church. They kept to themselves and loaned each other money at low rates of interest. It was difficult to identify them, they looked so like other Christian people. Their women were often extraordinarily handsome.

Westbrook had heard that Green who owned The Store Beautiful was a Jew; hearing it, he had wondered why it had

been said. Like all high school students, he had been required to read *The Merchant of Venice,* viewed by some as a
first lesson in bigotry, and he recalled from time to time Fern
Bell who later became a whore, who had pronounced "scepter" "skepter" in "mercy's scepter's way." He had been
impressed with Shylock's dignity and ashamed of the shabby
tricks of the Christians. A shame he was not ashamed of his
own shabby tricks. And yet Green had been pointed out as a
Jew. Possibly what rankled was that Green had established
himself in the largest house in town — once the proud possession of a Christian — and there did whatever Jews do.

And now Westbrook was going to the Jew Pollinger of
Pollinger & Son, Stamps and Coins, whose name he had
known as a boy, for Pollinger was an old, old man and perhaps the son of Pollinger & Son — Westbrook had seen no
younger man on his trips there — unless there had been a
tragedy. Here was another example of the inexorable ap-
pearances of the sixes and aces in a man's life. Long, long ago
he had hoped someday to go to Pollinger and buy his One
Penny Black. Sometimes he thought he would exchange his
entire collection for a One Penny Black. Now he would exchange everything to find his son or buy him a new pair of
shoes.

Twenty thousand was a good sum.

The shop was in a short street that runs between Tremont
and Washington, a squalid street prompting thoughts of
winos sprawled in doorways. The man in the bookstore to
the north sold valuable books, but the bins of hammock
reading and tattered paperbacks did not speak of the riches
inside. A casual search of the bins disclosed *Best Home Rem-
edies, Fun with Rocks* and a second edition of Gene Stratton

Porter's *Girl of the Limberlost*. Miss Porter wrote and wrote and wrote, but had at last been undone by a streetcar in Seattle. *So Big* by Edna Ferber who had lived in the apartment once owned by Kruger the Match King who blew out his brains shortly before Miss Ferber's occupancy. *Gone With the Wind* by Margaret Mitchell who was run down by a car on Peachtree Street in Atlanta, a larger city than one realizes. And so it goes.

To the south of Pollinger & Son is Daddy and Jack's Joke Shop where those bent on mischief might acquire false flowers that spurt fluids into friends' faces when a bulb is pressed, ashtrays shaped like tiny toilets; toy privies whose opened door reveals a doll squatting and straining, a reasonable gift for a man who lingers long in his anal days and is moved at the thought of bowel movements. Daddy and Jack's had supplied the clay Irish head that grew green hair in the Harp Bar and Grille. Rubber masks hid the true face and the wearer became Johnson or Nixon. Plastic pools of vomit; dice that never came up seven or eleven; disappearing inks mystified creditors. Scotties mounted on magnetic skids that moved them into lewd positions; powders caused itching and pills rendered the urine blue. Everything, everything to embarrass, to humiliate and to disgust. The infantile and the crude walk among us, elbowing their way. They vote, they breed and because they outnumber us they sit in higher places, and having sat there they rise to their feet and hand on heart are moved by the booming cannon in the *1812 Overture*.

Infinite riches in a little room.

Westbrook's entire collection, selected and culled over forty years, was contained in two Scott albums no larger than a volume of the encyclopedia. They fit neatly into his big briefcase, but once he had fitted them there it seemed that his entire apartment had a transient look, as if his next move might be to lock the door forever behind him. The familiar was suddenly unfamiliar, like objects seen through the eyes of someone with a ghastly hangover and the memory of a recent ugly incident.

On his first meeting with Pollinger Westbrook had announced his admiration for the old man's position in the world of stamps, that he had known the name Pollinger & Son for many, many years. But Pollinger had not responded to the small accolade, and his eyes behind glasses so thick they enlarged his eyes and made a sixth sense of them had not held a look of recognition when Westbrook said he was Tom Westbrook. If Pollinger had heard of "Midnight Line," he gave no hint, and Westbrook felt deflated. What had he meant in flattering Pollinger, what fragile thing in himself had he meant to strengthen? Had he hoped to involve the old man in his past or future and thus strengthen it?

He had had his albums with him — as they were then, ten years before.

Whatever he had imaged the shop to be — something like a neat bookstore or small bank attended by serious clerks in suits — it was certainly not this, a low-ceilinged hall-like room; light entered only from the street windows where the words POLLINGER & SON in ancient gilt were peeling.

Then transpired a painful scene.

He noted that Pollinger limped, and out from the ragbag of memory he drew the word "sinister," a word stuffed there from impressions of silent moving pictures at matinees at the Rex Theater, that the minds of the crippled are twisted. The covering shadows of the room suggested trysts and assignations and a routine receiving of stolen goods — and indeed there was in some places a traffic in stolen stamps and coins. The stamps on display here were relatively unimportant and under glass in two cases like those in the Pheasant Pool Hall where cigars were conditioned by a damp tan sponge in a heavy white oval side dish like those in which peas and carrots were served up at the Sugar Bowl Café, Mild White Owls for those who could ill afford to smoke and Antonio y Cleopatras for those who said The hell with it, we only live once.

Sinister, and the word was clothed again with the deepening twilight outside the theater that only hours before had been sunny afternoon.

"We've been in business many years," Pollinger said, referring to himself with the royal pronoun or to someone either absent or dead. "Have you something to sell?"

Westbrook savored the pride of one who need not sell. "I want an appraisal," he said, retreating from his first foolish enthusiasm.

"I'll need your albums for several days." Pollinger's thick glasses caught the movement of someone passing on the street. He reached out his hands.

Westbrook had assumed that a professional could appraise as rapidly as a conductor can read a score. Now he was troubled with the vagueness of the words "several days" and even "need your albums."

Pollinger returned his hands to himself. "You needn't

worry about their safety, Mr. Westbrook." And Westbrook was following the limping old man into a tiny room behind corduroy curtains. On a shelf was a hotplate and coffeepot, and on the wall a framed photograph of a young man of twenty or so. The safe was a Mosler the size of the Mosler in Westbrook's father's den. "Your albums will be quite safe," Pollinger said.

Again Westbrook hesitated; he felt his albums would be safe only in his own hands; never had they seemed more important. Indeed, they summed up his life. Pages pasted with pretty reminders of a world beyond Grayling, Montana — tickets to it, evidence of his determination, tangible ends of a lonely, inturned pursuit he had not understood and whose purpose was moot until he believed himself to be a father.

And Pollinger, the dusky light falling on his glasses, was saying, "Don't you trust me, Mr. Westbrook?"

"Of course, of course." Westbrook stood again on the street. The quality of the light had changed.

Twenty thousand, the old man had said. Now here he was again ten years later, this time to sell, a humbled man.

"Mr. Westbrook," Pollinger said. He was one of certain people who reach an age and remain there like Negroes and the Chinese and some women.

"You haven't changed," Westbrook said.

"Oh yes, we all change. We hope for the better."

"I am thinking of selling."

"Your collection is substantially what it was?"

"Yes."

"I can offer you ten thousand, cash."

"Ten thousand! But ten years ago you appraised my albums at double that!"

The old man was gentle. "It often takes years to get for your albums what they're worth. That is because people don't collect labels for profit, but for love."

"Yes, of course. But I feel I should get another appraisal."

And Westbrook was out on the street again with his albums worth ten thousand dollars, ten thousand saved in a lifetime, hardly enough to find his son, let alone help him.

We all change. For the better, we hope.

XI

AT THE WORDS "Maxine died" Westbrook had been so startled he had overlooked the sound behind the Voice — what he called hillbilly music.

But now (and his bathroom scales said he had lost seven pounds) he was often gripped with an emotion half nostalgia, half loneliness that centered around similar music and an image of him and his father shut together inside the old Chevrolet — strange, for he had never felt close to his father.

They were returning to Grayling (the feeling went) from the little settlement of Beech near which they had gone fishing in the river. Westbrook's father believed in fishing. Westbrook was no better at fishing than at other sports; his hook caught in the roots under the river bank. He had had to urinate and it embarrassed him to urinate in the vicinity of his father. Why was that? Because they were truly strangers? Later on they ate chili at the counter in the Pony Café across from the cattle pens by the railroad tracks. In his memory, three eating places had opened there — and failed. A restaurant had seemed to be a good idea to many cheerful failures who might otherwise have opened roadside stands offering mineral specimens, glass insulators from telegraph poles or homemade fudge. For in the fall cowboys came whooping in with herds of cattle and loaded them on the stockcars and then got drunk and then hungry. And all spring and summer tourists came to hunt and fish and they hiked up a draw to view drawings on the wall of a cave, stick men and stick horses fleeing some prehistoric horror. And Lewis and Clark had once passed by where Beech was now and the lovely Indian maiden Sacajawea guiding them. What a site for a restaurant! But the lonely winters doomed the Buffalo Lodge and then the Spur, and then the Teepee and later the Pony Café, for Westbrook and his father were the only customers that early fall evening, and only they and the waitress heard the end of a record on the jukebox.

Promise me that you will never
Be nobody's darling but mine.

Six wild horses grazed on the sides of the sagebrushed foot-hill out the window. Over the fancy cash register a white sign said IF YOUR WIFE CAN'T COOK EAT HERE AND KEEP HER FOR A PET.

His father's grammar was suddenly slovenly when he spoke to the waitress. "How long you been working here?"

She glanced at her wristwatch. "I guess about six months, now." She was blond and cheap and hopeful and kind and she had been wise in aging, letting fat fill in where the flesh fell away under the skin.

"Yeah? Oh, and this here is my son Tom. Tom, Vera."

". . . meet ya," Vera said smiling. "I din know you had a boy."

"Oh sure, Tom here's twenty, isn't it, Tom?" And his father reached to touch him.

Westbrook nodded.

"If I'd a thought," Vera said, "I'd a known."

Yes, he had secretely admired his father's ease with simple people; strange, it was one trait he had inherited from his father. As the Master of "Midnight Line" he had found that trait valuable.

"Tom here's going back East pretty quick," his father said.

Vera gave Westbrook a quick, suspicious look. "East, is he? Well, I gotta sister somewheres around Minnesota there." She looked out the window at the six grazing horses. "I wish to God sometimes she'd write."

"Oh — and what happened to Reeda?" his father asked.

Vera frowned. "Reeda? Oh, Reeda. That's how she changed it to. Well, one night she hightailed it."

"Hightailed it, did she?"

"Well, you know," Vera said. "But it was nice, of what you did."

"So she finally hightailed it." And now his father gazed out at the horses. And his father had once thought of hightailing it. Oh, yes. But hadn't. Why? His wife? Or had his father felt about him as he felt about a boy who no longer had a trailer?

That half-hour in the Pony Café was their farewell to each

other; they both knew it. A farewell as final as the last stroke of the Three Ones, as the last words of "Nobody's Darling but Mine."

What Westbrook called hillbilly music was now called country-and-western and those who made it popular moved in Cadillacs and dressed in sequined Levi's. Westbrook had once confounded a lover of baroque music by remarking that most of Bach and much Vivaldi resembled hillbilly music.

The lover of baroque had frowned.

But why? For the baroque was the musical heritage of those who had settled the hill country of America. When they took up their fiddles Bach tapped the rhythm and Telemann called the tune.

The music behind the Voice had been a phonograph record; when it stopped there was silence and not a disk jockey's patter filling dead air. The babble that floated into the silence was talk at a bar. Ten years before, Westbrook would have been correct in believing the Voice had been calling from the West, for it was there you found the rootless migrant workers, the sheepherders, the cowboys, the section hands, the hayhands, and it was they who cherished their harmonicas and guitars and sang the sad songs of death and the death of love, and of loss and the tragedy that shaped their lives. They were rejected, and their rejection they had in common; they were as moved by the song of a black man who had lost his woman to a slaveowner as by that of a blue-eyed child who sat in the coach of an eastbound train that carried her to her father who was dying in prison. The miner trapped in a cave deep in Kentucky was brother to him who read in a letter edged in black of his mother's death and of his father's longing for forgiveness.

> *Think of home, my boy,*
> *Think of home, your dear old mother's dead.*

Blistered bodies and the wrecks of locomotives; a dying man's request for a packet of love letters in a rosewood casket; a loved one dead in the baggage coach ahead. Those lost ones turned inward, but of horror and loss they fashioned a world of their own, and often it was beautiful.

When radio came to Grayling, Montana, the Victrolas and Columbias and Sonoras stood silent like upended coffins, something of an embarrassment for once they had meant so much and everybody had gathered around and now they meant so little; one had lied to oneself and had vowed that the music they reproduced was just as lifelike! And it was not, and who any longer cared for the Caruso and Melba records or gems from "The Runaway Girl"?

> *O sly Cigarette, O sly Cigarette,*
> *Why did you teach me to love you so . . .*

Now with the turn of a dial — well, three dials — you brought in the Street Singer who moved you close to tears and Ed Wynn who made you laugh and pretended to be a fireman. On ranches they cast out the old phonographs as they cast out old chairs and they came to rest in the bunkhouse. The day of the phonograph, like the day of the horse was done. Wasn't it?

But the mail-order houses knew a thing or two — that twenty million Americans in bunkhouse and shanty town, in tent and sheepwagon, knew that men are not created equal, that justice is not for all, that God is indifferent and only money speaks with authority. The pursuit of happiness leaves your pockets empty and your ass in a sling and you've got a dose to boot. So Sears, Roebuck and Montgomery Ward continued to stock records on the Silvertone Label about lost love, cheating women, paper flowers, last words, drunkenness and jails — life as so many knew it. A peculiar music for a peculiar people, a singular culture, lasting loyalty to buddies, to Mother, Father and Sister. Good women stood on pedestals; bad women expected to be used. That people knew hunger and cold and the last cup of flour and the empty coal scuttle. A violent and sentimental culture, it was like the laurel leaf: it was not for everybody.

Then how explain why thirty years later the young and the rich and the educated were picking out chords on bucolic instruments, struggling with progressions and the diminished seventh, and wearing costumes appropriate to the task, blue jeans, rustic footwear, beards and the hair long as God willed — and singing the songs of that peculiar people? Yes, pants of denim; the fabric of the poor was now the fabric of the rich. Who now could afford a pair of Levi's? The wail of the Horner harmonica was now heard in the very shadow of Main Hall, in the purlieus of the Art Center where never cowboy or peon had spat or set foot.

Here was a new generation who felt damned — felt

damned because they thought worthless their fathers' standards; their fathers had pressed stifling advantages upon them. They were uneasy, some said, with the atomic bomb; they were the first generation, some said, who had to accommodate the idea of sudden mutual death. To Westbrook, that idea was ridiculous; death is death, whether mutual or singular, and death is present from the moment we're born, and a sudden flash and sudden end is preferable to writhing under a flaming car or screaming with cancer.

To more closely associate themselves with those whose culture they had misappropriated, this new generation drank. Wearing Old Glory for jockey shorts and shaking their fists at those they were pleased to call pigs or fuzz, they got themselves put away, and remained overnight in the pokey. They acquainted themselves with hardship by thumbing rides across the country, sometimes easterly and sometimes westerly, and carried small money with them — and that only for dire emergency. They walked miles before they accepted rides and spoke of money as bread to prove they had become so simple they required but the staff of life. They split, rather than departed, and so declared themselves a special fragment — like those whose songs they played and sang, like those whose culture they had assumed but had not suffered to create. And like the laurel it was deathless and it was not for them.

But it belonged to Westbrook's son. The Voice had spoken. *"He got in jail. He shoplifted in the supermarket."*

XII

WESTBROOK FOUND AN ATTORNEY so obscure and so busy becoming less obscure he was unfamiliar with Westbrook's voice; he was not surprised at Westbrook's introducing himself as a Mr. Edwards. The sign DE WITT WILLIAMS, ATTORNEY-AT-LAW was a new one, printed in modified Old English, gold on oak, a reminder that the common law is of British origin. It hung over the porch by two hooks inserted in eye bolts, and its removal for regilding or against vandals in the nighttime would be a simple task. The small frame house was painted white quite as recently as the sign. Pretty soon De Witt Williams would hire office space in a tall building in town, and his present office could be used for what the architect had designed it — a living room? Pretty soon he would have a secretary and no problem of whether it looked better for his wife to pretend to be a secretary or whether it was better for him to greet clients at the door because his wife did not sometimes look like a secretary — as now: she greeted

Westbrook in curlers, a pretty young woman, very likely with a modest degree of her own, and she had a lovely smile and with that smile she held Westbrook until De Witt Williams could arrange himself professionally in his "office."

On the far wall which was not very far was a framed diploma from one of the wrong law schools. That Williams would take with him to the future office in the tall building along with the new metal desk of flat battleship gray, the desk set — an oblong of marble with holders into which were plunged two fountain pens, should it transpire that two people had to write at once — a brassbound perpetual calendar, and the two black Naugahyde visitors' chairs fitted with sturdy arms to give weaker clients a fighting chance to get to their feet.

The battered old Remington typewriter would remain behind.

"Nice to meet you, Mr. Edwards," Williams said, "and I hope I can be of good service."

Now, that was a nice thing to say. Williams was a thin, blond young fellow, lean and probably agile. Westbrook guessed he looked good on the tennis court, that he took more after his mother than his father, that De Witt was his mother's maiden name and that his mother came quite often with gifts and advice. He doubted that Williams needed the stern horn-rimmed glasses that outlined but did not enlarge his eyes; when he removed them he was quite without the naked look of the visually crippled. Like the diploma, the desk and the wall-to-wall carpeting, his spectacles were a part of a projected image of a bright young lawyer with his feet on the ground.

However, beyond the closed door that marked this room off as a place of business and dedication came the sudden yelp of a baby waking, outraged at finding itself still exposed to the world rather than sheltered by the womb. Quick concern flickered over Williams's face; his eyes slid to the closed door.

Williams now adjusted his spectacles and smiled. "Now what can I do?"

"Quite a simple matter. I want to know about shoplifting."

"You've been accused of shoplifting?"

"Not at all. It's an academic question. You see, I'm a free-lance writer. I'm presently doing a piece on crimes committed by the young."

The disappointment on Williams's face was fleeting, but was there. He had thought he had in that Naugahyde chair a rich kleptomaniac who could help with future plans. Instead he had a curious journalist seeking information that involved no courtroom. His wife would be waiting beyond the door with the baby, and as she later unwound her pretty hair from the curlers she would wonder what to wear, what about a baby-sitter, for this must be a night to celebrate. It was doubtful that many men so well dressed had sat in the Naugahyde chair.

"What do you wish to know?" Williams asked, dressing the wound of his disappointment with the use of the formal "wish to know" instead of "want to know." He had suddenly toppled from his lofty role of attorney-at-law to that of a simple man behind an information desk.

"What is the penalty for shoplifting?"

"That would depend on the amount taken. Up to fifty

dollars is petty larceny. Above that, grand larceny. The judge would consider that first."

"Wouldn't it matter where the — the shoplifting took place?"

"I would say that if it took place in a jewelry store it would very likely be grand larceny. It would scarcely be worth a thief's time to prejudice himself and face possible conviction for — for a few trinkets. Even a young thief would hesitate."

"Suppose the shoplifting took place in a supermarket."

"Food taken? Most judges would simply throw the case out. The judge would quite rightly feel that the thief was hungry. It's pleasant to say that few people starve in this country of ours."

Westbrook spoke without thinking. "Then I don't understand?"

"Don't understand?"

"I should have thought — would have said there must be some punishment, however light."

"A reprimand from the bench, I'm sure. I know of such a recent reprimand and then" — Williams removed his spectacles and smiled — "and then the judge, nice old fellow, took out his wallet and peeled off two ten-dollar bills and handed them down. I was there, Mr. Edwards. But certainly not jail. You see, if a thief were caught inside the store, whatever he had hidden on his person would simply be taken away, and he would be evicted from the premises and told not to come back and so on and so on. But if a young man got out the door with food, anything edible except for say — oh let's say so-called luxury items like Beluga caviar — but even then,

I'm quite certain the store would not want the bad publicity that prosecuting the hungry would cause. It is pleasant to think that in this country of ours there are so many to champion the needy. Unless, of course —

"Unless perhaps the thief had been apprehended at shoplifting more than once, several times, you see."

Westbrook saw, and Westbrook saw that the young man before him owned a fresh-painted white house, that he had a diploma and a lovely young woman in curlers who had a baby, who understood Beluga caviar and was going to be liked by many people in the future. And Westbrook saw the late sun flowing in through the clean window. It caught on Williams's wedding band.

Westbrook believed the woman living with his son was a wife and not a transient doxie. He was certain the other party was a wife because he himself would never have lived long enough with a woman not his wife for the world — and the Voice — to look on the arrangement as "they" and he assumed that neither would his son. He did believe so desperately in blood. On what else is a feeling for Family based? For what other reason would anyone honor his forebears except as those who had passed on blood?

But there was a mystical aspect, too. It would not have surprised him if a father and a son, strangers to each other, met and recognized each other because over each hung a telltale aura. He recalled an article — probably in the *Reader's Digest* for that publication liked materials that end happily — about a girl of twenty who as a child had been adopted, and who had suddenly known that the man who stood beside her at a counter was her true father. She had screwed up her courage and — she had spoken.

Beginning with his son and daughter-in-law, he began to piece together a picture of troubled domesticity at the point where their trailer was hauled off. A husband from the beginning has known that it is expected of him to kindle the fire with flint on steel and to fend off wild animals. The first woman was no more capable of rolling the protecting stone across the entrance of the cave than later woman is of getting the chains on the car or the top off the peanut butter. A man is proud of his ability to help and to protect. Because of his wife, how much greater his son's shame and concern at the hauling off of the trailer — her little house, her safe place, the haven he had provided. Within those thin walls they had laughed and whispered and made love and planned for the day she would be pointed out as she who had married him, he who ran a successful store or was on the way up in some small bank. Ah, they would look back with affection to those days in the trailer. No one lives who does not look back with affection on some shelter.

Yet there they stood, actors in a terrible comedy, their home gone, their little possessions naked on the stubble of a vacant lot under the awful sky. Whoever had allowed them to park their trailer there must now offer asylum — at least for a little while; and if Westbrook knew the world, this meant they must both now practise obsequiousness, as paupers, and must keep their voices down and be in little evidence in their borrowed space. For it does not do, even among friends, for two families to live under one roof. Privacy is first of all riches, and coldly defended. Sooner or later their host would suggest other arrangements, and then demand them.

The host's wife would have been at him. Another woman in the kitchen, another woman in the bathroom. Having to be furtive about sex. "I can't put up with it," the host's wife says, and sets her cup in the saucer.

He says he knows.

"Then do something."

He is torn between friendship and marriage, but not for long. He will do something.

And out of this Westbrook's son may have lost a friend, maybe his only friend. Feeling himself about to be ejected, Westbrook's son had thought to bring something acceptable into the house to placate his reluctant host, some little thing to please, and among the poor that may be only a chicken to roast or a steak to fry. And that accounted for the shoplifting so close on the heels of the vanished trailer.

But once his son had gone to jail, his friend would not wish to be known as an associate. The upright poor cannot afford to associate with — criminals.

One hope remained — that it was the Voice himself who had offered ground to accommodate the trailer and the Voice who had taken in the young people after its repossession. Westbrook saw this person as an older man, a childless widower who knew what life might be. And the Voice who went with the little wife to the jail for visiting hours.

Westbrook knew something about visiting hours. He often thought about visiting hours when going to work at midnight and passing again under the portrait of the Old Man. The Old Man's death had taken a long time and was played out in a hospital. You could not pass through the doors of a hospital, however colorful the lobby and engaging the items in the Gift Shop, without recalling those who do not leave alive. A ghastly cheerfulness prevailed. Priests trotted smiling to give Last Rites. Nurses pooh-poohed legitimate concerns and retired behind a healthy matter-of-factness born of long acquaintance with eschatology. With great good nature they suffered the inane inquiries about the time of day asked by the elderly who shuffled in the corridors.

It is not death that is the indignity, but punishing sickness.

And curious that both sickness and death should be to an accompaniment of flowers. For flowers in profusion there are. The thoughtful among the sick must reflect on the ephemeral nature of cut flowers and find more comfort in the potted plant, whether hyacinth or heliotrope. It might survive. But cut flowers there are, enough to fill a hundred silos, and offered to show affection or to appease guilt.

For all the Old Man's money, he shared his room with another. Perhaps he wanted it so, wanted company, and company he had, six or seven different men during the weeks he took to die.

Westbrook remembered a young man who attended his father, learning, with the use of an orange whose rind resembles the human skin, how to give injections to ease the agony of terminal cancer.

So he could die at home.

So his last vision would be of his own things, his last light would filter through his own windows, his last step sound on his own floor.

How deal with the fact of death? What should we have been, should be now? What should we have done to diminish death — how be remembered?

Money, for one thing. Set up a trust fund, and each month when the check comes in we'll be remembered.

Art, for behind the words, behind the notes, behind the brushstrokes stands ourself.

But what of the poor or the uncreative? Westbrook knew. You had a son. In him you lived on.

Westbrook had brought mints; the Old Man's teeth were in a plastic bowl; even the toothless can manage mints. In the early days of the Old Man's illness there were visitors, flowers, cards, magazines. But as week after week passed, only Westbrook and the Old Man's relative, a young man recently from California, were in attendance, and they the Old Man sometimes didn't recognize. The relative was the grandson of the Old Man's second cousin, and the Old Man's heir.

Blood.

On the two occasions when Westbrook saw him, the young man was dressed in a faun-colored suit, bell-bottomed, wide-lapelled, and constructed of something that looked like suede. His necktie was gorgeous, and his shiny blond hair hung well down over the back of his collar; he reminded Westbrook of a nervous sheep — he glanced first at his clean fingernails and then at his watch.

Nobody has time for the sick. A visitor comes, vows to remain thirty minutes and fidgets after five, shuffling excuses like cards. He must take the children to the Museum of

Science — you know how children are. He must meet a plane carrying important people from Florida. The store is delivering a deep freeze. A frozen turkey lies unattended in the car. He has forgotten to drop money in the parking meter; the police will be upon him.

But what is that to a dying man's need for company before he slips into the last dark, believing himself so loved he can command another's time? Let the children wait to see the stuffed mastodon; let those from Florida drink upstairs at the airport; let the deep freeze people cool their heels.

But all, all has been said. The patient has inquired of the outside world. Did Philips get his dog back?

Days ago.

Have you seen anything at all of Burgess?

None to speak of.

The visitor steers talk closer to home. Why, here's a card from Joe! You know, Joe's done pretty well for himself.

And the light filters through the window as inexorably as death itself, and picks out the innocent carafe of water.

"How about a little water?" And the visitor rises to proffer water before the patient can refuse.

In the hall the young relative spoke. "I've got to get back out West," glancing at his watch as if he meant "within the next few minutes."

'I hardly knew him," the relative said. "He said you were close to him. He's made all the — arrangements. I saw his will. He's left you his old microphone."

So now the Old Man had only Westbrook.

One afternoon the Old Man struggled up against his pillow in greeting. His cheeks were drawn in; his lips drooped from lack of teeth. He looked like a bum. But now the Old

Man smiled and made a swimming motion. "Hand me my teeth there." Then a thought altered his face as he installed them and ran his tongue over them to prove it. "Sorry not to be shaved. The young fellow didn't come."

So the orderly in white hadn't come. The time had come when coming was pointless. He would be shaving someone who had a chance. What does it matter if a dying man lies unshaven?

Westbrook said, "Let me shave you."

He sank in the elevator with silent people to the pharmacy for a safety razor.

"And a can of shaving cream."

"The large or the small?"

Westbrook was suddenly outraged that the Old Man had not been shaved, that the Old Man had no one but him and he had no one but the Old Man.

"Give me the big one," he said.

He filled a basin with water, found a cloth and a yellow soap said to dispell the human odor.

The Old Man lay back with his eyes closed.

Now, except for the touch of hands in greeting, Westbrook had never before touched a man's skin except his father's, as a little boy. Now he must proceed with an intimacy that had never crossed his mind and how horrible that age required one man to be dependent on another.

The Old Man sighed.

Westbrook escaped his distaste of his task by retreating into the detachment of the professional barber; before him was Grayling, Montana, and a barber unfolding a hot cloth over a customer's face, making a little tent over the nose to allow breathing. He smelled Lucky Tiger and Morning

After Rub, saw the colored lotions in bottles before the mirror reflected in the mirror opposite into infinity. Whitey Palmer who had the first chair in the shop in the Andrews Hotel building was saying, "You got your deer yet? Frisbee was in, got him a big buck up Black Canyon."

From under the hot towel. "The hell! The hell you say." About the last words he'd heard in the state of Montana. The last haircut.

The last he remembered of the Old Man was the feel of soap and slackening skin.

Next morning the Old Man was dead.

Our fathers saw signs in the guts of chickens. We seek answers in the drift of stars. Westbrook was not the first to believe in cryptic causes and effects, in deeds and punishments. Why should not a past impulsive kindness move the Voice to compassion?

The visiting hours in a jail? Short hours, and no flowers. From two until three in the afternoon, hours set somewhere into the day most convenient for police or sheriff or guards that did not interfere with coffee breaks, card games and perusals of newspapers.

His son's wife would dress carefully for the visit; the poor cannot afford to be casual. Her dress must make a statement, that she recognized the majesty of the law and the blue-coated police who upheld it. Her dress said she did not wish to offend by dressing as if she did not defer to authority. Pacified by her appearance — clean hair and pocketbook — they might be more disposed to treat her husband with kindness.

Her skirt and blouse, then, and her "good" shoes whose shape modishly deformed her foot and were worn so seldom the soles and heels did not yet show the peculiar marks of pressure from her style of walking. No hat. But her hair had been up in curlers since morning; she might have been preparing for a dance at some Roseland or Tivoli. But she would carry her purse — her "bag" — and although it held nothing but a compact, bobby pins and a snapshot of a young fellow now in jail, it might have had something in it, and it marked her as one who knew what to do and was ready for emergencies.

At the station house, men lounged, sat, stood, supported themselves off the horizontal by taking advantage of wall or doorsill. Men of power. But Westbrook knew them to be uneducated and so poorly paid they must stoop to petty bribes from whores and touts. The length of their pricks was important, how many broads they had laid, and if their team came through. Cheap politicians were their idols; they longed for twenty thousand a year, a vacation in California, freedom to fool around. They didn't know what they wanted and ended sitting and leaning, belching and farting like men.

And here she was before them, his daughter-in-law. Whoever had accompanied her waited in the hall. Here she was before them. It is remarkable how love and devotion never hesitate to run the gamut of scorn or pity.

She speaks, attempts a smile, and speaks. "I want to visit —" and she says his name.

"You the wife?" There may be rules against mere friends. A prisoner's right to see mere friends and acquaintances may be shadowy.

"Yes, I'm his wife," she says. "I am Mrs. Westbrook. My husband's great-great-grandfather discovered gold in the state of Montana and with it he bought the Westbrook acres and built the Westbrook mansion. A tall clock stands at the bottom of the stairs. My husband's great-grandfather was a judge and drove fast horses. The Copper Kings came to his house in Helena and drank his wine, and with them he rode in private cars. The voice of my husband's father is heard in thirty-eight states. He eats his food at the Ritz-Carlton Hotel and parks his cars in areas forbidden to others. Yes, I am Mrs. Westbrook."

But that she didn't yet know. Had she known, it would have been she and not the Voice who called him.

"Yes, sir," she said. "I'm the wife." A frightened woman with an empty pocketbook.

It is considerate of authorities, is it not, to spare a wife the knowledge of the cells in jails? If her man wants her to know about that — if he feels the need to express to her his humiliation, to walk through the cleansing fire of mortification, let him speak. But a wife need not know that attention there is accorded only the bare necessities — poor, starchy food on a tray, an iron cot for sleep and a toilet for defecation is what the wayward deserve, no more than beasts. So a wife waits in a bare room. She sits on a bench before a stout, fine screen of metal lest in love she hand him an instrument to harm himself or others. Beyond, a closed door.

That door opens.

And there he is. A shame about his eyes. His confusion is like that of one brought out of a hole into the sun.

Now only that screen separates them. They speak, but not

of plans or of friends, not of the past or future or even of love. For he may have lost his freedom and she her husband, but what life they had made of their years was yet inviolate unless they spoke of it and were overheard.

They speak in tongues. He speaks her name. That means, I love you.

She is saying, "I came as soon as I could." I love you, too.

"I'm glad." I was afraid you would be ashamed of me.

"You knew I would." I would never be ashamed of you.

"Is it all right, where you are?" Are the people who know about me being kind to you?

"Oh, yes. I would have brought magazines, but your eyes." What can I do?

"No, they wouldn't be any good, magazines." You're doing everything. He lifts his hand and touches the screen, smiling. She touches the screen. Their hands on the me al generate heat they both can feel.

Westbrook had often thought about his son's hands, and his son's eyes. He knew his son's eyes. But how were the hands. What did they look like? We fix attention on hands because we can't see the brain; those grayish tubes jammed into the human skull produce a Mozart or a Nixon. But the hands express the brain; ultimate nerve ends, they write or paint or touch a child, comfort a woman, remove trash, pick a flower, fix a carburetor.

Well, the time was near when his son need not wonder if anyone was ashamed of him; his son's wife would carry a pocketbook of the finest alligator and it would be stuffed with money. Do you hear? Stuffed. He would see to it. And he felt the heady power of one who can work a miracle. He felt something in his bones.

His bones did not deceive him. At one that Monday morning, the Voice spoke.

"Send fifty dollars cash to Box W, Fargo, North Dakota."

XIII

EXCEPT FOR HIS FATHER'S COMING THROUGH with a little more money, Westbrook might have remained for some time in Grayling, Montana, before he showed it a clean pair of heels. He'd never been sure whether it was his father's generosity or his father's sensitivity — whether his father wanted for him what he wanted — radio — or whether his father could imagine how painful Grayling would be after the Maxine Gates affair. He could expect pointless confrontations, loose talk in the Pheasant and at Skeet's Bar that might move some to believe the Hale appraisal of the Westbrooks was the correct one. Such would go on until John Gates wound up his local business and moved on east or west.

Check in hand, Westbrook could now in good conscience trace his journey across the country to Boston on the cloth-backed map of the United States that hung on the wall in the Circle W Insurance Agency. The map was a prominent feature of the office along with the rolltopped desk that had belonged to the sickly judge, a table littered with old copies of *Outdoor Life* and *The Saturday Evening Post*, chairs for loungers, and a brass cusspidor.

The purpose of the map was obscure; possibly it was meant to lend a national dimension to a painfully local business, but the purpose of the cuspidor was clear enough. More than a few men in town still chewed tobacco — Star or Horseshoe Plug — and the Circle W Agency was the last business establishment in Grayling that was prepared for their sloppy habit, and their money was quite as good as any other's. (It now crossed Westbrook's mind that since his father had had no janitor it was his father who had polished the brass and emptied out their casual spittle. That was something to think of.)

So thirty-five years ago, his finger touched the map. Pink Idaho, pale orange Montana, purple North Dakota, and his finger paused at Fargo, for that was the end of the West. Across the Red River lay Moorhead, Minnesota. Across the Red River were farms instead of ranches, timberlands instead of the open range, tales of Paul Bunyan instead of tales of cowboys and Indians and gold. That's where the East began.

Behind glass doors in a bookcase in the front hall of the Westbrook "mansion" were *Diseases of the Horse, Grasses of the Western United States* and a set of the encyclopedia bought long ago by the first Westbrook, who had doggedly educated himself. Between the covers were facts no longer facts, kings sitting on thrones long since toppled, boundaries described that no longer existed, assertions made in the name of science that time proved untrue.

Westbrook drew out Volume 19.

Fargo, N. Dak.

Fargo was still true.

. . . city, county seat of Cass County, at the head of naviga-
tion on the Red River, on the Chicago, Milwaukee and Saint
Paul, the Northern Pacific and the Great Northern railroads.
It contains a United States land office, Fargo College (Con-
gregational) the State Agricultural and Mechanical College,
Oak Grove Seminary (Lutheran), Sacred Heart Academy
(Catholic).

. . . brickyards, packing plant, creameries, bottling works
and manufactories of flour, harness, candy, corsets, bed-
springs and artificial limbs, etc.

Curious, Westbrook had thought, that the city that
marked the end of the West should be known for corsets and
artificial limbs.

"Yes, my corset came from Fargo," and "Yes, you can do
worse than get your leg from Fargo."

Early in the morning of his second day on the day coach,
the train stopped; the sudden silence of the sleep-inducing
wheels woke a baby; an old man across the aisle launched
into another coughing fit. The car was gray with dawn, stal
with the stench of sleeping flesh. Westbrook was cold, his legs
stiff from having been drawn up fetuslike against his stomach. Behind him a match flared. The baby sighed and was
silent; a woman whispered, "There, there, there."

Westbrook looked out the window.

The station was a long, low brick structure. A massive
chimney argued strongly for a fireplace inside; if the architect was worth his salt — a young admirer of Stanford White,

he had modeled his fireplace after the vaulted windows, and ordered andirons which for some reason had never come. A virgin fireplace, then, swept clean of dust; it had never known the leaping flames meant to warm travelers caught in a wild storm sweeping down from Canada.

The architect had kept his fancy in check until he de·signed the roof. There he fell under the spell of the Chinese. From its long, sharp spine, the corners of the roof swooped down and then tilted sharply up at the ends, pagoda fashion. Such roofs confound evil spirits; evil spirits, sliding down and bent on troubling those inside find themselves whisked up harmless into the air.

A sign hung from brackets.

FARGO

He had awakened at no other station. Why at Fargo? He had a strong leaning towards metaphysics and fate, more than half-believed that a man's life is laid out like cards; the aces, say, or the sixes turn up again and again. It is no accident that a man marries when he does or is suddenly drawn to a piece of music. When a man hears it he's ready for it. In reading about Fargo, he had made Fargo a part of him; his physical approach to it had perhaps set up a heightening awareness, like the movement of a magnet towards a bit of iron that had awakened him.

All but one of the vaulted windows of the station were dark; behind that single one a weak bulb glowed over the telegraph key.

No one stood on the platform. Nothing suggested corsets or artificial limbs.

It had begun to rain.

Then down from the front end of the train walked a man dressed in bib overalls and a denim jacket; he wore a train-man's cap and carried a cardboard suitcase, and his face was awry with anger, an emotion more often encountered at the end of the day when fatigue has brushed the emotions. A tall, thin, middle-aged man loping beside the train.

Westbrook thought, Revenge.

Thought it, and the man stopped under him and looked up, twisted his head on his long neck and looked up. Their eyes locked. The man's look was one of quiet appraisal. A long, reptilian look, and Westbrook was left wondering if a stranger whose opinion was unclouded by either love or hate was not a better judge of a man than either enemy or friend.

So the sixes and aces — and Fargo — were turning up again. Fifty dollars to Box W, an anonymous box like those briefly rented by persons seeking queer relationships or quick money. The word "cash" ruled out a check that would return with a traceable endorsement. But the amount of cash suggested that the Voice was precise, reasonable, and would be obeyed — exactly. Fifty dollars for a pair of glasses?

He sealed the envelope with his own spittle, and on his face was a faint smile. Maybe his patience was being rewarded. It appeared the crux of the Voice's operations was to reveal facts but never a location. Was this a first slip?

Once the general store was the local forum. Meeting there and talking was a pleasant afternoon, and comfortable where everything wanted was within arm's reach — food, should the stomach require it; tonics and salves, should you hurt yourself; clothing on racks and fuel in the cellar, should a wild blizzard strike and you be marooned there for days with friends. But the general store has long since fallen for reasons of economy to the chain store and the supermarket where you are lucky if they will cash your check. Gone is the cracker barrel and the pickle barrel; into the museums the pot-bellied stove and the chairs drawn up where sat the selectmen and the sheriff come down for the day to look into something he heard about, and the jokers and joshers and the bores and the liars who knew a thing or two.

The seasons are different now, the snow not so deep. Winter passed overnight. No sooner had the forsythia failed than the lilacs bloomed. Only yesterday the children crawled down over the rocks to the ocean, their laughter clear on the sudden east wind, and now here are the little yellow butterflies and the goldenrod. The children have all gone away. The woods where you walked are cleared and filled with houses, and called Fairview now. The people in the houses scarcely speak except at PTA. Those who knew the general store have died or come to terms with themselves. Great-grandfathers, they look amazed at the sons of the sons of their sons who must wonder why this old man wants to be loved. How could this have happened to them who played baseball in the far field and longed to be twenty-one and free to love and to carouse? Now they are urged to eat a little something and not to tire themselves, and have a little nap, for when they wake up everybody will still be there. What a mockery aging is. What do the young make of the old? What do the old with their wrinkles and spindly shanks have to teach?

Why, that is easy. The old teach that worry is worthless,

that you laugh and do not divorce, that you must not show a fear of death because the young will be watching, and that you put precious things away in little boxes because someone will want them someday, and that it is probably wise to save and not give money away unless somebody needs it — the payment on a house or a bill for teeth fixed or other things which are so difficult for the young who have not yet learned to be prudent because they have not had time, and above all, that you love and show it and end letters with Remember, I love you and your son and his son. For in these terrible terrible times there is nothing lasting but to be a Smith or a Burk or a Cohen or whoever you are, that's what the old have to teach.

The church is no local forum, for there you keep your voice down in case you should disturb God who is quite unpredictable and no one to count on as it turns out. There is no food except a bland bread at arm's reach and the medicines available there are bitter and, some think, worse than the sickness, and anyway churches are closed except on designated days. So now it is in garages and service stations that men gather and are pleased to be known by their nicknames, for men are comfortable around automobiles and the fuels that propel them and the lubricants that make them last. Men are free to speak their minds there in words they wish to use and to spit and fart in peace because women do not come there except for crazies on the backs of motorcycles and they don't count because they are not really women. Your ordinary women didn't understand cars except for getting behind the wheel and taking off; if something happens they throw up their hands and call somebody. There is no sense in talking to them about cylinders or bore and stroke and valves and distributors. When cars from funny places like Arkansas or Delaware drive in and stop the light from inside falls on the faces of the women in the passenger's seat. If they have to get out they get out and go around the side of the building. If the place is locked the man asks for the Ladies' key and he gives it to her outside and she goes around and comes out and gets back into the car and nothing is said. It is funny that the Ladies' is locked and the Men's not. Maybe women feel they are special and more special if it's locked.

You bet Bud is glad to see you because it's been a dead night and he's got through his paperback and is sitting there looking at the grease under his nails and then tearing off the page of the calendar because he had forgot to, and only twenty more shopping days. It's nice and warm in there. So if he has some little job to do, car coming in with a flat to fix or water in the gas in the winter, you can pump gas for him like you owned the place and anybody else there can stay inside and keep an eye on the cash register. If you watch close you can learn a lot about cars you didn't know so if you were out of a job you could get one because you knew.

Gasoline has a good smell and remember how when you were little you used to smell raw gas and nowadays they say that's wrong, smelling it raw. It is good to get under the hood of a car and wipe off the grease from a place and see what's wrong with her. You get at the truth that way. There is food at arm's reach, if you have a dime or whatever, candy bars and cheese-flavored crackers drop down from the machine into a place; cups appear behind little glass doors and liquids fill them. Let me tell you there are sure worse things than squatting against a wall with a cup of java and having friends know just about everything about you by this time, and still liking you anyway. You can treat your friends if it's your turn, and it's like a regular club or something. It's enough to make you think, so many people out traveling, and the things you see. Service stations are open the whole night long. Everything is different at night. People don't act the same. The night is private, like having it rain and you inside.

That son-of-a-bitching Bud likes to have you there because the other day some goon at another station came in like to ask for the key for his girl to take a piss and instead held the fellow up with a gun and took the key for the cash register and heisted two hundred bucks and the son-of-a-bitching company held the fellow responsible for what he had been robbed of. This didn't used to go on except when Johnson got in and everything went all to hell. Christ, you lock your doors at night and nobody did, you didn't even know where the God-damned key was and your wife at home and rape and just killing people for the fun of it, getting up on high buildings with rifles and shooting everybody and nurses in Chicago and old ladies with a stocking around their necks, talk about your law and order and Nixon and them with their prayer breakfasts and him talking like you wouldn't even with your friends and everybody going to jail and him pardoned by Boob McNutt who you remember from the funny papers if you're that old, and also Happy Hooligan.

So Bud told you, he had the paper right there under his java, and sometimes you thought about Bud, you knew he had a wife because of the picture of her in his wallet, but this one he said she hates because she's got her hair up in curlers, but she's pretty anyway, she was going someplace where you got to have your hair right. Why don't fellows have to have their hair right? And so when Bud goes off and the other fellow comes on at six, he's all right, too, but not so much fun as Bud — you think about Bud getting into his Chevy and going home, driving home, and getting out and unlocking the door where he lives and she calls down and says, Bud? And he says, It's just me, Bud. And she says I thought it was you. How was everything?

How is everything? What is everything?

Well, everything is how your sandwich was when you ate it, and that your friends see in you what she sees in you. You went back to work with confidence and the problem you had solved. Did you see anything that moved you, and did you find the right words.

That's the crazy things you think of at night beyond the dark.

And then the Voice was saying:

"*He's got himself a job in a service station nights.*"

*XIV*_____

TOM WESTBROOK SAYS God bless you whoever you
are to the judge who pronounced so light a sentence. Whatever you wish — to be transferred, to own a Cadillac or to
have land in Florida, to have your portrait painted and hung
in the capitol — whatever you wish, let that be what you get.
God grant that your children honor you and that when your
step falters and you forget things your grandchildren will
indulge you and fly to your defense.

And bless the man who hired my son because I understand
as anybody does understand that people shy away from hiring a man with a "police record" and you knew forgiveness
and understanding is the answer to everything, and you
hired him. And you made a girl happy who stood there with
an empty pocketbook, who loves my son.

To give something a secret name is to endow it with
magic. Thus Westbrook had once called those earliest hours

of the morning the Three Ones, when the bell in the tower threw out wave after wave of a special time, his own, but shared by those who sat beyond those windows where the last or the first lights burned. Removed, unanswerable to spilling sand or shifting star, it was a time when anything might happen.

But to give a name can make it threatening. And so were the next ten days he called the Long Silence.

He was apprehensive that now the boy was safe in a job, the Voice would abandon him.

Mr. A. said conditions in Upper New York State pointed to another Depression. Mrs. B. struggled along on a fixed income; when the government increased her Social Security it reduced her war widow's pension by the same amount. She was going to have to get somebody to help her put up plastic storm windows.

And now Hallowe'en was in the air. On that night children are allowed to be what their parents are, superstitious, destructive and cruel. It is not hard to believe in ghosts; it is hard not to believe in them; possibly it is the Holy Ghost as the third party in the Trinity who is responsible for the appalling acts of Christian people. Naughty acts are condoned on Hallowe'en. A cranky old man has his windows smashed; an old woman's roses are torn out and her dog is soaked in kerosene, just escaping becoming a torch. A widow of a certain age sees scrawled on her sidewalk a word she has no reason now to believe in.

Masked and garbed as grotesques, children roam the alleys to beg and blackmail and come to understand that society sets up certain times and conditions for which no one is held accountable.

Mrs. C. urged parents to keep children home on Hallowe'en; the previous year deadly candy was handed out.

Mr. D. chuckled, remembering simpler days when nothing worse happened than a privy toppled over or some farmer's Tin Lizzy ended up on the roof of his barn. But now the young people destroyed; and while some solicited food at the front door, their older friends, knowledgeable concerning precious metals, slipped around and carried away the silver. That was not to say that children should be routinely poisoned, but there were two ways of looking at Hallowe'en.

Mrs. E. said she had never grown up. She offered her recipe for candied apples.

The hours pressed on. Alert to accidents and human pain, Miss R. reported that a friend, preparing fish mousse, had pulled a pan of boiling water off the stove so burning her instep she was removed to the hospital where she couldn't endure the pressure of the sheet; they would graft on skin from her back. Nobody wore evening gowns now and the glistening scars where the skin had been peeled away would interest no one but the mortician or a lover drawn to scars.

Westbrook now regularly cut callers short.

Lifting a fork at his "dinner" he was struck by a mad little thought — the vanity of eating. And what is there in life except hope? That you will get rich and confound people? Put off the agony of death. People are lucky who die in sleep or coma. Leave something to the children. Shore up a damaged name. Be eligible for that last Social Security benefit that pays enough for cremation but not enough for a coffin.

Make someone proud. But life — as life? Oh, the awareness of the beating heart!

Westbrook used to give parties in the comfortable little apartment on West Cedar Street on the Hill; his first New Year's Eve party was well attended — eggnog and a fire of applewood in the fireplace. He believed people came because they knew of the Old Man's affection for him.

Someone had brought along a wealthy insurance broker whom he remembered for several reasons. One thing was the effect the man had had on the women in the room—he could have had any one of them, but he declined all gambits. He talked with Westbrook (they were standing near the fire) and had remarked that he, too, had come from the West, but his West was Chicago — East, to Westbrook. In Grayling, Montana, if you went "back East" you went to Chicago or you went to New York; if you went to Chicago you went to Marshall Field's and if you went to New York — well, where did ordinary people go in New York? His mother had known somebody who had climbed up inside the body of the Statue of Liberty and eventually looked out the eyes.

And then this insurance broker — what was his name? — brought out snapshots of his children. The girl, Westbrook remembered, was shockingly beautiful, much like the profile on a silver dollar. And the boy — just a boy with glasses, but something glowed in the father's face. This homely display of snapshots was so ingenuous Westbrook could not help liking the man, and he was appalled to hear later that the man had accidentally shot and killed his son. Westbrook had thought to get in touch with him, but what in the name of God could he have said? A man hesitates to intrude on another's trag-edy. It might be looked on as meddling at the least and morbid interest at the worst.

And the Lord said unto Cain, Where is Abel thy brother?
And he said, I know not: Am I my brother's keeper?

Westbrook wondered if sometimes pride or the horror of being pitied makes a brother wish to be his own keeper, and alone.

He stopped entertaining when he moved into his present fortress. His telephone number was unpublished and un-listed. He was jealous of his free time and important enough to protect it. He spent the weekends in New York at the Pierre and the Metropolitan Museum with the Egyptians on the first floor and *View of Toledo* upstairs — the first paint-ing to move him. The Egyptians appealed to his sense of dynasties and the past.

Few people knew where he lived. His fan mail was di-rected to the station, and leaving there each morning he stuffed it into his briefcase. He could not answer all of it, and this his people understood, but he did answer those cards and letters that showed the writers were sick or troubled or would profit in their neighborhoods by owning the signature of a now fairly famous man.

His generation dreaded the arrival of telegrams. Tele-grams, terse and laconic and impersonal as the Voice itself, brought either very good or very bad news, and usually bad, for good news can wait but people rush to bring bad news.

Who has left more men in despair than the boy who used to come in the ill-fitting uniform and the jaunty cap?

And here this early Sunday morning when he had not yet decided how to endure the day — here was a telegram in his hands. He laid it on the partners' desk and went in and washed his hands. He glanced away from his face in the mirror.

It was beyond him how the Voice had found his address — for the Voice it surely was. He would have been happy at any time to give the Voice his address and private number. It would have been far easier to deal with the Voice privately and not on "Midnight Line."

He opened it.

Why, the thing was from Frank. Frank?

Oh, *Frank*.

His driver. But he had seen Frank only two nights before. Why a telegram? Why not a letter? Frank wanted to see him that afternoon at two in a bar he had never heard of. Why the urgency? His mind flew to Frank's wife, whom he had never met, and then to the retarded son whose picture he kept. "He can do little things," Frank had said, "like rake the leaves at the place where he is. And he knows Christmas and his birthday, we think." Had Frank run out of money. Did he need a loan? Westbrook was grateful for an opportunity to be generous, to have something to do with this day.

On the side streets and back streets where the rents are reasonable you find the little bars, sexual, social and ethnic backwaters. Some are special-interest bars, bars for homosexuals or the sportsminded. In both the lights are low — in the one because soft lights flatter the skin; in the other because soft lights do not interfere with television. In the one are long glances and posings, exaggerations and compulsive superlatives. A transcript of the speech of homosexuals would reveal the underscoring of key words, but not the characteristic hiss of the sibilant. There are no social, religious or color barriers; homosexuals have little in common but their preference for the same sex, Tiffany glass and certain actresses whom they envy. They drink beer, the cheapest liquid that allows them to sit or to lounge against the wall where the view is better of the passing trade.

Most sportsminded fix on the peasant sports, baseball, professional football, basketball, hockey and boxing. In the half-darkness the intellectually wanting attend the shadows in the box, follow a ball to its destination, see big men hit each other until one falls senseless to shouts and groans. Golf and tennis have small place here for neither is violent enough to satisfy; except on rare occasions no one is so badly hurt he must be carried off.

Bars for Italians, for Poles and for the Irish who have nothing in common but a commitment to the Infant of Prague. In Italian bars the jukeboxes play opera, for Italians make no bones about a love of music and a view of the Bay of Naples made by a local whose art stops at the primary colors.

Poles polka and eat sausages in brine.

The Harp Bar and Grille was a convenient spot to relax after the exhausting Mass and cumbersome sermon and to get your wits about you. Above the bottles were tacked posters of recent elections that revealed the distinguishing features of the candidates and announced their promise to be honest.

At two o'clock in the Sunday November gloom a half-dozen young men sat at the bar, hands near their shot glasses. Rapt, they watched an old movie, watched two young men escort two young women into a lavish nightclub, watched the young men give up their black coats and white scarves and hats, watched the pretty hatcheck girl take the hats, watched as hauteur overcame the young women who arranged their evening wraps and preceded the young men into the festivities like lovely prows, watched all four seated at a table. With the help of the young men the young women had been divested of their evening wraps made of slick material and fur. The young women wore no hats.

From the bar they watched an empty stage in the lavish nightclub, a girl move out and make faces and move her arms and sing. They could see by the faces in the audience that it was enjoyed. Then suddenly the camera was back at the entrance and two bad men came in, one of them in a derby and one in a fedora. These hats they kept on, and with them on they spoke to the hatcheck girl who seemed frightened. She didn't ask for their hats. They walked on in. The four sitting at the table looked at them, and one of the young women screamed, and the girl who was singing ran off the little stage and there was a shot.

One of the young men at the bar drank from his shot glass and put it down as a sign he was going to speak. "My old man used to wear hats," he said.

Westbrook sat near the street. Beside him on the shelf in the window a clay model of an Irish human head not quite life-sized sprouted green hair.

A black Continental stopped at the curb; long, swift and glittering, it had carried him to work and to his New York extravagances. In this alien bar it now bore in on him that the car was hired, not his, as his apartment was hired, not his — he was a mere renter, only half in control of transportation or even the roof over his head; only half in control of his life. Half of him was here at a table and half in Fargo where the West begins, in substantial as a ghost whose fragile spine was his people on "Midnight Line" and his power to help.

Frank made himself felt. Here Frank belonged, as Westbrook belonged nowhere, neither at the Ritz nor at the Hotel Andrews in Grayling, Montana.

"Hey, Pete!" Frank shouted.

"Frank-boy!" cried the waiter. "You son of a bitch!"

"Go fuck yourself," Frank said happily. "You getting any?"

"Not what I can't handle," the waiter said.

A young man at the bar pumped Frank's hand. "Ya doin'?" he asked.

"You got a new kid," Frank said.

"Boy this time," said the young man.

"God love him," Frank said.

This was a different Frank. Westbrook had hired a different Frank. Frank now carried his unexpected personality with him to the table and lighted a cigarette. He lowered his voice. "Sorry I'm late. Traffic. They're all using Washington Street for a footpath as per usual. City Hall ought to stop it. I couldn't get your phone. I was going to write yesterday but it was late and now Sunday you wouldn't have got it, and if I wanted I wouldn't of gone through with it maybe."

Westbrook had imagined a more formal meeting, his

standing and Frank's standing, embarrassed, but here was Frank breezing over.

"Glad you went through with it," Westbrook said.

"Glad you could make it," Frank said. "What I've got to say is hard. I like to mind my own business, but sometimes it's better not to keep your mouth shut."

Westbrook felt this meeting slip out of control, but as a man with the power to help, he said "You're in trouble, Frank?"

"I don't want to — did I give that impression?"

"What's on your mind, Frank?"

"You Mr. Westbrook," Frank said.

Westbrook sat speechless.

Frank went on. "I've been worried about all the weight you've dropped."

Westbrook looked down at his stomach.

"I kept my mouth shut," Frank said, "then the other night I was over at your building. I get a lot of fares there now — people don't mind sitting in a car where a famous man has sat. I saw you standing and watching a new service station looks like a Howard Johnson's. Then about an hour later I get another call, and you were still standing there looking. My lights were on you. You looked lost, to me, Mr. Westbrook. If there's anything I can do . . . ?"

"You're very kind, Frank," Westbrook said. "No, there's nothing you can do."

Yes, he had watched the service station, wondering how much it cost, watched the young man there, and wondered about his son's hands and how the sun looked on him in the morning and the look of his face at night. Was it strange to stand there so? If you knew what went on before a man stood looking from the curb — even if you understood what went on before a murder, you might understand. They say a murderer feels no different from anybody else.

Yes, he had felt lost. Lost and a thousand miles away.

XV

EACH SEVEN YEARS the cells replace themselves. The nose that smelled, the eye that saw and the tongue that tasted find new qualities in the old objects; the finger is surprised by the once-familiar grain of teak. The ear perceives unguessed harmonies among the cellos. The brain is a different brain.

What you thought you no longer think. You are not what you were. What you did you did to no one, for that one is no longer. Your new self is recognized because it is seen with eyes that have changed with you. You are no longer who was born, but have been born again. You have the right to another chance.

Many of those who live on dreams are trapped by little schemes inside matchbook covers.

LEARN TO BE A TV REPAIRMAN!

STUFF ENVELOPES AT HOME. MAKE UP TO FIFTY DOLLARS A WEEK!

WRITE LYRICS TO SONGS!

The last bastion of the exclamation point is there among the desperate and the poor.

Westbrook's mother had failed at FIRESIDE INDUSTRIES because handpaintd china plates and satin sachets had not appealed to Grayling, Montana.

The schemes of others had. Scarcely a ranch house in the valley beyond easy reach of the fire engines but bristled with lightning rods supplied by salesmen who came to the door with tales of conflagration and death. Why, everybody knew somebody who had been struck down when moving between barn and bunkhouse, trees split by heavenly fire and forests in flame. Skeptics maintained that rods simply attracted lightning; they installed fire extinguishers, tall brass cans with hoses to point into the flames, glass globes of quenching fluids that escaped from brackets and shattered when rooms reached dangerous temperatures.

Ranch wives answered the knock of a tall man who looked so like Lincoln he was instantly trusted. He brought lurid stories of children who perished before the doctor could be reached. He sold small black coffins no longer than a fiddle-case fitted with tourniquets, flasks of fluid, vials of pills and jars of ointment to banish fever, expel worms, quiet the stomach, halt the flow of blood and revive the faltering heart. He demonstrated how the windpipe can be entered with a sharp knife and held open with a fountain pen to forestall death from choking.

The Fuller Brush man walked the earth with his bristly wares, and successfully. Brushes, except when seen in astounding variety and whisked out from a neat display case, though useful, are so straightforwardly dull they blunt desire, and are passed over in stores.

Oh, there are ways to augment the income. Prostitution in its several guises has served well, and few retire from politics without a little something, another house, a few sparkling stones to perk up the little lady. Blackmail works until the victim is bloodless as a turnip and threats to hurt or maim him are pointless.

Medical schools have more than a cursory interest in the human corpse; there is a brisk traffic in blood and human hair.

Celebrities appear on *The Today Show* hawking books they have written or had written for them. Twice their books are held up to the scrutiny of the camera, should the viewer have been nodding the first time. Sometimes the book is held up by a delightful clown with a mad celebration of both cranial and supralabial hair.

And sometimes by Barbara Walters. She rises from her bed God knows when to greet those anxious for the latest moves of Tricky Dick or his now-ruined vice-president whose name suggests a terminal disease of youthful sheep. Wise to the short attention span of her audience and its need for novelty, Miss Walters projects each morning a slightly different image. Now we have the Peter Pan collar; then the mildly décolleté. The next morning, pants. Extraordinary spectacles lend her ever a new eye.

Earnestly she questions aging beauties whose hands falter. How is it to grow old? For her, old singers sing; their voices crack. How is it to have been young? Miss Walters asks a First Lady if her husband strays.

It is the clown who interviews authors of lighter books about tulips, how to be a superstar, to make a million before you're thirty. Miss Walters handles the seamier books. She speaks with a piglike man who has denounced a brother for a price. A criminal who has set down his crimes for profit shakes his head at what he once was, before he found God. From another author we learn that many animals are on their last legs. Elephant children stumble and die beside their mothers, those great, good beasts. Women who wear fur and men who encase their feet in alligator are denounced. We learn how to tell antiques from fakes, something about the subsequent thoughts of rugby stars who have eaten their companions.

In being "who he was" Westbrook had what his mother might have called "another string to his bow." He was a celebrity, the Master of "Midnight Line." No other talk-master had a larger audience — until just now. No priest heard more confessions, for he heard atheists as well as believers, Jews and gentiles. No hired psychiatrist was more acquainted with the twisted paths and tortured ways than he — for his ear cost no more than a dime telephone call.

He knew the space between the open parenthesis of birth and the closed one of death: Mr. A. spellbound before the Northern Lights. Mrs. B. begging for a second chance. Under the often tragic line of conversation the little hours flowed like counterpoint; he knew the themes, the developments, the codas, and that the man who wakes is a stranger to him of the night before. We are changed by dreams. Something new is understood and the old rejected.

Changed for the better, we hope.

"How is it," Miss Barbara Walters would ask, "to be first among talkmasters? How —"

He had another string to his bow.

As the Long Silence continued, he moved to clear the air for the Voice, and before Thanksgiving he changed the format of "Midnight Line": six times each session for five minutes he played old jazz records, hoping to hoodwink his audience with the charm of nostalgia. Many were not hoodwinked; he could not now bring himself to care. He would woo them back later. Music was a shabby device used by lesser men to cover up dead air. It was a device he used hoping for clues to reduce the price of finding his son.

Three hours before midnight, two weeks before Christmas, Westbrook stopped at an unfamiliar bar off Boylston Street, sat down and ordered Scotch from one who appeared silent as a ghost. When his eyes had accustomed themselves to the gloom, he saw, past the handful of beer drinkers at the bar, a Christmas tree — a symbol of family and religious faith and inappropriate there. A plastic tree; the false needles in the shaded light had a fairy glow. But it was not the composition of the tree that drew his attention but that it was trimmed only in paper roses.

The sweat from his glass printed a ring on the table. Act! Move! It was required to return the glass to that exact spot each time. The figures at the bar were shadows and they spoke so softly — like penitents confessing their sins at the rail, softly lest they wake themselves to what they were in daylight. Darkness shows a different face in the mirror, a new man for whom one is not responsible. Darkness invites intimacies, for darkness is a netherworld where one is anonymous, as behind a mask.

And yes, someone had slipped into the booth across from him, and was saying, was speaking, "Are you lonely?"

Lonely? Westbrook was alert at the word. A strange word for a man to use — it was a man. Lonesome, possibly, not lonely. And because it was the moment it was, himself transformed by the gloom, and now grateful for the comfort of the human voice, he said, "Yes, you could say I was lonely."

"Have you a light?" the man said, and put a cigarette to his lips and leaned forward as a flower leans to the sun.

"I have a lighter," and Westbrook produced his silver Zippo. The little flame caught in the smoky atmosphere over the man's head, like a halo.

"And I have a place to go," the man said.

For a second their eyes were locked. The man smiled faintly. Westbrook clicked the Zippo shut. Now he understood. "I'm sorry," he said. "I'm waiting."

"Yes," the man said. "We wait, don't we."

The Voice spoke early that morning.

The Jews in Grayling, Montana, had neither temple nor synagogue to their name; there were too few Jews to support such luxury and anyway it is said Jews think seldom of an afterlife. For Christians, the matter of prayers and miracles was attended to by the Methodist Church and Saint James Episcopal Church, among others.

Westbrook had been baptized a Methodist, but it was the Episcopal church that attracted him, for those families he envied worshiped there, those who were a reflection of what the Westbrooks might still have been. The Episcopal church was considered better than the others because it had been the church of the British upper classes whom the American upper classes secretly believed to be their betters. People who became Episcopalians without already being Episcopalians were thought to be social climbers; strangers who moved to Grayling and said they were, maybe were not, but hoped by moving to Grayling to leave the tatters of embarrassing old faiths behind, and to start anew. Many Episcopalians cared very much what they wore, and some did not care at all.

They wouldn't let you marry anybody you wanted, nor would they bury everybody, either.

The Hales were, and of course the Burbanks, and the Barts when she wasn't drinking. The Burks would have been except they were born Roman Catholics who never went because the ranch was so far away but sometimes they had the priest out in his Buick and he did it out there in the big living room with all the stuffed heads on the walls, all of them kneeling. Old Adele Burk used to send him five hundred dollars for the church and another five hundred dollars for himself at Christmas because he liked a drink or two; and roasts of beef whenever she thought of it. For some reason they couldn't marry but housekeepers were all right.

But there were poor people who were Episcopalians like

Miss Ruby Wyatt who taught piano, whose pupils played in recitals in Grayling High School gymnasium. She heated up soup on a hotplate. She played the organ in church and was asked everywhere and she went in her old gray crepe de chine and jet beads or down the river on their picnics in an old tweed skirt and a green eyeshade. Yes, they had brass vases on each side of the altar that Mrs. Hale put a towel around her head and polished with her own hands like her own hired girls, and brass candles and robes and red plush. They didn't have a steeple. When they got through with their flowers they gave them to the children at the hospital where a lot of them worked for nothing. They had dances in the Guild Hall where tickets were on sale for anybody but if you went you might get snubbed. The minister went to people's houses and drank and his wife smiled. It only took them ten minutes to get a funeral over and they were not sad about it, never got up and said anything about him and the casket was closed so you couldn't tell. Sometimes they had, well, parties after funerals and talked and laughed. They showed up with ashes on their foreheads in the early spring because that's what they did. How did they get so grand, including Miss Ruby Wyatt?

Westbrook's mother called the Methodist church "the Old Westbrook Faith," lending it dignity by handing it a name as he himself did with the Three Ones. In the early days there were no Episcopalians. They did not wish to match wits with outlaws and Indians. They were quite comfortable where they were until later when the trains came and the Indians were off on reservations and the outlaws in jail, or dead. The Old Westbrook Faith — an angry God and a slight, pretty Jesus as painted by Holman Hunt in *The Light of the World*, sad eyes questioning, and from Him the soloists took their cue and tempered their quaver'ng, hopeless voices. The best they could hope for was to be overlooked in the final scuffle. A faith at once harsh and sentimental, as man himself is said to be, as Old Westbrook had been, a gun in his scabbard, a Bible in his saddlebags and in his purse a lock of his wife's hair.

No one important in Grayling embraced the Old Westbrook Faith or even recognized it as such. The church was a white frame building so poorly constructed the steeple would not support a bell. From time to time a plan was set afoot to strengthen the steeple and buy a bell to ring out the glad tidings, but money was short among the Methodists and so were the glad tidings, and what was raised went into the Fuel Fund, for Montana winters were long and cold, and many Methodist coats threadbare. The raised, timid faces of the congregation resembled those of the sheep they were sometimes likened to from the pulpit. The anemic spirit of the establishment was reflected in the grape juice they sipped at the communion rail instead of wine.

"Faith or a Bell?" had once been the subject of the Reverend Ricketts's sermon, and Mr. Ricketts concluded that since both bell and a faith "ring out" and faith is longer lasting than a bell, it is wise to forget the bell. As for the "useless" steeple, it was not at all so, but a symbol thrusting up at God, as we all must, he said.

Underneath was a basement where the Sunday school met in dampness smelling of lime. Of that place, Westbrook remembered the cold and the piles of slatted folding chairs so cranky to erect, and movable partitions of beaverboard to isolate one grade from another. He was through with it at fourteen and he refused to join the Young People's League, for the Young People's League like the congregation upstairs was largely female; he was uncomfortable in groups of any kind, but especially in groups of females. He loathed associating with failures, though he knew himself to be one.

The young don't much hold with religion. Some look back with affection to when they were very young and believed God to act probably much like their mother's father who was gladder to see them than anybody else was. God was associated with crayons, library paste and next with maps of Palestine, all that brown space. Later on, the educated recognized God in portraits of the elder Brahms.

Few of the young have yet gotten themselves into scrapes that cannot be handled by their fathers, and the idea of death, except for that of pets, is ridiculous. By the time their time comes it is likely science will have done away with death and so death need not trouble anybody. Ministers and priests labor, organizing outings and dances and clubs to attract the Young People who are expected to give the church a visible continuity. Young women are often tractable, fancying the idea of dances no matter under whose auspices, and some are drawn to the idea of a gentle Jesus although he never married and couldn't have been much fun and called his mother "Woman." But to organize young men is next to impossible, even Roman Catholic young men. When Pope John and the council opened up the windows, the fresh air rushed in and the drama and the magic rushed out and the priest now faced the wrong way. Young men wished to be elsewhere than in church and to be associated, rather than with Judaism or Christianity, with the New York Jets.

But as the years pile up and begin to totter on their base and as the shadows lengthen, things change.

In Grayling, Montana, men wanted miracles to retrieve failure in business, to reestablish a good name lost under the influence of some wild whim, and to insure life after death. Not that life as they knew it had been a bowl of cherries but when there's life there's hope, like the man says, and another life might be better, couldn't be any worse God knows and anything is better than being nothing forever underground or thrown to the winds as ashes, as some fancy as being not quite so final. But when the final ash falls from cigar or cigarette and the last sports scores are chalked up, what then? A man they had played cards with has toppled over; a woman they had held in their arms at the Legion dance is getting rouged up downtown for her last appearance.

But until men got very old and the time of decision was near, they ordinarily left salvation to their wives who had nothing better to do with Sunday morning and who are one flesh with them and presumably acceptable substitutes for you yourself. A man who has all week added up figures, argued the merits of this mowing machine, gathered up other people's dirty clothes for cleansing or butchered countless beefs needs his sleep once a week, requires a time for himself, an hour or so to inspect and to oil his guns against the hunting season, to lave his golf bag with saddle soap. He wants to descend into the basement and look around in case something's happened. He wants to be alone long enough to see himself in the mirror. No man wants to be seen looking at himself. Wants time to consider what has been. It is appalling what has been.

His daughter whose picture as a child he carries in his wallet has cried out against him. His son possesses stolen goods. His wife promised, but she is drinking. She misses her mouth with the lipstick. In innocence, he and she married and found that it was not enough, sharing each other, for neither she nor he knew who the other was. How could they have known in so short a time, so brief a courtship? They had both dissembled. She might have died when he pushed her, for behind her was the sharp back of the cast-iron chair. Or she did die, and now —

He turns to God for miracles. That is what He is supposed to do — miracles. He is supposed to have a man's welfare in mind. But alas, suppose He is an invention of those who cannot justify themselves, their occupying space, holding up a line in the supermarket, requiring the attentions of a harassed doctor, disputing ownership of a lot in Mountain View Cemetery and so have no right to expect help from Whatever It Is and must turn to cards, to tea leaves and ceremonies or to a God as they would have Him.

So Westbrook knelt in the only church he knew, whose old priest had once cleaned him out. One by one like garments we cast off ambitions and desires until we stand naked with but one request.

Save the one I love.

He sat far back in the early morning gloom. Beyond, over the altar, was a mural of Christ ascending.

Not an hour earlier the Voice had said his son had been shot defending a cash register and now lay in a hospital.

XVI

TOM WESTBROOK had not raked leaves except his father's leaves, nor shoveled snow except his father's, nor even delivered the *Grayling Examiner* folded hard in on itself and hurled from a bicycle. He had not distributed the bright-colored fliers advertising coming attractions at the Rex Theater for a free ticket to Pearl White in *Plunder*. There was nothing seasonal about the colors of the fliers — purple, say, for Easter or green and red for Christmas; no, each week all the colors went to all the houses, yellow to this and orange to that. He had then been quite as attracted to colors as to words. Moved once by the brilliance of the orange when he was nine or ten he had written on the back of a flier his only poetry, an ode to Thanksgiving, and handed it to Miss Egan whom he loved.

> *We thank Thee for the corn and wheat.*
> *We thank Thee for the pumpkin's meat*

It is likely he had just learned that the flesh of pumpkins is termed "meat," and the pronoun "Thee" reflected the Old Westbrook Faith.

One time in New York he had left his fancy quarters in the Pierre for the Museum of Modern Art to see for the second time in forty years the silent movie *Beau Geste*. Once the name was bold on a yellow flier, a yellow like the shifting sands around Fort Zinderneuf where desperate legionnaires fought off howling Arabs on horses. Around and around the fort they raced, shooting their rifles up into the parapets of the fort as Indians the week before had raced around a log stockade bearing similar arms.

COMING SATURDAY!

And now on Saturday afternoon at two in the Rex Theater it is Miss Pegram who first comes, leaning back against the sharp tilt of the floor, already shrugging off her fur-trimmed coat as she treads on down to the console of the organ in the pit. She sits. She opens the lid over the keys. She flicks on a shaded lamp over the sheet music. The pages rustle. And she plays.

The music insists on a Persian market, but beyond Montana boundaries are vague and ill-defined, and this music means we are anywhere east or south of Suez, out there where everything is more or less the same with their funny music and drums and gongs and what they do in their robes and things.

Now the lights dim, and the brain is drawn along after the retreating light.

Darkness. Then a shocking beam of light hits the screen —
the projection man has not got the film right.

That's better.

Here now is the cast of characters, and opposite, the actors
playing them. After the first two or three names nobody has
ever heard of them. And now the credits, composed of names
unknown in Grayling but belonging to people so competent
they are in charge of lighting, subtitles, music, wardrobe research and screenplay — Verna Ispanell, Jobas Berne, Homer
Osping, Bud Le Boeuf, Van Krumpf, Jon Flaught. Yes, the
Jons of the world had surfaced way back then, if not the Jacs
and Tomies, names assumed in flight from mediocrity.

BEAU GESTE.

Miss Pegram's music now implies a vast, impersonal sky.
The broad cold eye of the camera encompasses an uncom-
promising desert. Of oases there are none but sand in smooth
dunes merges with sand and shadows. And now the camera
moves towards a speck out there, and that becomes a fort
built of whatever they use — stone, concrete, stucco.

But Miss Pegram has stopped playing. Silence. A closeup
of Fort Zinderneuf shows it shocked in silence. The little
party of whites who have come to inspect it are puzzled.
Reining in their steeds, they look at each other and shake
their heads.

Subtitle: *Something strange is going on here!*

For in each parapet a legionnaire mans a post.

Subtitle: *But they are all dead!*

Dead men propped into place up there. The guardians of

the fort are all dead. Tom Westbrook was deeply impressed by the dead playing the living, and twilight in Grayling was never the same again.

Now once again on the screen in the museum was Fort Zinderneuf — but what had happened in forty years? Why hadn't he questioned the makeup on the actors, the rouged lips, the powdered cheeks — not seen that Fort Zinderneuf was constructed of chicken wire, two-by-fours and plaster. It was not merely that he as a child had believed — for a child believes what he wishes — but grown-ups had believed it, too. Did man today briefly discard his reason before such lack of style? Back then you accepted the conventions: you saw a fort, it was a fort, no matter of what it was constructed. Just so the Greeks accepted masks. At the Rex Theater a whiskey bottle meant somebody was drinking. Empty, it meant somebody was drunk; trouble was in the offing. The tray of stubbed-out cigarettes meant somebody was nervous. The tray overflowed, somebody was desperate.

If a candle lighted a scene — watch the candle. For some in the world are so poor they must forgo the electric current and even kerosene and settle for tallow. For the poor, prepare your sympathy.

A candle flame might mean somebody is waiting for somebody and had lighted the candle so the person he was waiting for would know he was waiting because if it were dark the person wouldn't know anybody was waiting.

And a flame might mean a vigil in the house of someone poor, and that someone was sick, or having trouble having a baby. Watch the candle carefully, for there will be a crisis.

Sickness approached a crisis because underneath in words the doctor said so.

We won't know until the crisis.

And after the crisis everything would be all right — or it would not, and the person would die. The candle said this. If the flame leaped up the person lived; if the candle guttered out, as candles gutter, the person died.

You "kept" a vigil.

And now Westbrook was moving once again into the glassed-in cubicle. The aces and the sixes were conspiring: he kept a vigil with a ghostly Voice; as a ghost himself he now so often walked the streets of Grayling, Montana.

Often the little hours were peppered with violence — scenes recaptured, tales remembered and refined in the privacy of darkness. But that last session began quietly enough. The first callers were in a relaxed if fey mood and bent on acquainting others with their peculiar lives as night-people, which no more resembled those of day-people than what transpires under mossy stones resembles what happens in sunlight. Under their talk the night moved like a pedal point: a weak light showed the way to the bathroom; a faucet dripped. Two casual lovers briefly locked together turn away to separate worlds. On the coast a light flashes a warning.

A rose folds the twilight in upon itself.

Here on the windowsill are two earrings discarded because they had troubled the earlobes. Small sounds explode — a twig snaps under a cautious foot. A mouse nibbles, seeking entry — the bait in the trap is but food to extend its life. The life of animals alone is not compromised by a fear of death. The old beagle never dreams that one day in tears you will deliver him up to be put away.

Yes — a red light retreats and disappears around the corner.

They speak of marathons of checkers playing and cooking, midnight walks along the quiet streets questioning the stars and risking arrest by baying at the moon, walking into houses of other night-people bearing food and drink. The shades go down and the music goes up. Innocent brushes with the police who as night-people might understand but sometimes don't and come at the call of neighbors suspicious of the flitting shadows against the drawn shades and the re-peated rhythms. But sometimes the police join the night-people for a drink and sit and talk until the radio alerts them to other mischief.

Mrs. P. maintained not as an admission but as a fact that she drank a good deal during the night but usually not too much. Often she copied poems into a notebook and could hear her husband in a far room running the vacuum cleaner. How she and Mr. P. underwrote their gentle madness was not revealed, but many wondered how Mr. P. could operate a vacuum cleaner the livelong night and work gainfully in the daylight so that Mrs. P. could copy down *The Girl in the Blue Velvet Band* and occasionally drink to excess after dark and he could get to his cleaning. Either he or she must have a private income that freed them to live life as they fancied. So few do.

"I'm having some dental work done today," Mrs. B. said, "so I won't be able to talk to you tomorrow," suggesting that dentists are as brutal today as when they moonlighted as barbers.

Mrs. S. attributed her insomnia to her having slept as a child with her older and heavier sister who each night wet the bed and then rolled over to her sister's side to escape her incontinence.

Mr. J. wondered if anybody had noticed around Christmas how there was not so much bitterness. "I lay down," he said, "and I rest. I change jobs a lot, but I don't need to. I have a good frame of mind. I've got a car. I walk along the beach."

Then the first drama of the morning shaped up.

Mrs. L.'s dog had but moments before gone into labor, a black Labrador retriever of some six summers; to Mrs. L.'s knowledge the dog had not been earlier with another dog or even in another's vicinity, but God works in a mysterious way. Mrs. L.'s past had not prepared her for this emergency. As a little girl she had not known anything because her father had adored her and they lived in Baltimore then at a time when things were much easier for a little girl in the South. Her voice at the word Baltimore grew more aggressively southern and now the letter "e" was "i" and "when" became "whin" just as "men" become "min" not twenty minutes south of Philadelphia. Southern, like swimming, once learned is never forgotten. Her friends had repeatedly urged her to have her dog altered — all theirs were — distant though her dog was from compromising companions; she had demurred, not having the stomach to admit her dog into a hospital where an operation would thwart Nature's intentions and change her dog's personality. And they got fat. Foolish though it may sound, Mrs. L. was of the "old school" and balked at changing God's plans. But now the immediate problem was upon her. Her dog roamed the house like a banshee. What should she do?

The console before Westbrook was alive with little lights, the voices behind them anxious to help a woman and a bitch in labor.

Mr. R. said Mrs. L. should at once put her dog in a room apart, a room bare except for a box with sides so low it allowed easy entry and lined with whatever wool blankets were dispensable. When "her time had come" the dog would enter the box and deliver there. In the meantime, let Mrs. L make herself a cup of coffee.

Mr. F. said dogs sometimes went an hour between puppies. Mrs. L. might be dealing with puppies all night. Dogs, he said, clean up after themselves. His experience was with hunting dogs but now more as pets than hunters since age had slowed his steps through the woods where once he had strode whistling, a young man, sixty-five now, going downhill like everybody else, he guessed, looking forward to his daughter and grandchildren at Christmas. She was a real peach, his daughter. Her voice on the telephone made people feel good.

"But don't let her bite the afterbirth too close," said Mrs. K.

Mr. A. knew a dog that ate her puppies.

Mr. J. said pigs did it. Pigs.

In Vermont the boars, not the sows, watched and then did it, Mr. B. said.

Mrs. G. had lived on a farm back then. Pigs the only animals with human eyes. You know? Follow you with their eyes? Not turn their heads? Human.

In New Hampshire a little boy wandered into the pigpen. A pig got him, mangled his arm. Those teeth. The father jumped in with a pitchfork, the pig crazy with the smell of blood took after him and he jabbed it with the pitchfork, got both the eyes and it ripped around the pen blind, smelling where to get them. The little boy in the mud and screaming. The pig stood smelling and the father got the little boy out.

The father and the mother got divorced over the pig. The father, you see, was supposed to be watching the little boy. She had warned and warned the bad pig would get him. The man began to drink after that and the woman went off somewhere with a truck driver who wouldn't take the little one-armed boy.

The console was alive with callers eager to offer tragedy.

It was the Long Silence that had prepared Westbrook for tragedy. He could not have prevented the death of Maxine Gates even had he married her, but like a boulder in the middle of the stream he could have altered the current of her son's life and the boy would not now be lying near death in a hospital the Voice refused to disclose.

He glanced at the clock and prepared to play more music to invite the Voice.

Devices that reckon time are prized; without them no man knows the interval of a minute, let alone an hour. The young with their life before them judge time too long; the old, their life behind them, too short. Whatever these instruments depend on for credibility — the reversal of polarity, the relaxing of springs, falling weights, dripping water, shadows or consuming flame, all relate to distance — the tour of hands about a face, the depth of water in a basin, the extent of shadows, the length of the remaining guttering candle.

Certain devices strike a bell.

It was now 3:29, Eastern Standard Time.

Westbrook reached for the tape of music.

It was never played. He was drawn to the last little light to the left of the console. He took that line off the air, and listened.

The Voice spoke. *"Westbrook. Stand by."*

Westbrook heard the miles, and something else. He rose, removed his glasses and steadied himself.

Many lives revolve around a single image as a wheel around an axle — a whiff of coal smoke, say, the taste of apples or bare, black branches motionless before the moon.

At the center of Westbrook's life there was a sound, one of peculiar loneliness — the bell in the courthouse tower telling the Three Ones. Even as the Voice spoke, that is what he heard and as clearly as if he and not the Voice stood in a booth three thousand miles away. There was no mistaking it. His ear responded in sympathy as a wine glass sings when a certain string is plucked.

The liquid sound fell like the asperges over the vanished Westbrook "mansion," over the Crystal Rooms where the whores arranged what there was of their lives, over a rented room in the rectory where poor Miss Snodgrass lived with her ugly nose; paused over the high school where once in a toilet stall he had drawn his feet up against discovery, over the Matador Apartments where they heated soup on a hot plate, high over a rotting verandah where an ancient abortionist considered drifting constellations. It washed over the Cabbage Patch, over the crooked paths traced by aimless, drunken feet, where ryegrass whispered and the forgotten died in shacks — and trailers.

The bell was silent; the last of it fled like mist beyond the town where the highway veers south near the Hale Memorial Hospital. But the bell had told him what the Voice had not.

Listeners in thirty-eight states were puzzled by the silence. Some suspected a blackout. Some were startled by thoughts of death, for the dead air seemed a harbinger of Eternal Silence. How will you deal with death? Emulate someone who has gone before? Beethoven shook his fist at heaven. What will your last words be, the last syllable?

Your children stand there who once watched how you bore shame and disappointment. Will your death be an example of courage, or will you go sniveling into the dark? And when the time comes, remember that birth is as frightful as death; the fetus as well as the corpse stands amazed at the unknown. Oh, five minutes was time enough to think.

When death came to Tom Westbrook, a son would stand beside him. Until then, he would stand beside his son. Five minutes was time enough to call the hospital.

Then he dialed the airport.